Bad to the Bone

The Dogfather · Book Five

roxanne st. claire

Bad to the Bone
THE DOGFATHER BOOK FIVE

978-0-9981093-7-4– ebook
978-0-9981093-8-1 – print

COVER ART: Keri Knutson (designer)
and Dawn C. Whitty (photographer)
INTERIOR FORMATTING: Author EMS

Critical Reviews of
Roxanne St. Claire Novels

"St. Claire, as always, brings a scorching tear-up-the-sheets romance combined with a great story: dealing with real issues starring memorable characters in vivid scenes."

— Romantic Times Magazine

"Non-stop action, sweet and sexy romance, lively characters, and a celebration of family and forgiveness."

— Publishers Weekly

"Plenty of heat, humor, and heart!"

— USA Today's Happy Ever After blog

"It's safe to say I will try any novel with St. Claire's name on it."

— www.smartbitchestrashybooks.com

"The writing was perfectly on point as always and the pace of the story was flawless. But be forewarned that you will laugh, cry, and sigh with happiness. I sure did."

— www.harlequinjunkies.com

"The Barefoot Bay series is an all-around knockout, soul-satisfying read. Roxanne St. Claire writes with warmth and heart and the community she's built at Barefoot Bay is one I want to visit again and again."

— Mariah Stewart, New York Times bestselling author

"This book stayed with me long after I put it down."

— All About Romance

Dear Reader:

Welcome back to the foothills of North Carolina where the Dogfather, Daniel Kilcannon, is once again pulling some strings to help one of his six grown children find forever love. On these pages, you'll find my favorite things in life and fiction: big families, great dogs, and lasting love. And, I am delighted to inform you that a portion of the first month sales of all the books in this series is being donated to Alaqua Animal Refuge (www.alaqua.org) in my home state of Florida. That's where these covers were shot by photographer Dawn Whitty (www.dawncwhitty.com) using *real* men (not models, but they are gorgeous!) and *rescue* dogs (now in forever homes!). So you don't only buy a terrific book...you support a fantastic cause!

I couldn't publish a book without help. In this one, I had massive support from Dr. Linda Hankins, a talented veterinarian and one of my favorite readers. Also major thanks to my content editor, Kristi Yanta, who clears the obstacles I create for myself; copyeditor Joyce Lamb, who is truly without equal in this business; proofreaders Marlene Engel and Chris Kridler, who have eagle eyes and unparalleled comma skills; and cover designer Keri Knutson, who helped bring Trace and Meatball to life on this book. Again, props to photographer Dawn C. Whitty who captured a moment so beautifully, I had to write a scene for it. My love and gratitude to all of them, and my family, writing pals, and the doggos who snore (loudly) at my feet while I write.

I hope you love the Kilcannon clan! Don't miss a single book in The Dogfather Series:

Available now
Sit…Stay…Beg (Book 1)
New Leash on Life (Book 2)
Leader of the Pack (Book 3)
Santa Paws is Coming to Town (Book 4 – a Holiday novella)
Bad to the Bone (Book 5)

Coming soon
Ruff Around the Edges (Book 6)
Double Dog Dare (Book 7)
Old Dog New Tricks (Book 8)

And yes, there will be more. For a complete list, buy links, and reading order of all my books, visit www.roxannestclaire.com. Sign up for my newsletter on my website to find out when the next book is released!

xoxo
Rocki

Dedication

For Roxy, one of the sweetest puppers I've ever
known and loved, and not just because of her cute
name. A friend to my own dogs, Roxy had a spirit and
a smile I'll never forget, and she is missed every day
when we take our walks. (And much love to her
owner, Chris Schumacher, who has a heart for doggies
and is a true friend and great neighbor.)

Chapter One

November, 2003

Molly gripped the steering wheel of the seven-year-old Plymouth Voyager she'd managed to parallel park, trying to channel some of the Kilcannon magic that her whole family seemed to possess. She sucked in a deep breath, but that only filled her lungs with the lingering scent of baby powder and vanilla, the signature fragrance her mother sprayed in the minivan to combat the scent of the dogs she carted to and from shelters and new homes. And that simply made Molly realize how far short she fell in her desire to be exactly like spectacular, serene, sweet-smelling Annie Kilcannon.

Mom had encouraged her to come to this party tonight. She was sure that Molly's mood would improve by seeing her old high school friends. Well, yes, if Molly were like her older brothers, a party would be just the ticket. If she had Shane's swagger or Garrett's good looks or Liam's classy cool. But she had none of those gifts and wasn't even sure why she'd been invited to a gathering of former high school friends during their first Thanksgiving break since graduation.

Closing her eyes, she dropped her head on the steering wheel and felt the weight of her unfashionably curly hair over her face, covering this morning's new arrival of two lovely zits on her forehead.

Oh God, why wasn't she as fine and flawless as the rest of her family?

That's right. Molly "got the brains"—which made her a nerd stuck in the dead middle of Kilcannon perfection. Even her two younger siblings fit the mold, with Aidan's golden-boy charm and Darcy's stunning beauty.

That left Molly, middle child, odd man out, not...amazing. Yes, she had the supersmarts and was going to be a vet like her father, but on nights like this, when the home of one of the popular, pretty girls from her high school class was packed for a party? Amazing would be nice. Sure, these kids all stayed home and went to Vestal Valley College while Molly had gotten into UNC-Chapel Hill. But sometimes, tonight for instance, she'd give up an IQ point or six for some gorgeous skin, straight hair, and one of those Cover Girl smiles.

She peered into the darkness, noticing that Kaylie's mom had already put some Christmas lights on the bushes, sparkling like stars around the two-story house on the outskirts of Bitter Bark. She knew Kaylie's neighborhood well, having spent plenty of time here after Jessie had moved away to Minnesota. Girls like Kaylie and her crowd had been fun to hang with, especially after her best friend left, but Molly suspected they were more interested in the three older Kilcannon boys than Molly herself.

So, why wasn't she excited about this invitation?

Because she didn't feel the least bit pretty? What nineteen-year-old girl wanted to walk into a party alone when she felt unattractive and unappealing and un—?

"Hey! Molly Kilcannon!" She almost jumped out of her skin at the loud slam of a palm on her window and the high-pitched screech. "I'd know that doggie van anywhere!"

Yanking out of her thoughts, Molly eyed the girl on the other side of a slightly fogged window, recognizing Isabella Henderson immediately.

"Dizzie Izzie!" She rolled the window down, getting blasted by unusually cold November air and the impact of Isabella's cascades of blond hair and skin that looked like it was poured out of a bottle of heavy cream. She even wore the silly nickname Molly had given her like a jaunty cap, with style and pride.

"Where have you been all winter break?" Izzie asked, her long lashes nearly touching her perfectly arched brows as she widened her eyes. "We've been drinking at Bushrod's every night and haven't seen you."

Bushrod's? "I can't go drink in a bar yet," she said. And neither could they.

"Kaylie and I have fakes," she explained, no doubt reading Molly's expression.

"And you think Mr. Duncan doesn't know you graduated from Bitter Bark High six months ago?"

She gave a classic Dizzie Izzie shrug. "He serves

3

all the college kids, and our parents don't care that we drink."

Molly was raised on sips of Jameson's, and getting wasted with crazed freshmen held zero appeal for a chemistry major at a tough university. Kaylie and Izzie hadn't even decided what their majors would be, but they'd made it to college, so it was time to party hard. Meanwhile, Molly was acing Chem 2 and had her whole life planned down to the color of scrubs she'd wear on her first day at work for the Kilcannon Veterinarian Hospital.

"God, you look great, Molly," she said, gesturing toward Molly's face with a mittened hand.

Immediately, Molly shook her head to argue. "Please, I'm a wreck."

"I love your hair all wild like that."

Was she serious? She'd tried to straighten it into submission, but ten minutes in the snowfall and it was nothing but curls again. "No, it's a mess," she said, shaking off the compliment.

Izzie dipped down to look into the van. "You alone?"

"Yeah."

She seemed vaguely disappointed, but gestured with her mitten. "Well, come on. You going in, or you want to sit here all night and freeze?"

Sitting there sounded like a good option. "I'm not going to stay long," she said. "I just wanted to say hi to Kaylie."

"You might change your mind," Izzie said in a singsong warning. "Kaylie said there's a ton of her brother's friends here. Speaking of brothers, is Shane home for Thanksgiving week?"

Oh, *that's* who she was looking for. "He's on a date tonight," Molly said.

"There's some lucky girl. How about Garrett?"

Yep. She'd been invited in the hopes that a Kilcannon boy would come along. "He and Liam had somewhere to go."

"Oh, too bad."

Wasn't it, though? On a sigh, Molly grabbed her keys and pushed open the door. At least she had someone to walk in with now, and someone who virtually guaranteed no one would notice her.

Their boots crunched in the half inch of fresh snow as Molly and Izzie navigated the sidewalk and turned into the driveway. The notes of a familiar Dierks Bentley country song blared from the house.

"What was I thinkin'?" Izzie sang, shimmying in a little dance and playing air guitar.

"What was *I* thinkin'?" A male voice stopped them both, coming from the shadow of Kaylie's front lawn. "Letting Molly Kilcannon slip through my hands in high school."

She recognized the voice almost immediately. Low, rich, and insanely sexy, that voice was capable of so much more than talking. A voice that caused shivers, quivers, and plenty of panties to fall with happy sighs from girls who lusted after Bitter Bark's homegrown bad boy. Not Molly's panties, of course, but she'd certainly had a few fantasies.

"Trace Bancroft!" Izzie moved toward the shadow. "I heard you were making an appearance tonight."

"Hey." Stepping out of a dark area, Trace moved into the soft white of Christmas lights strung on a bush, eyes the color of the night sky locked on Molly

5

so intently that his bottlebrush-thick lashes nearly touched. His hair was still black and long, his jaw always set at a defiant angle, his mouth...oh Lord above. *That* was a mouth. A bad, bad mouth that said bad things and could probably do even badder things.

Molly's stomach sailed into her throat like she'd been thrown down a roller coaster without a seat belt at the sight of him. Under her jacket, an unholy heat curled through her, warming her from the inside out.

"I heard you went to Chapel Hill," he said, adjusting his leather jacket on his shoulders like it might be too tight for how broad they were underneath. He nudged her. "Always knew my chemistry tutor was Miss Smarty-Pants."

She swallowed, and nodded, not trusting her voice and not willing to sound the least bit excited that he'd bothered to find out where she'd gone to college. All she knew about him was that he'd managed to get into a vocational program at Vestal Valley and still lived at home with his mother, Bitter Bark's one and only astrologist.

"You coming in, Trace?" Izzie had flipped off her mittens and put her bare hand on Trace's shoulder, drawing Molly's gaze to the size of him, making her wonder if he had even more tattoos than he had in high school. She'd seen a few in the library, when he'd flirt with her and she'd tried to teach him in chemistry for community service hours. There'd been plenty of chemistry, but not the kind he needed to pass the class.

When he didn't answer, Izzie inched closer. "We're shotgunning tonight."

He barely glanced at her, as if the idea of poking a

hole in the side of a beer can to suck it down faster sounded as stupid as it was.

"I might." The two words were spoken directly to Molly and as much an invitation as if he'd said her name. "Not a big party guy," he added.

"Me neither," Molly said, unable to look away from the magnetic grip of his gaze.

Izzie glanced from one to the other, her eyes narrowing imperceptibly. "Come in with us, Trace," she said, cozying up to him. "I'm freezing and need a big strong guy to hold on to."

He barely reacted, his attention on Molly. "Or you can hang out here and teach me some chemistry, Irish."

The old nickname and the invitation nearly took Molly's breath away, but Izzie bristled and stepped back. "Irish?"

Molly gave a self-conscious laugh.

"Cute," Izzie added in a tone that said she thought it was anything *but* cute. "Well, I'm going in. You two can stand out here and play doctor for all I care, but I want to party."

"Bye," Trace said, completely without humor, irony, or interest.

Molly glanced at her friend. "I'll come—"

Trace reached his hand out. "Stay."

Izzie raised one of those perfectly arched brows with the slightest air of defeat. "See ya. *Irish*."

When she left, Molly stuck her hands deeper in her jacket pockets and turned to Trace Bancroft, the most *off-limits* guy in the town, who was looking at her like he had *no* limits. Didn't know the meaning of limits, in fact, and was born to break every one.

7

And it made Molly feel sexy and beautiful and daring.

He inched closer, still silent. He smelled a little like the woods, like snow, and maybe beer, but his eyes were clear and pinned on her. The effect was dizzying.

"So," he said after a minute, a whisper of a smile curling that magnificent mouth.

"So."

"Long time no tutoring."

She laughed softly. "Yeah, long time. I'm a chem major, though." God, why did she add that? It sounded so nerdy.

"You always were combustible."

"Look at you, knowing your vocab. Glad you remembered something from all those sessions."

"I remembered you." He reached up and touched her cheek, making her flinch because his finger was hot. And she didn't like to have her not-silky-smooth complexion examined so closely. Except, the way he was looking at her made her completely forget her skin or hair or whatever she'd been so worked up about twenty minutes ago. "And believe it or not, some of that stuff still sticks with me at work now."

She inched back, surprised. "What do you do that requires chemistry?"

"I'm a welder. An apprentice, actually, at McQueen's Machine Shop. Every once in a while, I have to think about chemical changes and such when I'm working on something." He leaned into her. "And then I think about you, my tutor from local royalty."

Royalty? Oh, yes, now she remembered the many comments he'd lobbed at her during their tutoring sessions. He'd frequently taken the occasional dig at her well-known family name, or commented about the hundred acres of prime property they owned. He'd often referred to her father as Dr. Kilcannon, with too much emphasis on "doctor," as if she were the daughter of a renowned brain surgeon, not the local vet.

He angled his head toward the darkened lawn. "Take a walk with me, Irish."

She hesitated, torn between how much she wanted to and how much she shouldn't.

"It's cold," she said, delaying the decision. But he put his arm around her, and he felt so warm and strong, the debate in her head immediately ended. Nestling a little closer, they walked into the shadows of tall trees and thick bushes of the oversized lawn.

She glanced up at him, a little startled to find him staring at her and not ahead. "What?" she asked.

"You got even prettier."

The statement, so simple and honest, eased everything. The pain, the self-doubt, the sense that she wasn't all that her siblings were...that all disappeared with four words. "Thanks."

"I like your hair all wavy like that," he said. "Brings out the red."

She laughed again, less nervous this time. "You *are* trying hard tonight, Trace."

He slowed and turned her to face him, the only light from the moon now. But it was enough to show his chiseled features and intent gaze. "You're still out of my league, though."

"I'm not—"

"Where the hell is Trace Bancroft?" The man's voice boomed from the street, punctuated by the thwack of a car door slamming. "Where is that son of a bitch?"

Trace swore under his breath and backed deeper into the darkness, horror suddenly etched on the features Molly had been admiring.

"What?" she asked, turning toward the street and the loud footsteps coming up the drive. "Who is that? What does he want?"

"Probably to kill me for something I didn't do." He closed his eyes. "I knew I'd have to pay a price."

"For what?" she demanded.

"Hey!" the man bellowed. "Somebody better give me that prick Bancroft so I can bash his head into the sidewalk!"

"Who is that?" she asked.

"Bart McQueen. My boss."

His boss wanted to kill him?

"I'm gonna get you, Bancroft!" he yelled, a drunken, violent sound that sent chills up Molly's spine.

Trace backed up some more, looking one way, then the other, then at Molly. "I didn't do anything," he insisted in a hushed whisper. "I swear to God, Molly, I didn't do *anything*. And that's what got me in trouble!" He spat the last words.

Some kids came out of the house, adding to the noise and confusion, but the man looking for Trace still had the loudest voice. "Bancroft! You're gonna die for what you did to my wife!"

Trace's face melted at the words, as close to tears as Molly could imagine this tough kid ever being. "I didn't *do anything*!" Trace repeated. "I turned her down. And God knows what she said about me." He swiped his hand through his hair, panic flashing in his eyes. "I gotta get out of here."

"I'll help you," she said, the words out before she could really stop herself.

"He'll see me if I go in the driveway," he said, the genuine fear in his voice twisting at her chest.

"I know another way." She grabbed his arm and headed to the side of Kaylie's yard, to a path she remembered that ran along a separate garage building.

Bart McQueen's earsplitting threats grew distant as they ran in the opposite direction, holding hands, zipping around the garage, then to the street where Molly had parked.

"Over here!" She fished her keys out of her bag, unlocking the passenger door with shaking fingers. "One word about the minivan and I'll send you back to him."

Trace managed a laugh. "Right now, I'd get into a shopping cart with you to escape that lunatic."

She stole a look at him as he climbed into the passenger seat, her heart flip-flopping as she caught his sweet and sexy smile.

"You better be innocent," she whispered.

"I am." It was sincere, and for reasons she'd never understand, she believed him. She pushed his door shut, darted around to the other side, and as she climbed in behind the wheel, he leaned close to her.

"Irish." He took her face in both hands, easing her to him. "How can I thank you?"

She looked at him for a long moment, vaguely aware she held her breath while her heart hammered at her ribs and every double X chromosome in her body hummed with kinetic energy. Without giving it too much thought, she closed the space between them and pressed her mouth against his.

He froze momentarily, then intensified the kiss. "That'll work," he murmured against her lips.

"More," she whispered.

"Thought you'd never ask." The contact seared her lips as he clasped her face a little tighter until their lips parted and tongues touched. Light-headed and lost for a moment, Molly kissed him back, giving in to the sparks of pleasure and twists of raw desire that ricocheted through her body.

"Where should we go?" she murmured into his mouth.

"Someplace where I can kiss the holy hell out of you all night long."

"It's cold outside."

He threw a look into the back. "It's a van, sweetheart. Let's rock it."

"There's a dog crate back there."

"We can make it work." He lifted her chin and planted his mouth on her neck, and somewhere, in the back of her mind, she thought she better not get a hickey, because if one of her brothers saw it, she'd be dead.

She shoved the thought away, not caring, because right now, with this boy in this van on this crazy night, she suddenly felt unutterably beautiful and desirable and ready for whatever Trace Bancroft had to offer.

Chapter Two

"Shhh. Molly, baby, stop crying."

"I c-c-can't." She shuddered, turning her face to wipe tears on Mom's jeans, not caring that she'd soaked them as she wept. Molly's head felt like it would explode from crying, her chest ached from the weeks of pressure she'd finally unleashed, and her stomach was, as it had been since Christmas, on the brink of a full toss.

But the truth was out now. Mom knew. That hurdle, one of the hardest in her life, had been crossed. But there were so many more ahead.

"You have to." Mom lifted her by the shoulders and handed her another tissue. "Crying isn't going to stop what's happening."

She nearly collapsed again. "Don't you see what I've done? I've messed up my entire life! My whole future. My dreams of becoming a vet like Dad. My scholarship, my hopes, my life. All for one stupid night of…oh God. Mom! What was I thinking?"

"You weren't." Her mother's narrow shoulders straightened, her hazel eyes, so much like the ones Molly faced in the mirror every day, took on a greenish hue as she narrowed her gaze. It was the first real sternness since Molly had found the nerve to make her confession.

Mom had been shocked, of course. Speechless after Molly had slipped into her mother's bedroom on a quiet Sunday afternoon while Dad was out back doing an exam on a new foster dog. Silent after Molly whispered two horrible, life-changing words.

I'm pregnant.

After a few seconds, Mom's stone-faced disbelief had morphed into a flash of disappointment, gone so fast anyone else might have missed it. But not Molly. She knew this woman inside and out. Knew every expression in her pretty, loving eyes, every emotion that tugged at sweet, soft lips. She saw that split second when she'd broken her mother's heart, and that's when Molly started to bawl.

It took a good fifteen minutes of slobbering and sobbing to tell enough of the story so that Mom got the idea of how it happened, and with whom.

"You need to calm down and listen to me," Mom finally said.

Molly sniffed, staring at her, grateful her mother wasn't crying or screaming, not that either one was in her repertoire. No, she was being Annie Kilcannon, calm in a crisis, steady as a rock. Everything Molly never could be.

"It's not about you anymore," Mom said. "You better get used to that."

For the millionth time since Molly first realized her predicament, a now-familiar punch of terror and regret slammed into her gut. Right where her "predicament" had been growing for twelve weeks.

"Mommy, I'm scared," Molly whispered.

Her mother nodded, caressing Molly's cheek. "I know. God, I know exactly how you feel."

"Is that why you're being so...so...*nice*?" Because Molly had put this conversation off for as long as she could, but by mid-February, the lady at the clinic assured her nothing was going to change. A baby would be born on or about August twenty-third, scant weeks before Molly was supposed to start her second year of college. "Why don't you yell at me and tell me I was stupid?"

"Because you already know you were stupid."

She flinched. "He had a...you know."

"Oh, I know. Ever count the months between our wedding anniversary and Liam's birthday? We also had an 'I know' on hand another night about six months after Shane was born, and now we call him Garrett."

"*Mom*."

"Sorry, you come from fertile stock, Molly. Next time, you'll be more careful."

"Next time?" Molly almost choked on the words. "There isn't going to be a next time! My life is over. I'm going to have a kid at twenty and...oh!" She slapped her hand on the settee cushion, sending a sharp pop of noise through Mom and Dad's bedroom.

"When did you find out, Molly? Were you alone? Scared?"

Of course Mom would worry how Molly felt at that moment. It was so like her to not want one of her children to be unhappy.

"I was up in my room on New Year's Day, that celebration of new beginnings." She let sarcasm and bitterness darken her voice. "Peeing on so many sticks I could barely wrap them up and hide them in the trash."

Mom's eyes widened. "Molly! Why didn't you tell me then? I'm your mother. The one you've always gone to when you needed something."

"I couldn't bear to hurt you, Mom. And what was I supposed to do? Waltz into the family room, wave my stick at the football-watching Kilcannon clan, and announce, 'Guess what, team? I'm officially the dumbest moron in the family.'"

"Don't ever say that again," she whispered. "This child is a gift."

"This child is a *mistake*," Molly shot back. "And the father is a bad-to-the-bone, scum-of-the-earth, no-good loser whose mother is a freak from the wrong side of town. I'm sure that announcement would have gone over great with the *uncles* who can't stand that guy."

"Have you made any effort to contact Trace Bancroft?" Mom asked when the tirade ended.

Molly cringed at the sound of his name on her mother's beautiful lips. "He's gone. Disappeared without a *trace*." She emphasized the last word with hatred. "My guess is he split the next day because Bart McQueen was going to kill him. He's fallen off the face of the earth, and that is *fine* with me."

"He has to know," Mom said. "He has to take responsibility for this."

"Mom, he didn't assault me. I mean, things got out of hand fast, but I was a hundred percent on board. It was mutual. I'm sorry."

"You don't have to apologize for being a normal

young woman, Molly. Or even for your choice of partners. But a man does have a right to know, and an obligation to help you."

"Pretty sure he'd rather not know and is in no position to help." She eyed her mother again, still not able to believe this response. "You're really not mad at me?"

"I'm worried about you, concerned for your health and the baby's, and wondering if I'm up to raising another one."

"You?"

"Together, with you."

Molly frowned. "What do you mean?"

"You think I'm going to send you out in the world to fend for yourself and my grandchild? There's plenty of room at Waterford Farm, and I'll help you exactly the way Gramma Finnie helped me."

"You were married to her son."

"Not when Liam was conceived." She tipped her head and added a smile. "Plus, I have six times the experience you do in the child-rearing department."

Molly's eyes filled again. "How can you be so...so fine with it?"

"First of all, I'm not fine with it, but it can't be changed. Second, I know what you're going through, because I went through the same thing at the same age, which tells you it can all work out well."

"Sure, if you're pregnant by the most awesome man on earth who thinks the sun rises and sets on you."

"That helped," Mom conceded. "But third, and this is the most important reason, so listen to me: I'm your mother, Molly." She put both arms around her and pulled her in for a warm embrace, so tender it only made Molly sob again. "My mother essentially wrote me off when this happened to me. I won't do that. And when you're a mother, you will learn what I mean when I say you're only as happy as your least-happy child. Until you are happy again, I won't be, either."

Comfort poured over her heart with every word of her mother's heartfelt speech, soothing in a way Molly hadn't thought possible. For the first time since New Year's Day, she felt a tiny ray of hope. "I was so scared I'd have to do this alone."

"Alone?" Mom leaned back. "We are family."

"But Dad..." She bit her lip. "He's going to be so disappointed."

"He'll get over it."

"And the boys are going to kill me. And...him."

She inhaled slowly, thinking. "I'm going to do what I can to find Trace Bancroft, but until we do, Molly, you have every right to keep his identity private until he knows. I'll make it clear that it is our secret and we are handling it. After a while, they'll forget."

She very much doubted that, but if Mom wanted to take on the problem of Trace Bancroft, then it was one less thing Molly needed to worry about. Mom could make Dad accept anything, and that fourth foster dog he was with outside was proof of it.

"But what about Darcy? She's only fifteen, and I'm her idol. And Aidan is a junior in high school. He'll get teased."

"You'll show them both how you handle it when life throws you a curve ball. We all will. That's what Kilcannons do."

Overwhelmed again, Molly dropped her head on the strongest shoulder she knew and let out a sigh. "Will that be my baby's last name? Kilcannon? I don't have to use...Bancroft?"

"Of course not. This child..." She put her hand on Molly's stomach. "Is a Kilcannon."

"This child is a mistake." How could it ever be anything but?

"Please don't say that ever again, Molly. Promise me."

Molly just stared at her, not willing to make a promise she might not keep.

"What you did was a mistake, Molly, but the result is a precious child we will love with all our hearts and souls."

Could she love this baby? Her mother made it sound so easy. Made everything—including motherhood—seem easy. "I don't know, Mom."

"I know," her mother replied with the utmost confidence. "Molly, you are not the sum total of one mistake you made in your life." She added gentle, loving pressure to Molly's stomach. "You never want this child to think he or she was a mistake that defined your life. You make mistakes, but no one *is* one."

"My mistake was a hot guy who melted me and used a faulty condom. The next day, I thought my only mistake was losing my virginity in the back of the minivan."

Mom inched back, a tiny bit horrified. "The dog van? What did you do, move the crate?"

Molly managed an embarrassed smile. "Kind of."

"Lord. The Plymouth Voyager. *That* you better not

let your brothers know. You'll never hear the end of it."

Was she really able to find humor in this situation? God, Molly needed to be more like her mother. In every possible way. The need was never stronger than right now. "I'll never hear the end of it anyway."

"Yes, you will. When you have an adorable son or daughter toddling around here, all wrapped around Grandpa Daniel's baby finger, and playing with the dogs, and riding piggyback with Uncle Shane, and running wild with Aunt Darcy? The only thing they'll say is thank you."

Molly studied her mother's face, drinking in the beauty on the outside and the peace that shone forth from the inside. "Sometimes it makes me crazy that you're so perfect, Mom."

One pretty brow lifted.

"And sometimes I want to fall on my knees and thank God you're the mother I got."

This time, Mom's eyes filled with tears. "I am always, always here for you. And my grandchild."

"Grannie Annie," Molly whispered.

Mom gave a soft hoot. "Grannie Annie. I love that."

"I love *you*," Molly said. "I'm sorry I went from Superkid to stupid, worthless teenager in one night."

Mom shook her head. "You are still Superkid." She brought one of Molly's hands to her lips and placed a kiss on the knuckles. "And you'll be a super mom. I know it."

Molly wished she knew it. "But I won't be a super vet like Dad."

"Why not?"

She snorted as if the question was simply too wrong to answer. "That's the saddest part to me. I wanted to graduate from UNC and go to vet school and be Dad's partner. It's all I've ever wanted."

"You will, but your path will be different. It'll be longer and filled with more…diapers."

Molly closed her eyes like she'd been shot. "What will I do?"

Mom didn't hesitate, brushing back a silky lock of her auburn hair as if she'd already thought all this through. "You'll finish this year, have a baby in August, start up at Vestal Valley in the spring semester, and take it one step at a time until you are a vet and Dad's partner. I know you can do it. You're much stronger than you realize, Molly."

"But that wasn't what I wanted to do." She knew her whining sounded childish, but letting go of her dreams was hard.

"You make your plans, and God laughs at you," Mom said.

Molly looked skyward. "Now you sound like Gramma Finnie and her Irish proverbs."

"I can hear her now when we tell her," Mom agreed. "'Prudence has a man prepared for the unexpected,'" she said with Gramma Finnie's Irish brogue.

"Prudence," Molly whispered. "I wish I had exercised some."

"You will, when you have your own child. Nothing matures you faster, believe me."

"Still…" The word rolled around in her head. "Prudence Kilcannon. That's kind of pretty and old school and Irish, don't you think?"

"Yes!" Mom's face lit up. "We can call her Pru."

"I like that." That tendril of hope tightened around her chest, and the strangest, most unfamiliar sensation rolled through Molly. Happiness. Just a glimmer, just a sliver, but there it was. She'd forgotten what happiness felt like. "Pru Kilcannon."

"Come on, honey," Mom said, standing up. "Let's tell your father the good news."

Only Annie Kilcannon could see this that way. Only Annie could turn this mess into something positive. Only the greatest mother in the world could love her kids the way this woman did.

"Mommy." Molly slipped her fingers into her mother's hand and squeezed. "I hope I'm half the mother you are."

"You'll be twice the mother I am," Mom assured her.

She'd have to be, since she was doing this alone. On a sigh, Molly closed her eyes, making a silent vow. She would love this child the way her mother loved her children. She would find her way, become a vet, and still be a great mother. She would do all that for Annie Kilcannon, who deserved nothing less.

"I hope it's a girl," Molly said softly as they walked out of the room. "Because I know exactly what I want to name her."

Mom went ahead, shoulders squared, delicate jaw set for battle with anyone who'd get in the way of one of her children. Behind her, Molly lightly touched her belly.

I'll do right by you, Prudence Anne Kilcannon, I promise.

Chapter Three

Fourteen Years Later

"Pru! Look at this handbag." Molly snagged the pink leather shoulder strap from the rack and held it up against herself. "*J'adore.*"

"*J'adore?*" Pru rolled her eyes and eased the bag out of Molly's hands. "First of all, you're no more French than Fifi L'Amour over there," she whispered, throwing a look at the vixenlike owner of the newest boutique in town. La Parisienne catered to the tourists, and the prices were sky high, but Molly loved bringing Pru in here when they did some Saturday shopping.

"And second," Pru said, in her best General Pru voice. Her uncles had given her the nickname when she was three and started to show her unwavering penchant for rule-following and corralling the family to do things exactly as they should be done. "We are shopping to purchase new sweaters for our trip next weekend. Not Kate Spade bags that don't go with anything you own."

"It's the kind of bag you take on a date," Molly said, giving the pretty purse a reluctant look.

Pru's mouth opened to a little *o*, showing both disbelief and a mouthful of braces. "You have a date?" Her voice rose in thirteen-year-old drama-shock, her eyes—the same chaotic blend of green, brown, and gold as Molly's—widening.

"Would that be so awful?"

Pru did a little fake choke. "You're kidding, right?"

"It would be awful," Molly guessed. "Men are awful."

"Mom!" Pru laughed, shaking her head so some of her insanely thick, black hair fell over her narrow shoulder. "Don't be a manhater."

"I am not a manhater."

"Then why *don't* you date?"

"Because my standards are very high."

"No kidding. If perhaps you scratch 'noble bloodline' and 'heads charitable foundation' and 'looks like that guy on *Outlander*' off your list, you'd have a shot at a date."

Molly laughed. "I was kidding when I made that list. And you'd hate it if I dated. Admit the truth, girl." Molly tugged playfully at some of that thick hair.

Pru backed away and crossed her arms. "The truth is that I have been telling you for a year that you should get out more. Have I not?" She lifted one brow, making the most of the fact that she'd been allowed to have them waxed for her thirteenth birthday, and the new look had definitely matured her young features. Her face still had the very last remnants of childish softness around the jaw, and the

24

orthodontics made sure her appearance stayed firmly prepubescent…for now.

Truth was, her baby was blossoming into a teenager and then a young woman. And then Molly would be the one hating the idea of dating.

"You should go out with a guy sometime," Pru said.

"I know you say that, Pru, but if I did meet a guy, you'd lay down so many rules, the guy would run for the hills."

"Not true." Again, she shook her head with that vehement know-it-all way she'd had since birth. "I even talked to Grandpa about it."

Molly drew back. "You talked to my father about me dating?"

"And Gramma Finnie," she added.

Well, Molly understood that. The only person who could rival Molly for closeness with Pru was Molly's own grandmother. Mom and Pru had been close, too, which was another reason Molly had abandoned the idea of dating. Her mother's unexpected passing a little over three years ago had rocked all of their worlds. And although no one could ever fill the void of losing Annie Kilcannon, it was no surprise Pru grew even closer to Gramma Finnie as everyone mourned the loss. The eighth-grader and the octogenarian made a strange but beautiful friendship.

"Why would you talk to my father and my grandmother about me dating?" Molly asked.

"Because it's Grandpa's gift," she said. "He's the force behind three marriages in our family."

"Oh, please. He was in the right place at the right time." Although Molly did give her father credit for the matchmaking, nothing would have stopped the

25

power of her brothers' new relationships. They'd have all found their soul mates with or without help from the man they jokingly called the Dogfather.

"And if you think my standards are high?" Molly gave a soft hoot. "No one on earth could be good enough for me in my father's eyes."

Pru laughed. "You might be right about that. Still, you're not right about me not wanting you to date. You are totally allowed."

"Good to have your permission." Molly picked up a peach-colored top with holes where the shoulders should be. "Could this style go away, please?" It was always easier to joke with Pru than talk about things like dating.

"Mom."

Or not, if Pru wanted to stay on topic. Relentless little thing. "Honey, don't push Grandpa into trying to fix me up. I can do my own dirty work."

"But will you?" she challenged.

Maybe. After…the weekend. The trip to the Outer Banks that she and Pru planned was much more than the "girls' getaway" they told the family. It was…the talk. The truth. The time to tell all.

At the thought, Molly swallowed and shifted her gaze to a pile of sweaters on a post-Christmas sale table. "Were you thinking of something like that for the trip?"

Pru studied her mother for a moment, but then turned to the table of sweaters. "This is pretty." She picked up a soft heather-gray pullover and held it against her narrow frame.

"If you're a nun," Molly said, hating the dreary thing.

"Or if you appreciate a classic," Pru retorted, making Molly smile. "Can I try this on, Mom?"

Molly had long ago accepted that she and her daughter had polar-opposite tastes in clothes. And decorating. And food. And movies. And how to organize a pantry, library, or to-do list. For Pru, rules and structure made the world go round. And Molly couldn't love her any more for it if she tried.

"Of course you should try it on," Molly said, getting a kick of maternal affection that was as instinctive as breathing around her daughter. "I'm going to look around."

"At expensive handbags?"

"At sweaters for our trip," she promised.

"Good idea." Pru leaned closer. "You'll want cozy clothes for when we're walking empty beaches having meaningful mother-daughter talks."

For a second, Molly just stared at her, dread at the impending weekend making her stomach feel a little queasy. "Is that *all* we're going to do? No spa time? Fancy dinners? Maybe some serious shopping?"

"Mom." Pru made a face. "You know why we're going. You *promised*."

Yes, she had. On that snowy Christmas Eve a few weeks ago when the whole family secretly orchestrated one of the best holiday surprises in history. But the real surprise was the conversation she'd had with her daughter that night, when Pru essentially said...*it's time*.

And it was time. Pru had every right to know her father's name and the circumstances of her birth. Molly had solemnly sworn that she would tell Pru everything after the holidays, which had come and gone as the days of January started to slip by with alarming speed.

"Try the sweater on, Pru. I'm not going to renege on a promise."

Satisfied, Pru turned and headed toward the dressing room, and Molly took a few steps back to that handbag.

"Isn't it beautiful?" The store owner, a middle-aged, overly made-up woman named Yvette, came out from behind the counter. "Pink really is a neutral color."

Molly shook her head. "My daughter nixed it."

That made her smile. "Since when do we listen to our daughters?"

"Since...she was born," Molly admitted. Pru had always been her sounding board, even when she was a wee little girl and the only thing anyone was sounding about was what to have for dinner.

"I noticed how close you two are when you come in here," Yvette said. "You seem to have so much fun together."

"We do." Molly couldn't help beaming. "She's special."

"Most kids that age would die a thousand deaths before shopping with their mother."

"Well, I do have the credit card," Molly joked, not wanting to brag about their extraordinary relationship. She knew she and Pru had something wonderful—a friendship and a tiny immediate family of two.

"It's more than that," the woman mused. "You're doing something right."

Molly smiled. "I hope so. Thanks."

The door opened, taking the woman's attention to a new customer and leaving Molly to meander to some tops at the front of the store, imagining what she'd pack for the trip to tell all. Not much, since she was already bringing all the emotional baggage a person needed.

Maybe Pru was right. Maybe when this was all behind her, she would start dating again.

She wanted to, no question about it. Yes, Pru was the best thing in her life, and her job as a vet with two offices was busy. But Molly often woke in the middle of the night so profoundly alone that she couldn't breathe. She ached for a man's touch, and the kind of companionship she saw her brothers all enjoying as they fell in love last year, one by one.

Pru would be off to college in five years, and then Molly would be in her late thirties. Too old to find Mr. Perfect.

She smiled, remembering the list Pru had her make a few months ago on a night when she was feeling a bit lonely, not long after Liam and Andi married in the living room of Waterford Farm. Yes, her standards were high, but how could they not be? She was surrounded by her awesome brothers and wouldn't settle for less than what they offered their wives. She wanted a decent man. A good-hearted, kind, loving, compassionate man who could hold his own at the Kilcannon dinner table.

She looked over the rack of clothes, out to the side street of Bitter Bark, which wasn't exactly bustling with tourists and townsfolk in the middle of January, but there were quite a few people—and dogs— enjoying a crisp Saturday afternoon.

Her soon-to-be sister-in-law, Chloe, engaged to Shane, should be congratulated on a job well done in building tourism. It had been Chloe's idea to have the town rename itself Better Bark for one year to brand it as a dog-friendly vacation destination in the foothills of North Carolina's Blue Ridge Mountains.

The canine push was a boon to Molly's business, of course, as one of her vet offices was a few streets away on the other side of Bushrod Square. But it also meant more bodies in town, more jobs, and more…men.

She glanced from one to the other, noticing that most of the men between thirty and fifty were with women, since Better Bark was marketed heavily to families. But there were a few. As her gaze skimmed the passersby, a man across the street caught her attention. He was walking along the square with an unleashed but extremely obedient dog, both of them moving in concert.

Someone like that, she thought. With broad shoulders and a confident stride that matched his dog's. A strong jaw and close-cropped hair, who was both clean-cut and sexy. He paused for a minute, right in Molly's line of vision, adjusting a navy wool jacket so it sat more comfortably on his shoulders in a move that was…oddly familiar.

She watched as he interacted with the dog, getting him to sit, then reaching in his pocket for a treat. She couldn't tell the breed from here, only that it was a mix and beautifully trained. Lab and Staffy, maybe.

But for a moment, Molly forgot she was a vet and remembered she was a woman. The man angled his head, then turned, glancing in the direction of this section of storefronts. She wanted him to come closer, maybe head into the sandwich shop across the street, then she'd go in with Pru and strike up a conversation about the dog. One thing could lead to…something.

He started walking toward her, making her heart kick up enough to be a little embarrassing. She was staring at a perfect stranger, at a…

Or *was* he a stranger? Frowning, she watched him walk, swipe back his hair, look around, adjust that jacket again. He was too far away to make out his features, but there was something oddly familiar about him. Had he been to Waterford? Adopted the dog from the canine rescue and training facility her family now ran? Or brought the animal into her office?

Not possible she would forget a man that effortlessly attractive.

She watched as he crossed the street and came closer, and she could finally see the square strong line of his jaw, the deep ebony of his hair and lashes, the shape of his…

She sucked in a breath, all of the blood suddenly draining from her head.

Trace Bancroft.

He turned just then and disappeared into the hardware store, leaving Molly gripping the rack of clothing for support, dizzy and stunned and blinking away the ghost she'd just seen.

Of course, it was impossible. Trace was dead. Her mother had never succeeded in her efforts to track him down, but when Pru was very little, not even two, Annie Kilcannon had come into Molly's room with the first and only concrete information they'd ever had on him.

She had it "on very good authority" that Trace had been killed in a bar fight in West Virginia. She didn't have any details or information, but Molly hadn't cared. In fact, she'd felt no sadness at this news, only relief.

In the years since, Molly had gotten totally comfortable with the notion that Pru's father was dead. When pressed, she told very close friends over the years that Pru's father had passed away, though she hadn't revealed his name or that he was from Bitter Bark.

As her mother had predicted, her family forgot all about the secret of Pru's father, or at least, they never mentioned it. Molly knew in her heart that her mother had taken their secret to her far-too-early grave. But once Pru found out his name, she'd probably do research and learn that—

"What do you think?"

She spun around at Pru's question, rooting for stability and sense when it all seemed to disappear at the sight of one man. She blinked, seeing her daughter in the sunlight, her hair that same deep, near black as...the man she'd just seen.

Pru's shoulders shook in a silent laugh. "Wow, based on the look that says you might heave, I'm gonna say it's a no."

She actually might heave, if that had been who she thought he was.

"Mom?"

"Oh, I'm sorry, Pru. It's...it's...it's the color of dull," she said, forcing herself to be normal and sarcastic, not a shell-shocked lunatic who saw ghosts on the street.

Pru tugged on the bottom of the sweater, which, in truth, was lovely and, yes, classic. "I kind of like it."

"Well, okay," Molly said brightly, knowing she sounded fake and her cheeks were probably bright red but hoping Pru thought it was all because of sweater-hate.

"Are you?" Pru stepped closer.

"Am I what?"

"Okay." She searched Molly's face as if looking for an explanation. "You look weird."

Because I just saw a dead man. "I'm fine. It's hot in here." She glanced over her shoulder at the window as if longing for an escape but really hoping for a glimpse that would confirm she was wrong about who she thought she saw.

"Oh, come on, Mom. You think I don't know?"

Oh Lord. Did she? "Know...what?"

"That you really want that designer bag."

Relief swamped Molly. "I do like it," she said, seizing on the subject change.

"So get it. Maybe you *will* have a date one of these days."

"Yeah, maybe." Wanting to only stop thinking about that man, Molly spun around to the purse and picked up the tag. "Ugh. Too rich for my blood. But you should definitely get the sweater."

"I don't look like a nun?"

Molly took a good long time staring at her daughter, at her slender body that would soon blossom even more, and at her sweet face that was much more Kilcannon than anything else. This child, this miracle, this gift.

Channeling her inner Annie Kilcannon, she reached forward, put both hands on Pru's cheeks, and said, "You look like the angel you are. Let's buy it."

"I love you, Mommy." She leaned closer and smacked a kiss on Molly's cheek, then turned to skip back to the dressing room. For a moment, Molly watched her near-ebony hair swing, her coltish body moving gracefully. Her words echoed, sounding very much like ones Molly had said to her own mother daily...until the last day.

"See?" Yvette said from behind the counter. "You two have something special."

"I know," Molly agreed. And hopefully, their special thing wouldn't change when she told Pru she was conceived in the doggie van by a guy who really did die in a bar fight.

She never wanted anything with Pru to change. Ever.

Chapter Four

Molly's father scanned the jam-packed dining room table, a grin reaching his blue eyes as he lifted a water glass in a mock toast. "We're reaching capacity for Wednesday night dinners," he announced. "I love it."

"Well, Mom and I won't be here for Sunday dinner," Pru said brightly, referring to the other night of the week the Kilcannon family usually ate together.

"Oh, that's right." Gramma Finnie scooted her petite frame closer to the table and to Pru. "It's your big girls' weekend at the Outer Banks. What do you have planned? A mani-pedi date? Maybe a museum or art show?"

Molly opened her mouth to answer, but Pru beat her to it. "We're going to talk, Gramma. Lots and lots of talking."

"Oh?" Gramma raised a brow behind her bifocals. "That sounds like fun."

"That sounds like hell," Liam, Molly's oldest brother, muttered from his seat next to Dad, making them all laugh.

"Anyway," Pru said, ignoring him. "We can get a

bigger table if there are more Kilcannons someday, right, Grandpa?"

Molly looked over at her daughter in time to catch her give Dad a meaningful look. Was Pru really pushing that hard for the Dogfather to do his matchmaking on her very own mother? It was a dumb plan, but the sentiment touched her.

Daniel Kilcannon loved all six of his kids equally, but Molly knew he had a very soft spot in his heart for her. He'd made enough jokes about the man who'd be good enough for Molly to know that such a man didn't exist in her dad's mind. Honestly, Molly was safe from his meddling. And, as the youngest, so was Darcy. Aidan was overseas, though he'd definitely made it clear he was thinking about getting out of the Army soon when he'd been home last month. Maybe Dad could match-make him then, but now the three oldest boys were off the market.

Truth was, if Dad should be getting dates for anyone, it should be himself. Which was about as likely as snow in July.

"That's why we built this great big dining room," Gramma said, snapping her napkin onto her lap and bringing Molly back into the conversation. "Seamus and I wanted it filled to the brim."

"And Annie and I did our part," Dad added. He shot a playful look to Garrett. "Plenty of room for high chairs, though."

"Subtle, Dad," Shane cracked.

"Really," Garrett added with a laugh, looking tanned and insanely happy next to Jessie, the woman he'd married a few weeks earlier on New Year's Eve. "We've been back from our honeymoon for two whole days, and he's pushing for grandchildren."

Jessie looked skyward, shaking her head. "Nothing really is sacred at the Kilcannon dinner table."

Molly beamed at the green-eyed, strawberry-blond beauty, remembering when Jessie was ten or eleven and a constant fixture at this table as Molly's best friend.

"You know, Jess," she said, "sometimes it's like you never left." Although their childhood friendship seemed like a lifetime or two ago, Jessie Curtis Kilcannon's marriage to Garrett meant she was back forever. "I'm so happy you came back to Waterford, Jess."

"Me, too," Garrett added with a wink to his bride.

Jessie smiled easily, completely part of the Kilcannon clan now. "Maybe after my first book comes out, Daniel," she said in answer to Dad's unsubtle hint. "Until then, the next wedding is April eighteenth. Pressure Shane and Chloe."

Those two shared a look of mock dismay. "You sure you want to marry into this mess?" Shane asked his fiancée in a stage whisper.

"Extremely," Chloe assured him.

"Well, I did my part to fill the table." Liam put his arms around his pregnant wife, Andi, seated on his right, and his stepson, Christian. The six-year-old was always as close to Liam as he could get, and Molly would bet a million bucks that Christian's beloved German shepherd, Jag, was at his feet.

Inching back to take a peek, Molly confirmed that guess, spying the big dog with his face flat on the floor, staring at Rusty, Dad's setter and constant companion. Despite Jag's imposing physique, Rusty was situated under the head of the table, his paws crossed, his head up, his message clear: *I'm in charge*. Under Darcy's feet, Kookie, the crazy Shih Tzu, snoozed, unconcerned about the rest of her pack.

"It's getting crowded below deck, too," Molly joked, smiling at the beasts they all loved so much.

"That's why we left Lola in the kennels," Garrett said, nodding to Shane across the table. "I put her in with Ruby since it's so crowded in there."

"Good call," Shane replied. "While you were on your honeymoon and Lola stayed with us? Those two were inseparable."

"The kennels *are* crowded," Dad noted. "We don't have a spare inch over there."

"Don't complain about booming business," Shane said. "That was always a big side benefit of the Better Bark campaign." He glanced at Chloe with pride. "Which, folklore has it, was actually my idea."

Chloe laughed, pushing back some long, dark hair to give Shane an elbow. "You *inspired* the idea," she clarified. "But if you want to change history to win some imaginary competition, go right ahead."

"I already won," he said under his breath, leaning close to her.

"Y'all are killin' me," Darcy said on a sweet chime of laughter. "Some people want to be single forever."

"You do not," Shane fired back.

Darcy sliced him with a look, lifting her delicate chin to look down an aquiline nose. In a family of stunners, Darcy was quite possibly the most beautiful of them all. She didn't know it, though, at least not in the way Shane did. They constantly ribbed each other, too.

"You don't," Shane insisted. "You just haven't met the right guy."

"Too much of the world to see, dear brother. Too many people to meet and experiences to have." She practically sang the mantra that made Darcy the tumbleweed she was. Here for a few months, then on a trip somewhere, then back, and gone again, usually with her close cousin, Ella, in tow.

"Too many dogs to groom," Liam added, giving her a serious big brother look. "You were wall-to-wall in there today, Darce, and every one came out as pretty as you are."

"Oh, anyone can do my job around here." She flicked off the compliment. "It's not like I'm some super-talented dog whisperer like the rest of you."

Dad gave her a look to stop that modesty. "You could be, though, Darcy. You know we're desperate for good trainers with Allison leaving. We're literally turning business away."

Shane grunted and faked a dagger to his heart, expressing what they all felt—a true investment in the family business.

In the little more than three years since Dad had the idea to transform the homestead and property into an elite canine rescue and training facility, Waterford Farm had grown exponentially, thanks to all of their hard work and determination. Dad's idea might have been a way to bring his far-flung pack home and heal the grief that cut them all in half when Mom died, but it turned out to be brilliant and lucrative.

Five of the six Kilcannon kids lived in Bitter Bark now, and they each had a role in the business. Darcy's grooming shop might not have been as high profile as the others, but it was as important, and it brought outsiders to Waterford every day, which increased the training business and rescue operation.

"We need trainers, Dad," Shane added, lifting his fork. "We've had dozens of requests for service dogs that can be certified by a national service dog organization. I know it can take a few years to train service dogs, but it's really the one end of the business we don't have covered."

"My rescue operations are going gangbusters," Garrett said. "Did you see those golden pups Marie brought in the other day?"

"Oh my God, so cute," Darcy exclaimed, balling up her hands. "I wanted to *eat* them."

"They are therapy dogs in the making," Shane agreed.

"Therapy dogs aren't service dogs," Dad said.

"I know that." Shane leaned forward. "But in two years, they could be. With the right trainer doing one-on-one or one-on-two intense, focused training. That someone isn't me."

Liam nodded. "Hey, I wouldn't mind another set of hands on the law enforcement end, too. We've got cops and dogs lined up for months of training, even in winter."

"Maybe Aidan really will come home," Garrett said. "He sure sounded like he wasn't going to re-up when his enlistment is up this year."

Dad nodded thoughtfully. "He hasn't made that decision, though."

"You train trainers, Shane," Andi said. "Don't you ever find someone who stands out and could be brought on board to start a service dog program?"

"I've had a few, but they were either not from around here or didn't want to make a two-year commitment. It takes a long time and an incredible bond, especially if you're training a dog for the blind or a specific illness."

Dad put down his dinner roll, frowning in thought. "Funny this would come up," he said. "Because I ran into a guy in town today who was exactly that kind of trainer."

"Really?" Garrett turned to him. "Is he looking for a job?"

Dad angled his head, considering how to answer that. "He's looking for...something."

The vague answer intrigued most of them. Not Christian, who was trying to secretly slip food to Jag, and not Gramma and Pru, who were having their own quiet conversation, not that interested in Waterford Farm business. But her father had everyone else's attention.

"Turns out he's recently out of prison."

Now he had Gramma's attention and definitely Pru's. "An ex-con?" she asked. "I don't think so, Grandpa."

Dad's look was stern. "Don't judge people, Prudence."

"Sorry," she muttered, glancing at Molly, who happened to agree with her father and was long used to sharing the discipline of her daughter. Tag-teaming her had obviously worked, since Pru had lived in this very house for the first six years of her life and had turned out mostly magnificent.

"In many prisons," her father continued, "there's a program called—"

41

"Puppies Behind Bars," Shane interjected enthusiastically, inching closer. "I know it well. They do amazing work and put out some truly impressive therapy and, in some cases, service dogs."

"Exactly," Dad said. "I bumped into this…young man at Linda May's bakery."

Molly smiled at the "young man" phrase that Dad had hesitated to say, probably looking for the right, nonjudgmental word. Her father wouldn't say anything negative about anyone, and she loved him for it.

"We should talk to him," Liam said, gesturing at Dad with his fork. "See what he can do. I've had more than a few police officers and sheriff's deputies mention the program to me. They pick the most reformed prisoners, or they get reformed after working with the dogs."

"Of course," Shane added. "Training therapy dogs *is* therapy."

"That's what I think, but…" Dad took a sip of water, while the rest of them were silent and waiting for more.

"But what?" Garrett prompted when Dad didn't finish. "We don't have issues with someone who's served time."

"We just need a rock-solid trainer," Liam said.

"And this guy is." Dad ran a finger along the water glass, thinking. "But perhaps not confident enough to walk into a place like Waterford, even though his dog is sick."

Molly put her fork down. "He has a sick dog? What's wrong?"

"My guess is lepto," Dad said. "But I can't be sure."

The symptoms of leptospirosis flipped through her head. "Lethargic? Drinking a lot? Vomiting and urination?"

"Uh, excuse me," Pru interjected. "Eating dinner here."

Gramma Finnie gave a look over her bifocal rims. "Aye, lass. Take the doctoring to the vet office, please."

"But a dog is sick, Gramma." Molly turned back to Dad, her focus on a dog that could be wandering around with lepto. "Was the guy in the woods or camping recently? Somewhere the dog could have had a drink of contaminated water?"

"That's possible," Dad said, sounding purposefully vague. "Dog was well trained, though. Amazing, really."

"Breed?" Molly asked, knowing that would affect treatment and how the dog would handle the illness.

"Mixed. Staffy. Maybe a little Lab in the blood. But a gorgeous dog," Dad added. "Very regal and warm. Meatball."

"We're eating ham, Grandpa," Christian chimed in. "But we had meatballs at home last night."

Dad chuckled. "Meatball is the dog's name."

That got a belly laugh from the little boy. Everyone had to smile, though they'd heard every imaginable dog name at this place.

"Actually, I'm not sure about lepto, and I asked him to come and see you, Molly."

"Sure. Here or at the office in town. I'm happy to look at the dog."

Dad's lips pressed together, and he shook his head slowly. "Not sure if he'll do that, though I offered to take Meatball in for observation, only for a few days, but…" Again, that vague unfinished sentence that was so unlike Molly's father.

"But what?" she asked.

Dad exhaled. "He's lived in Bitter Bark as a kid," he finally said. "And he's hit hard times. I really think he's ashamed to take what might seem like a handout."

The very first thread of worry wove up through Molly's belly, featherlight and barely noticeable, like the opening note of a song she didn't remember or recognize, but she would if she heard more. A song she didn't like.

"Who is this guy?" Garrett asked. "You say he's a local?"

"Long-ago local. Served his time for a crime up in West Virginia and has been gone ten, fifteen years now."

West Virginia? That worry thread tightened a little, adding pressure on her chest and the first real tangible thought that…no, that was impossible. It was her imagination. The pressure of the talk this weekend.

"What's the guy's name?" Liam asked. "Do we know him?"

"Possibly," Dad said, his attention shifting to his food. "Not sure if he wants his name or past bandied about town."

"This isn't town," Shane reminded him.

"Anything you tell us won't leave this table, Daniel," Chloe assured her future father-in-law. "Do you think it's the new dog program that brought him back?"

"I don't know," Dad said. "But I told him we could treat his dog, do a workup, and administer some fluids or antibiotics if needed, and that my girl is the best vet this side of the state."

"Thanks, Dad," Molly muttered, the words caught in a throat that had gotten increasingly tighter.

"But he didn't want to take me up on that."

Why not? Her palms felt damp, too, and the sight of that man she'd seen on Saturday was flashing in her head like a neon warning sign. A man with a Labrador-Staffordshire terrier mix who was definitely…regal.

I have it on good authority that Trace Bancroft is dead. Killed in a bar fight in West Virginia. She could still hear her mother's voice, whispering the words over a sleeping baby Pru.

"What did he do time for?" Liam asked. "Can you say?"

Dad swallowed his bite. "Murder."

That brought every mouth, fork, and person in the room to a frozen halt.

"Well, manslaughter," he added. As if *that* made it okay.

"Murder?" Pru's voice rose along with her shoulders and eyebrows. "*Grandpa.*"

"He served his time," Dad said. "Man's gotta have a new life once he's rehabilitated."

No one answered him, as every one of the eleven other people in the room let that sink in and maybe formed their own opinions. Molly tried to breathe.

"I expect more tolerance from you, Prudence," Dad said, breaking the moment of silence.

Her daughter squirmed a little and glanced at Molly for help, but she was in no shape to chime in on a life lesson at the moment.

"'Kay, Grandpa. Sorry." Her color rose, reminding

everyone at the table that Pru didn't like to break rules, especially those set by her beloved grandfather.

"Really, Dad," Shane said, jumping in to give his niece a reprieve. "We ought to know his name. No one in here is gonna rat him out all over town."

"He doesn't hide his past," Dad said. "He told me straight up over a cup of coffee. It's that…" He looked from one of his children to another. "Apparently, some of you went to school with him."

Oh God. Sweat tingled on Molly's neck, and her arms went numb. It wasn't possible. It wasn't. Her heart hammered so hard, she couldn't believe the rest of them didn't hear it, but the way they all moved and turned, maybe they had. Blood was thrumming in her brain and swishing so loud, she actually felt light-headed.

It wasn't possible that—

"I got the door!" Crystal, the housekeeper who always made them Wednesday night dinner, called from the kitchen.

The *door*. That's what was banging. Not her heart. Not her poor, terrified heart.

"I'm happy to talk to this guy," Shane said. "I don't care if I knew—"

"Excuse me, Dr. K?" Crystal came into the room and stepped close to the head of the table. "There's a man with a very sick dog at the door. He only wants to see you and no one else."

Dad was up before Crystal finished her sentence, and Molly felt every other head at the table turn toward her. Of course, when there was a vet emergency, she'd be up, too. Running to the door, caring about the animal, ready to do what needed to be done.

"Don't you think you should go out there?" Liam asked, looking quizzically at Molly's face, which was no doubt as white as the tablecloth.

"He said no one else." Her voice came out like she was being held under water, which was exactly how she felt.

"Molly!" Dad's voice bellowed into the house. "We have an emergency!"

She launched to her feet, a little unsteady, vaguely aware that more chairs pushed out to follow. She moved on autopilot, with one thought: *I have it on good authority that Trace Bancroft is dead.*

She stepped through the open door to see her father crouching over a dog. A man in a dark jacket stood with his back to her.

"Exactly when did this start?" her father asked, moving his hands over the dog's belly.

It couldn't be him. *It cannot be him.*

"What's going on?" She croaked the question, making the man straighten and slowly turn to her. His gaze was dark, direct, and one she'd seen in her memory a million times.

A sharp stab of shock nearly pushed her back into the house.

"GDV!" her father announced.

Molly stood, utterly frozen, the acronym for a deadly condition echoing in her head.

"We have to operate now, or this dog is going to die."

She blinked at the man, trying to process her father's words and the pure impossibility of the situation, but nothing made sense.

Pru's father was standing in front of her.

"Molly," Trace mouthed her name, raw desperation in his eyes. "Please save my dog."

Of course. Of course. She wasn't sure if she said the words or thought them, but somehow, by the grace of God, Molly flew into action.

Save the dog. Save the dog.

Save the dog.

She couldn't think beyond that.

Chapter Five

She remembered him. Exactly as he'd feared.

The realization rocked Trace a little, making him more uncomfortable than he'd already been. But then two men came barreling out of the house behind Molly, headed toward Meatball, who lay writhing in pain with a belly so swollen he looked like he could give birth to a giraffe any minute.

Trace cut them off as he realized they were going to pick up his dog. "Whoa, whoa. I can get him." He tried to muscle past the taller one, who shot a quick glance at him.

"We're professionals," the man said. "We'll get this dog into surgery while Molly and Dad start tests and prep the room. You wait."

The two men moved in perfect concert, raising the seventy-pound dog as if he weighed nothing. But more than that, they lifted him with care and tenderness. That alone made Trace take a step back and let out a long, agonizing exhale.

This had been the right decision, after all.

Just then, a third guy joined them, and in the yellow light of the porch, Trace caught a quick glance of a man he recognized. Older, bigger, but that was definitely Garrett Kilcannon, who was in Trace's high school class. Different worlds, but the same class.

Garrett added his arms to the human stretcher, easily taking hold of Meatball's horrifically distended middle. With one word and a view ahead, he ordered the three of them to move in unison, the trio carrying Meatball away without so much as a glance his way.

Trace froze for a moment, still reeling from the panic of realizing Meatball was really, really sick. His instinct might be to beat them all away from his dog, but this wasn't Huttonsville, and they weren't hurting his boy. They were saving him.

He followed them, taking a quick scan of his surroundings. He'd never been to Waterford Farm, of course, but always imagined it was big, beautiful, and idyllic. Even in the dark, he knew he'd imagined correctly.

The other day, when he'd had that unexpected conversation with Dr. Kilcannon, he'd found out the family had transformed the property into some kind of big-deal canine facility, which was obvious from the huge training pen and sizable kennel. There were other structures scattered around the area, but the men carrying his dog followed a path around a fence and headed toward a small, well-lit building.

He could hear them talking to one another, taking the two steps up to a small, covered porch. On the clapboard, a hand-carved sign read Kilcannon Veterinarian.

The door opened, and he saw Molly inside hastily tying on a scrubs-style top as she ushered them in. She stepped aside to let them pass, and as they did, she peered into the darkness, a slight frown pulling at her features.

He wasn't sure if she could see him or not, since he hung back in the shadows, but he could see her. She'd always been pretty, but grown-up Molly Kilcannon was nothing less than beautiful. She still had rich brown hair that gleamed with hints of red in the soft curls. Her eyes narrowed, and he was too far away to see, but he remembered them as constantly shifting from brown to green, like those mood rings his mother used to wear. Her face was heart-shaped and delicate, but she carried herself with confidence, with the security a girl who'd grown up with protective brothers and a big, fancy house would naturally have.

She'd made him laugh that night...and made him crazy.

Way too crazy. No wonder she'd come out of her house and looked at him like he was Satan himself, invading her world and dragging his dog...

His dog.

Meatball was all that mattered. Not some long-ago chilly night when he and Molly had sex in the back of a minivan. He stepped forward, into the light, seeing her whole body stiffen as he came into her view.

"Is he going to be okay?" he asked, not caring that he sounded pathetic. If anything happened to that dog, a piece of Trace would die, too. The only piece of him left after fourteen years in hell.

"I don't know," she said, her voice as icy as the January air around him. "We'll do our best to help him."

Minimally encouraged by that, he took a few steps closer, coming to the raised porch, looking up a foot or two to meet her gaze. Her eyes were more brown than green tonight. More mad or scared than...than the last time he looked into those eyes.

"Do you know what's wrong?" he asked, aching for one word of reassurance that Meatball would survive this.

"With this? Everything."

What the hell did that mean? "What's going to happen to my dog?"

"Molly!" a man's voice—Dr. Kilcannon, he presumed—bellowed into the night.

"You can wait in here," she said. "This might take a while."

With that, she turned and disappeared, leaving the door open and Trace standing with his jaw unhinged.

What might take a while? Surgery. Garrett said they were taking him into surgery. Would that save Meatball?

Letting out a grunt, he landed a booted foot on the wooden porch with more force than necessary. Inside looked like a typical warm and friendly reception area in a vet's office. But he glanced to the porch at a small bench where he imagined patients—or their owners—waited on warmer days.

He considered sitting in the cold like the outsider he was. He hadn't wanted to come here, not at all. Even after a candid conversation with a kindly vet who was the first person in town to make him feel welcome, Trace didn't want to come to Waterford Farm.

And when that man mentioned that his daughter Molly was also a vet? That he thought maybe the dog had a little problem he called...lepto something? Even the worry of Meatball being sick wasn't enough to get him here at first. The last person he wanted to see in Bitter Bark was, well, the last person he had seen in Bitter Bark.

And now Meatball's life was in her hands. His question had been simple: What's wrong? What was the diagnosis? What did it mean? Would Meatball live? *What's wrong?*

Her answer baffled him. *Everything.*

A chilly wind blew down from the Blue Ridge Mountains, cutting through the thin coat he'd picked up at Goodwill the day he'd walked out of Huttonsville Correctional Center, a free man. Shit. Forget pride. He was freezing and needed to accept Molly's invitation to wait inside, no matter how unenthusiastically it was issued.

He stepped into the golden glow of the undersized room, closing the door behind him, letting the warmth penetrate his bones. On one side was a desk surrounded by a granite-topped counter and on the other, a waiting area with two chairs and a table. Taking a seat, he stared at the closed door he assumed led to treatment rooms.

The only sound was a bubbling fish tank, where a lone betta swam from one side to the other, reminding him of some of the inmates pacing the exercise grounds.

Above that, the wall was covered with framed pictures of dogs—all Irish setters, he noticed right away—with some of the yellow-tinged photos looking like they dated back to the fifties. Almost all of them were posed in front of a yellow clapboard house, which he was pretty sure was the house he'd just left.

Trace let his head fall into his hands, closing his

eyes and not moving as time ticked by. Waiting for time to move had been how he'd spent the better part of the last thirteen and a half years. Until the dogs. Until Meatball. Before that, prison had been exactly the way people described it, no different than the life lived by that fish.

Doing time. An action of complete inaction. He had no idea how long he sat there, eyes closed, waiting.

"GDV, is it?"

He looked up, not expecting the female voice, and even more surprised that he hadn't heard the front door open.

A girl, a little slip of a thing with dark hair pulled severely off her face, stood in the doorway, massive eyes the color of oxidized copper staring at him.

"What is that?" he asked, suddenly remembering the letters Dr. Kilcannon had used when he yelled for help. "What is GDV?"

"What your dog has. At least that's what one of my uncles said when he came back in."

Trace frowned, sitting up straighter to look at the door that led to the offices. Had those men marched right by him while he sat here *doing time*?

"There's a back way out," the girl said, clearly a mind reader. "But Uncle Liam stayed with them to do the anesthesia and tubes."

Anesthesia and tubes. On Meatball.

He shook off the worry and tried to place all these people, but the acronym was the loudest question in his head. "What does that mean? GDV?"

"Gastric dilatation and volvulus," she said, the impossibly big words rolling out of her little mouth with ease. "Most people call it bloat."

54

"Oh, bloat." Trace stabbed his hand in his hair and dragged it back. "That doesn't sound too bad. Like a bad stomachache."

"Way worse," she said. "It can be fatal."

The word smacked him, making him blink at her. "Fatal?"

She gave an apologetic smile, revealing a flash of what looked like cobalt-colored braces. "Your dog's in good hands, I promise."

He nodded at that, not sure what else he could say to this little intruder. But she didn't move from the doorway, her eyes locked on him as if he were some kind of weird animal in a zoo instead of a bereft man in a vet's waiting room.

"He must have eaten something pretty serious," she finally said. "Usually, they get into a whole bag of kibble or food for humans, like popcorn. He might have gulped air or even played too hard after eating a lot. It doesn't take much for the stomach to flip."

"Flip?" He tried to visualize that, and failed. "What does that mean?"

"The stomach gets all blown out of shape from food, and it loops around..." She made a twisting motion with her hands. "And flips." She turned that same hand. "That's when it blocks the flow of gas and stuff and can trap the spleen."

Holy shit. That did sound serious.

She took a tentative step inside, eyeing him as if she were having some kind of internal battle over her curiosity and the need to get closer. "They want to throw up, but they can't because the stomach is stretched."

He stared at her, mesmerized by this child who

knew so much about veterinarian medicine, but his mind kept going back over the last few hours as Meatball had gone downhill. "Yeah, yeah, you're right. He ate a lot today. I got some dog food, and he loved it. Hadn't eaten for a while…" His voice trailed off, realizing that sounded like he hadn't been feeding his dog. "But not 'cause I was starving him."

"Because he had lepto symptoms, right?"

Despite himself, he let out a dry laugh. She couldn't have been eleven or twelve, but she was so serious. So strong. So…something he couldn't pin down. Familiar? He wasn't sure, but the effect was oddly comforting.

In fact, bathed in this sweet light of a welcoming lobby, resting on this leather chair, listening to a wisp of a girl explain complicated veterinarian issues, he felt…okay.

"Anyway," she said. "That's why his stomach got big. Was it huge?"

He held out his hands in front of his own belly like Santa Claus himself. "Massive."

"Oh." She took a few steps closer, a mix of pity and knowledge on her elfin features. "That's not good. When the stomach expands, it can actually squish the lungs."

He wasn't even able to respond to that. Meatball's lungs were being *squished*?

"Of course, it depends on how long he was sick," she said quickly. "They might get in there before any of the, you know, squishing goes on."

He didn't know. He didn't *want* to know. He just wanted Meatball to survive. "It went on for a few hours," he said. "Is that bad?"

"I don't know," she said. "I'm not a vet."

"Coulda fooled me, kid."

That made her smile again as she closed the door behind her, never taking her gaze off him.

After a second, she perched on the edge of the other chair as if she wanted to be there, but might need to jump up and run at any second.

"I'm Pru."

He frowned, not sure what she said. "Umproo? Is that another dog disease?"

"No, but that's funny. Umproo." She giggled the word. "I meant my name is Prudence Kilcannon. Everyone calls me Pru."

He tried to place her in what he knew was a big family. Kilcannon as her last name meant her father was one of the brothers, the ones who took Meatball away. Yeah, she said one was her uncle, so—

"What's your name?"

There was a directness about her that was both refreshing and off-putting, and there was no way to ignore her. "Trace," he said. "Trace Bancroft."

She swallowed, that subtle inner strength shining through her eyes again as he could see she was weighing all the things she could say next, but wasn't sure which to pick. "Well, welcome to Waterford, Mr. Bancroft."

He almost smiled, and not because he couldn't remember the last time anyone called him that. Lawyers and a judge, but that's about it. "Thanks."

"We're the largest canine training and rescue facility in the state." She sounded like a brochure, but such a cute one that he smiled.

"I heard. I met…" He tipped his head to the door.

"Dr. Kilcannon," she supplied. "He's my grandfather."

As he suspected. "He's a nice guy."

"Oh, the nicest," she said. "Everyone loves him." Her eyes sparked with pride, giving him a weird kick of…what was that? Jealousy? Because he'd never had a grandfather everyone loved? Only a loony-bin mother and a father mired in shame.

"They call him the Dogfather."

"The Dogfather?" he asked. "Like the Godfather?"

"Only we're Irish," she said with a huge grin that let him see the braces were actually clear, bound by bright blue rubber bands. "And he doesn't, you know, put hits on people. But he does pull some strings to get people to do what he wants."

"Yeah, I can see that." He glanced at that office door that stayed firmly shut.

"I know you're worried," she said softly. "That's why I came over here."

He drew back at the unexpected kindness. "That wasn't necessary." But it was really, really sweet.

"I thought it was the right thing to do."

"Thanks," he muttered again, taking in the strange little creature. "You always do the right thing?"

"Always," she answered without a millisecond of hesitation. "They don't call me General Pru for nothing."

That made him let out a wry laugh. "General Pru."

With her little hands clasped like a high school principal, she leaned closer, all serious. "I keep this whole clan marching straight, you know?"

He laughed again, shaking his head. "How old are you?"

"I turned thirteen in August."

"You seem older." He frowned, inching back. "Or maybe younger." What did he know about thirteen-year-olds anymore? He'd been on the inside since before this kid was born.

"Gramma Finnie says I'm small but mighty and wise beyond my years."

"She's right," he said, realizing that for about two minutes, he actually hadn't thought about Meatball. "Thanks for the distraction, Umproo."

The nickname made her laugh again. "I know what it feels like when a dog is sick." Reaching out her hand, she touched his jacket sleeve for one second, startling him. Contact with anyone was still so foreign. He looked at her narrow hand, so precious and perfect against his cheap, rough jacket. That was foreign, too. But, like everything else about her, comforting.

"I come over here a lot when people are waiting, so I—"

The office door popped open, followed by a loud gasp.

Trace whipped around to see Molly, her eyes wide in horror. "What are you doing?" she demanded.

"I'm only trying to make him feel better, Mom."

It took a second to realize Molly was talking to Pru and not him. That she was...*Mom*? So Molly was this girl's mother?

He shook off this news, more focused on the blood splattered on Molly's scrubs than her personal life. "How's Meatball?" he asked.

She glanced at him, then Pru, then him again. "Just a second," she said stiffly, as if trying to center herself. "Pru, you need to go back to the house now. It's getting late. Uncle Shane will drive you home. I'll be home later, but it's a school night."

He stole a glimpse at the girl, catching the dismay in her eyes. "I was just...jeez, okay. No need to be weird, Mom."

"Pru."

"She wasn't bothering me," he said, feeling an inexplicable need to rise to her defense. But it wasn't Pru who needed defending. He could see the look of disgust in Molly Kilcannon's eyes as she took him in.

Although no one in Bitter Bark knew where he'd spent the fourteen years, since his mother moved away right after his sentencing in West Virginia, Trace had told her father. No doubt Daniel Kilcannon had filled her in, and she didn't want her precious daughter anywhere near an ex-con.

"Bye...Mr. Bancroft." Pru backed out, giving her mother one more look. "Hope Meatball's okay."

Molly let out the softest sigh, one that he couldn't begin to interpret. Impatience skittered all over him as he turned back to her, anxious for news.

"Well?" he demanded.

She waited until the door closed tightly behind Pru. Which, if you asked him, was a pretty shitty bedside manner.

"We tried to release gas by puncturing his stomach with a needle, but when that didn't work, we managed to get one X-ray and could see we had to operate."

He cringed a little, knowing Meatball was a big baby with zero ability to handle pain. Clipping his nails sent him into a whining frenzy.

"His heart rate was two twenty with occasional

VPCs." She held up her hands at his look of confusion. "Premature heart contractions."

He closed his eyes for a second, hating the sound of that. Of all of this.

"We had to do surgery."

"Did you fix him?"

"My father and I did," she said, holding up her hands as if to say those narrow fingers alone couldn't have done a job like that. Only then did he see the blood rimmed around the arms of her surgical scrubs.

At what must have been a look of horror, she eased her arms back. "I didn't take the time to change, sorry."

Why would she apologize? She'd been that deep into Meatball's guts. His heart turned over, a wave of affection and gratitude and admiration nearly knocking him over.

"We were able to get in there and flip his stomach back into proper position," she told him.

"Oh, thank God."

"But there was a problem with his spleen."

And he fell down that roller coaster again. "What kind of problem?"

"We had to take most of it out. The GDV obstructed blood flow, and the organ died."

"The organ." The words came out like a groan. "But not the dog."

She slowly shook her head. "He can survive nicely without a spleen. Meatball is in recovery now. Still coming off the anesthesia."

He finally sighed, letting his head drop and his eyes close again. "I don't know what to say."

"It's our job."

He lifted his head, studying her, finally able to think about this woman who he'd once—one night only—had known so intimately. That girl had been so light and bright and wild and wonderful. With a dry wit and quick tongue. More like her daughter than…

"We'll keep him overnight and under close observation for a few days," she said.

"A few days?" Oh *hell*.

"He'll need to be on fluids and pain meds. Also antibiotic injections, of course. There are some numbers we'll run overnight to make sure all is well in there. We have to watch his stomach. It wasn't the best color, and we need to monitor his vital signs very carefully and slowly introduce regular food back into his diet."

So much to be done, he couldn't even imagine how he'd pay for it. Or how that poor animal would endure it all.

"Okay," he finally said. "Can I see him?"

She hesitated a quick second before nodding. "Yes, yes, of course. My father and brother are back there with him." She gestured to the door as an invitation, but she didn't move.

Despite her cool attitude, he wanted to thank her. Wanted to acknowledge this weirdness between them and somehow clear the air, especially if Meatball would be in her care for a few days.

But how?

"I had a nice chat with your daughter," he said, hoping that would soften her a bit.

Instead, he could have sworn every drop of blood in her cheeks drained straight away.

"She knows an awful lot about vet medicine."

Still pale, she nodded very slowly, and the complete silence threw him.

"She seems really smart and...looks like you."

Jeez, how deep would she let him dig himself without even responding? A few awkward seconds ticked by, answering his question. *Very* deep.

"Anyway, thank you," he managed, walking by her.

He pulled open the door, assuming he'd find his way since this ice queen wasn't going to tell him a thing. He faced a small area with more doors and hallways and no clue where the hell he should go.

He turned as the reception area door was closing, in time to catch Molly Kilcannon drop her head into her hands and give in to a full-body shudder. *Really? Now she shows emotion and compassion and a human side?*

The door closed, and he stood there, stone-still, trying to understand...anything.

He picked a corridor and started walking to the light coming from one room, trying to shake off Molly, but man, she'd needled him with that attitude, that chilliness, and the fact that she acted like he was committing some kind of crime by talking to her daughter.

He stopped midstep. He swallowed against a dry throat. He felt his heart literally cease to beat for a second.

I turned thirteen in August.

Which meant she...had been conceived fourteen years ago in....

He squeezed his eyes shut and did some quick mental math.

November.

He reached for the nearest wall, suddenly needing support because the world tilted sideways and Trace Bancroft damn near fell off.

Chapter Six

Oh, she didn't like this. She did not like this at all.

As Molly slipped out of her jacket the next morning and hooked it on the rack in the reception room, she reread the vital sign chart that Cara Lee, the nurse who'd come in for overnight duty to monitor Meatball, had just handed her.

"Eleven." Molly felt a tightening in her stomach as she stared at the PCV percentage. "That's not good."

"Poor guy had a rough night." Cara Lee narrowed blue eyes, her brows pulling as she examined Molly with the same scrutiny she'd give a sick puppy. "Looks like he wasn't the only one."

"Oh, yeah." Molly brushed back some of her hair, wild and unruly today, remembering the shadows under her eyes that had met her in the mirror that morning. "Well, I didn't expect to perform surgery last night."

"Your father said you were done by ten," Cara Lee said. "I figured you got a good night's sleep."

She figured wrong. "Not really. I stressed about the dog." And his owner. "Is he still in Special Care?"

"Of course." Cara Lee gestured toward the room on the left that served as their ICU when needed. Unlike the office in town, which used to be her father's practice, the Waterford Farm vet office was a small operation, used primarily for checking on the many dogs housed and trained at the facility. On the rare occasion they had serious treatment, they had two rooms that could be used for high-level monitoring and long-term recovery. Thank goodness, because they'd need both for this case.

"I'm going to see him now." She took a few steps and reached for the doorknob. "I don't want him to be alone long."

"Oh, he's not."

Molly felt her breath catch, already knowing what Cara Lee was about to say.

"His owner's in there."

Molly froze and slowly turned to look at the nurse. "He is?"

Cara Lee grinned at the reaction. "I know, right?" she mouthed the words. "He's *hot*."

Oh God. "Really?" The word came out like a croak. "I hadn't noticed."

They were too good of friends for Cara Lee not to lift a *you can't be serious* brow, but Molly ignored it and headed in.

Trace didn't turn when the door opened. He stood next to the large cage, both hands braced on the bars, staring down at Meatball, who moaned with every inhale and shuddered on the exhale as he slept.

Trace wore faded jeans and a white T-shirt that clung to well-developed muscles, both arms completely covered in colorful tattoos. His dark hair was tousled on top, but cut short along the neckline and around the ears. Facing his profile, she could see his jaw was clenched, and one vein in his neck throbbed in a steady beat that perfectly matched the one pounding in Molly's chest.

"He's a wreck," he murmured, still not looking at her.

For a moment, Molly wondered if he meant him or the dog.

"He's struggling," she acknowledged.

Finally, he tore his gaze from Meatball, turning his dark eyes to her, shocking her with the red rims of someone who might have been crying. Or maybe he had the same crappy night she had.

"The nurse said I should talk to you." He sounded like the very idea bothered him.

Molly lifted the paper in her hand. "Meatball's blood test shows a low PCV, or packed cell volume. That means the percentage of red blood cells to serum is low, and he might need a blood transfusion."

He murmured a curse and threaded his fingers through his hair, pulling it back and making it even more tangled. "Then what?"

"Then..." She hated to make him agonize any more. One of the many reasons she'd barely slept was shame for how she'd treated him. Even taking Pru and the past out of the picture, she should have been more compassionate. "Then there might be more surgery," she added softly. "If he doesn't respond to the transfusion, we'd have to look for a vessel that isn't ligated completely, or maybe a complication that happened during the splenectomy. Something affecting the red blood cells."

She took a few steps to the cage and carefully unlatched it, but Meatball didn't stir. His left paw was outstretched with the IV stuck in his shaved skin. Reaching in, she stroked his smooth brown belly, feeling for any new distension.

Meatball's closed eyes fluttered at the touch, and Molly drew back, looking up to meet Trace's gaze. He was silent, with agony carved on to every feature.

"He's a great dog," she said, knowing that if he were any other person on earth, she'd add a gentle touch to his arm and a lot more sympathy. He deserved that, no matter who he was. "He has very intelligent eyes," she continued. "Even as miserable as he was last night, he was sweet." His tail had thumped the operating table as if to express his trust. And she should have told his owner that last night.

She should have taken two minutes while Liam and Dad did the X-rays and pre-op tests to sit calmly with Trace to explain what they were going to do, why they had to, and what the possible outcomes were. As she would have with any other dog parent in that situation.

Instead, she'd been a stone-cold bitch to him.

"He's the best," he agreed.

"I think we can fix him up," she said. "I don't want you to worry too much."

His expression flickered, not revealing anything except that her words affected him. "I didn't think you cared much about the owners," he murmured.

Ouch. Well, she had that coming. "I do."

He repositioned himself in front of the cage, leaning closer and reaching his arm in where hers was, his skin brushing hers and sending a crackle of electricity through her. She slid her arm out and took a full step away.

"Hey, bud," he whispered. "You'll be out of this cell soon."

Cell? Molly tried not to react to that, but might have failed. One corner of Trace's lips curled in a wry smile.

"I know what you're thinking," he said softly. So softly, she wasn't sure if he was talking to her or Meatball. "It's like an elephant in the room."

Oh Lord. *Here we go.* "It…is?"

He looked directly at her. "What's protocol? What's right? Do you acknowledge the past or try to ignore it?"

Molly inhaled sharply. "I guess you—"

"I say face it head on," he interjected, saving her. "It's uncomfortable, yeah. But I think it's best to get it out there and endure the discomfort, because honesty is the most important thing."

She nodded slowly. "I was going to—"

"So, yeah. Protocol says it's okay to admit you know and I know."

He did? She waited, breath trapped, her gaze dropping over his face and landing on a cleft in his chin that looked like a man's version of the tiny dimple in her daughter's chin. *His daughter's chin.*

"I spent the last fourteen years in prison."

And all her breath came out in a whoosh. *That's* what he was talking about? "My father told me," she said. "He said that's where you've been."

He shifted his attention back to Meatball, and only then did Molly notice that for the entire conversation, he'd kept a hand on his dog's head. She stared at that

69

hand, at the size and strength of it, the dusting of dark hair and the clean, blunt-cut nails. The tats stopped at his wrists; his hands were ink-free and masculine. And, God, she remembered to this day what he could do with those hands.

"Did he tell you what for?" Trace asked.

Get a grip, Moll. He wanted to talk about prison...not Pru. She could handle prison. She could handle anything but the inevitable truth she had to tell him. Today.

"Not in great detail."

He stood up straight and let go of Meatball. "I want details," he said solemnly. "And I want them now."

"Details." She fisted her hands at her sides. Did he mean Pru now? Obviously, he had to wonder or suspect. "Details about..." She added him a questioning look.

"About when you're going to do a transfusion and what will make you decide to do surgery again. And what kind of surgery would it be. What are the risks?"

With each question, she felt herself relax a little, back in the zone of veterinary medicine, not talking about the child they shared. Still studying his expression and holding his gaze, she let out a sigh and made a decision. She would tell him later. She'd explain the process with Meatball, get the transfusion going if he needed it, and after they knew for certain whether there'd be another surgery, she'd tell him about Pru.

"Would you like to sit down in my office and have a cup of coffee?" she said. "I'll go over everything, from beginning to end. I have some pictures of his stomach from the surgery, and I can tell you where my concerns are. He's fine for now. I want to run another PCV test in an hour and then decide. We have time to talk." *And rock your world.*

He didn't answer right away. For a long moment, he held her gaze, silent. Her heart hammered so loud, it was a wonder he didn't hear it.

"Do you have any other pictures?" he whispered.

She drew back an inch, not sure she understood. "Pictures?"

"You know, baby pictures? First day of school? On Santa's lap or with her first puppy?"

"Oh." It was barely more than a breath.

"You see, I've missed so much."

She closed her eyes against the sting of tears. "Yes," she admitted. "You have."

Wally would be proud. In fact, Jim Wallace, certified shrink to the cons and officially the best friend Trace had ever had, would jump up from his chair, give a high five, and hoot out loud in the most undignified, untherapistlike way.

Trace might have made a few false starts in the conversation with Molly, mentally backing off and changing the topic without her actually realizing that's what he'd done, but he reached his end goal.

Do what needs to be done, Trace. He could hear Wally's voice. *Can't get a goal if you don't know it. It's going to make you uncomfortable, Trace. You can handle it, just do what has to be done no matter if it hurts short-term. That's how you grow. That's how you change.*

And last night, sleeping in a hovel that now legally belonged to Trace, he was plenty uncomfortable, but it was nothing like this morning waiting for Molly to show.

He'd wrestled with the facts all night. Dealt with the horror of possibly losing Meatball, which would be one of the many cruel ironies that plagued Trace's life. Like the fact that he accidentally killed a man while defending a woman. Or that he spent his life loathing his inmate father only to become an inmate himself. And the twist of fate that, after a war with the prison system that he'd ultimately won, the dog he'd been allowed to keep was at death's door a few weeks later.

And now...this. Because of the biggest mistake he'd ever made in his life, he'd missed out on a mistake he hadn't even known he'd made.

Umproo.

Of all of life's cruelties, the realization that he had a daughter took precedence and even offered a much-needed relief from worrying about Meatball. And now what? How the hell would he ever convince Molly Kilcannon to let him—with his murder rap and prison time, his inked-up body and run-down spirit—be anywhere near a little girl who was so completely and totally *perfect*?

Molly Kilcannon had all the power here.

"If you don't mind, can we take this outside?" Trace held up his coffee cup with a remarkably steady hand. "After fourteen years, I can't get enough fresh air."

"Oh, of course." Molly looked a little surprised by the request and glanced toward a coatrack in the corner of the lobby where they'd come to get coffee. "Let me get my jacket."

They put their cups down, and she reached for a pea coat on a hook.

"I'll get it," he offered, opening the jacket and holding it for her. That earned him a quick look over her shoulder. "To prove chivalry's not dead," he added. *And to stay on your good side.*

She slid into her coat and went back to get the coffee while he pulled on his Goodwill special. When she handed him the cup, he couldn't help but notice the slight tremble in her hand.

Okay, she might have the power, but she was scared. And he didn't want that, not at all.

She stepped to the desk and waited a second while the receptionist finished a call. "I'll be outside for a few minutes," Molly said. "Cara Lee's going to run another test on Meatball in a bit, and I'll want the results as soon as possible."

"Sure thing, Dr. Molly. I didn't think you were going to be here today."

She shrugged. "I'm supposed to be at the other office, but they're covering for me. I wanted to check on Meatball and talk to…" She gave him a glance. "To Trace."

It was difficult for her to actually say his name. The realization torqued him a little, but he'd become pretty good pals with humiliation over the past fourteen years. What was one more sidelong glance? He'd killed a man. He was used to the dubious looks that came along with that.

A moment later, they stepped out into the cold morning air. Trace sucked in a breath, as he did almost every time he was exposed to fresh air, especially this clean, mountain air he'd taken for granted his whole life before it was all stolen from him.

He sipped the hot coffee and let his gaze travel over the property currently bathed in winter sunshine. He hadn't been able to see details last night, and this morning, he'd been hell-bent on getting to Meatball. But now, he drank in the full glory of Waterford Farm, a sprawling place behind fancy gates he'd only ever heard about.

What those gates protected was nothing short of stunning. Foothills, covered in frost and darkened by pine forests or bare trees, rolled all the way to the horizon before giving way to the Blue Ridge Mountains in the distance. Closer to where he stood, a massive backyard went on for acres and acres, filled by a huge kennel, several outbuildings, and training pens. At the heart of it all, across a wide drive, sat a grand yellow farmhouse with green shutters and smoke puffing out of multiple chimneys. From here, the back porch was completely visible, furnished with rocking chairs and chaises, trimmed with white railings like comforting arms to hold everyone close and tight.

Molly had grown up here, he knew, with her big, happy family who now must all work at this facility they'd built.

And he'd grown up in a hole on the other side of Bitter Bark with a "missing" father and a fruit loop for a mother.

He shook off the thought and looked at a training pen where six or seven sizable dogs were running around while two people tossed orders at them and threw bright green balls that they weren't supposed to chase.

"Distraction training," he mused.

"Yes, that's exactly what they're doing today," Molly answered.

"The whole town is so dog-friendly now," he said.

"You can thank my soon-to-be sister-in-law for that." She nodded toward the two people in the pen. "That's Shane, one of my older brothers, doing the training. His fiancée came up with the idea to build tourism."

"It's nice to be able to take Meatball into stores in town," he said. "People don't even flinch that he's part pit."

She smiled and blew into her coffee cup to cool it off. "More thanks to Shane."

He took a few steps toward a grassy area, not really interested in talking about her brother, but wanting to let her set the pace of the conversation. He waited a beat, wondering if she'd be direct or coy.

"When did you figure it out?" she asked softly.

Yes. Direct. He so appreciated that. "Last night, she told me she turned thirteen in August."

She let out a long, slow sigh and led them toward a wide path where some benches were situated in the sunshine, a perfect distance to watch the training in the pen or drink in the scenery. And talk about the daughter he hadn't known he had.

"What have you told her?" he asked.

She turned to him, her eyes softening as she considered the question. "Thank you for asking that first," she said. "About her. It wasn't what I was expecting."

"What were you expecting? Demands for shared custody?" He added a dry laugh so she knew that wasn't his endgame. His goal was to know Pru, plain and simple, and not upset her life. Beyond that, he had no idea, other than to inflict the least amount of pain for everyone.

"I wasn't sure," she admitted. "And as far as what I've told her? Nothing." She paused when they reached a bench. "Oddly enough, I was planning to tell her everything this weekend." She plopped down, making the coffee splash a little on her bare hand. She wiped it as if the second of pain was nothing compared to what was evident in her eyes.

"This weekend?" He frowned, thinking about that. "Because I showed up?"

She looked up at him. "No. Because she's thirteen, and I've been beating around the bush about who her father is for a while, and it is time. She deserves the truth. But now?" She closed her eyes. "I hadn't planned on having living proof."

"What have you told your family?" he asked. "Your friends? Your...husband?" The last one was a wild guess, but he'd thought about who that might be and how he'd take to Trace. Or not.

"I'm not married," she said.

"Ever?"

She shook her head.

"You've raised her alone." He sat down next to her as the weight of that hit his shoulders.

"No, not really. I've had the entire Kilcannon clan behind me and, up until a little over three years ago, the world's greatest mother."

Her mother was dead? His heart hitched, for her

76

and little Pru. "So you had your family's help, but no one else?" While he'd skipped town, killed a man, got locked up, and left her to raise a child alone. "Shit. Sorry."

She blew out a breath, giving up on the coffee and setting the cup on the ground to turn to him. "Look, I really tried to find you. I mean, my mother did. But no one knew where you were, or your mother, either."

"My mother moved to be near me when…it all happened. And she did come back, but I guess she didn't stay long. We didn't communicate much after I was incarcerated." And really, could he blame her? His mother looked at him and saw…his father. The *other* con in the family.

"I guess I could have hired someone," Molly said, swallowing visibly. "But I was consumed with a new baby. Then, when Pru was a little over a year old, Mom told me you were killed in a bar fight in West Virginia, and I accepted that as the truth."

He snorted softly. "Where'd she hear that?"

"I never knew. She said she had it on good authority."

"Don't know how good that authority was but, like any good rumor, there's a thread of truth to it."

Her brows drew together in confusion. "You're obviously not dead."

"There was a bar, not quite a fight. A man died, but not me. The West Virginia part was right." He looked down at his hands, the *deadly weapons*, as that prosecutor had called them.

"That's why you went to jail," she surmised.

"There's a price to pay when a man dies." His voice sounded flat even to his own ears. He'd long ago stopped telling anyone within earshot the truth of what happened that night. Wally had convinced him that he was trying to make himself feel better, but a dead man was a dead man, regardless of the circumstances. Let her think he was drunk, stupid, and pummeled some innocent bystander, or whatever she saw in her head when she heard the words *bar fight*.

Except, he'd sure like to tell his daughter the truth. If he had the chance.

"When did it happen?" she asked.

"The night after I left Bitter Bark. I had to get out while Bart cooled down and didn't want to kill me."

"For turning his wife down."

His lips lifted in a smile. "You remember?"

"Of course I remember. You told me what happened. That his wife came on to you and you turned her down and she told her husband you tried to…to attack her."

For some reason, it gave him a boost of confidence and hope that she remembered the truth and, based on the way she relayed the story, believed him. It had been so long since anyone believed anything he said.

"Yeah, I figured Bart would come to his senses eventually, so I took off. If I hadn't, I wouldn't have been in that bar in West Virginia, and instead of going to prison, I would have…"

"You'd have known about Pru," she finished for him.

"If you told me."

Her jaw loosened. "Of course I would have. You had a right to know her."

"Have," he corrected, aware that the closer they got

to this, the more it mattered. "I *have* a right to know her."

She shut her eyes like the words hit a target. "I know that, but this is Pru we're talking about," she said. "It won't be…simple."

His laugh was quick and wry. "Think that's the point of this conversation."

"She's not an ordinary girl, Trace."

"I figured that out in about five minutes," he said, hearing the gruffness in his voice and praying it didn't crack with emotion. "She's incredible."

Her features softened at the words and the fight he hadn't even realized was in her eyes disappeared. "I *really* didn't expect this."

"Since you thought I was dead."

She managed a smile. "I meant that, after last night, I knew you'd either figure it out, or I'd tell you, and then you'd…you'd…" She lifted her hands, at a loss for words.

"Make demands? Tell her I'm her father? Drag you into court? Blackmail you? What kind of man do you think I am? Wait, don't answer that."

Again, she sort of smiled, looking up as if she appreciated the tiniest bit of humor in this humorless situation. He stared at her, seeing, not for the first time, the way her eyes matched her daughter's perfectly, that incredible mix of amber and gold and copper and tinges of green. They were wide, with long lashes, framed by eyebrows the same color as her hair, like burnished mahogany.

"Molly, I killed a man about twenty-four hours after…after we were together."

She flinched, but held his gaze, an act of bravery

that touched him somewhere he didn't even know could be touched anymore.

"You think I'm so cocky I would blow in here with a half-dead dog, discover I'd made a baby girl with you, and expect you to upend both your lives so I could start playing Daddy?"

"I honestly had no idea what you would do when I saw you last night. But I'm really happy it's not any of those things."

"All I want is to be part of her life."

She blinked at him. "How?"

"I don't know, but that's what I want."

"But you don't know Pru. I know, I know." She held off an argument with one hand up. "That's the point. But she's really…" She stared ahead, thinking. "She does everything by the book, Trace. She's obsessed with being right and good and on time and perfect and structured."

"Wonder where that came from."

She inched back. "What's that supposed to mean?"

"It's a legit question. Everything about us comes from some experience or incident in our lives."

"Did you study psychology in prison, too?"

He smiled. "A little."

"Well, I don't know where her personality comes from, because she was born this way. And the whole idea that she…that you…that we…" She dropped her head and pressed her fingers against her temples. "I have to think through how I'm going to tell her."

"But you were planning to this weekend," he reminded her. "What were you going to say?"

"That you were dead."

The words hit hard.

"But obviously, I can't now."

Because he'd shown up and stolen the chance for her to do that. Now the little girl who liked everything good and right was about to find out what the legacy was on the other side of her muddy gene pool. And that would hurt her.

Something twisted in his gut, a pain as sharp as what Meatball must have felt last night. But this wasn't a flipped stomach. This was a flipped heart and a need to protect that child no matter what it did to him.

"Then that's what you should tell her," he said simply. "Tell her that her father died, make up a name if you have to, and I'll...I'll..." This time, his voice did crack.

"What?" She choked the word. "I'll do no such thing," she said. "I'll tell her—"

"Molly!" The nurse came running out with no jacket, and Molly and Trace instantly popped to their feet.

"It's Meatball. His PCV has dropped to seven, and he's vomiting. We need to transfuse and do an ultrasound, stat."

"On my way." She turned to him. "Just...wait. Don't do anything. Don't...don't leave yet."

She took off, long, wavy hair flying in the breeze, leaving Trace holding a cup of cold coffee and what felt like broken pieces of his past.

Don't leave yet.

Okay, he wouldn't. *But save my dog, please.*

Chapter Seven

"'Scuze me. Trace, is it?"

Trace had just stepped back outside from the vet's office after returning the coffee mugs to find a man walking across the frosty grass toward him. When he reached the steps, he extended a hand to Trace.

"Shane Kilcannon. Not sure we've ever officially met."

"Trace Bancroft." Trace shook his hand, not surprised that a strong and confident shake matched the spark in eyes the same greenish gold as Molly's and came with a broad, genuine smile.

After the greeting, Shane stuck his hands in jeans pockets, sizeable biceps visible under thermal sleeves that stuck out from a fleece vest. With temperatures hovering near fifty in the sun, he looked a little warm with the vest. Training dogs would do that, Trace knew.

"How's Meatball?" Shane asked with real concern in his expression.

"Getting a transfusion." Which sucked. "Maybe needs more surgery."

"Don't worry, man. Molly is the best vet in the county, and I'd say that right to my dad's face." He grinned. "Heard you've done some work with dogs."

"Some." He wasn't going to lie. "In a prison dog training program."

Shane didn't so much as flinch, which didn't surprise Trace. The whole place and the people in it were pure class.

Wally would have told him that's why he didn't take Dr. Kilcannon up on his offer to help Meatball in the first place. And Wally would have also told him that's why he should have. The crafty shrink would have called it "exposure therapy" or some such crap that always worked.

"Want to see some of our dogs?" Shane asked. "We just got a few new ones in for on-site training. Come and give me your professional opinion."

"The prison programs aren't professional," he said. "I'm self-taught from books and videos."

Shane didn't look convinced. "Still, I heard you trained service dogs."

Trace searched the other man's face, wondering if this was a test of some kind. He'd already told Dr. Kilcannon what he'd done with two dogs in prison. "Yeah," he said. "A couple."

"And they passed certification?"

"I don't know," he admitted. "I think they would have, but in prison they don't let you go out and finish the job. So I trained the dogs up to a certain point." And, man, those had been a couple of shitty goodbyes.

"And Meatball?" he asked. "You got to keep him."

"I did."

"That's unusual, isn't it?" Shane's gaze was direct,

83

unwavering, and Trace met it with one of his own.

"Yep."

"So you must have been a model prisoner."

Trace lifted a brow, not at all sure how to answer that. He didn't have to, since Shane gestured for Trace to follow as he trotted down the stairs.

"I want you to meet a couple of new arrivals. Come on." When Trace didn't move, Shane turned around, then nodded as if he understood the hesitation. He pulled out a phone. "I'll text Molly and tell her you're with me. She'll find you. Otherwise, all you're going to do is sit there and stew about your dog."

True. He went along, silent as they walked around the training pen toward what he assumed from the shape and windows was a massive kennel. Shane opened a heavy door, and instantly Trace felt the temperature warm to a perfect seventy-something he suspected they maintained in here year-round.

The structure broke off into a few different corridors, each one a wide hall of gleaming white tile floors all washed in sunshine coming through skylights and windows.

Like prison paradise, he thought with a wry smile. At least a thousand times better than the place he'd spent the last fourteen years.

The echos of dogs barking at various pitches and speeds ricocheted through the hall, sounding like music to Trace. They passed several large individual kennels, almost all with sleeping, eating, or barking dogs. He recognized some as the ones that had been in the training pen earlier, now resting.

"We have rescues and training, and the training consists of us doing the work or training the trainers,"

Shane told him. "My brother Garrett is in charge of the rescues. You know him?"

"We went to high school together," he said. Not that they ran in the same circles.

"He got two puppies from the same litter last week, brought over from Greensboro from a family friend who volunteers in shelters." Shane slowed his step as he reached a corner they were about to turn. "I have a feeling about these dogs," he said.

"A feeling?"

The other man's mouth slid into an easy grin, one that Trace imagined he wore a lot. Why not? Life had been kind to this tall, good-looking guy. From his expensive haircut down to his pricey boots, he was pure confidence.

"I do know dogs," Shane said. "Maybe better than anyone else here. Oh, my brother Liam can turn a German shepherd into a beast of a guard dog, and Garrett's got a knack for finding the right homes for rescues. Normally, we'd get these two out for adoption, like, yesterday. But I think if we held on to them, trained them for therapy first, and tested them, we'd have top-notch golden retrievers ready for intense service training."

Trace stared at him. "Not every dog qualifies."

"I know, that's why I want your opinion on these goldens."

"Purebred?"

"Sure looks that way. Our friend, Marie, was at a shelter when a very pregnant mama was abandoned about ten minutes from delivery."

Trace winced.

"I know, people suck sometimes. Anyway, Mama

had four pups. The minute they were old enough to separate, Rocky and Bullwinkle got adopted. Marie snagged the other two and brought them here for special training. Come on, meet Natasha and Boris."

At Trace's look, Shane laughed and nudged him around the corner. "Hey, we don't name them, Marie does. My guess is she had some old-school cartoons on that morning. Be glad she didn't pick *Underdog*."

Twenty minutes later, Trace realized he hadn't thought about Meatball once. He'd been on the floor of a kennel with two of the most incredibly sweet and ridiculously cute golden retriever pups with soft yellow fur and fat little paws and brown eyes that looked through a man's soul and saw only good.

He lay down flat and let the dogs climb over him and played a little hide-and-seek with Natasha, who was clearly the top dog, and stroked Boris's belly every time he rolled over and begged for love. Shane had gotten called away a few minutes earlier, and Trace was relieved he wasn't asked to leave.

Both of these dogs were born for therapy—they were giving comfort right now. And one of them, Natasha, had that magical combination of calm but outgoing, a clue that she had that innate ability to connect, which was key for a service dog.

So if—

"Excuse me, Trace?"

He rolled over and turned, looking up, way up, at Daniel Kilcannon. Shane stood behind him, and both of them wore serious expressions.

"I've come from the vet office."

Still clasping one of the puppies, he automatically stroked his thumb over the little head in his hand, desperate for reassurance but getting none from the look on the older vet's face.

"Meatball's taken a turn for the worse," Dr. Kilcannon said. "Not only did his numbers drop, but he vomited a brownish fluid, which tells us we need to go back in for more surgery."

"To do what, exactly?" Trace asked.

"We need to take out part of his stomach."

"Good God." Trace gently set the puppy down, not wanting her to pick up the sudden trembling in his hands. Very slowly, he stood and opened the kennel gate, the little dogs he'd just met forgotten as he tried to imagine the hell the one he loved was going through. "How can he live like that?"

"He can," Shane assured him, stepping next to his father. "It's like bariatric surgery in humans for weight loss."

Trace looked from one to the other, feeling his whole shaky world fall out from under him.

"He will function just fine without most of his stomach," Dr. Kilcannon assured him. "Though I'll be honest, it's a difficult recovery. He'll have to be under very close observation, fed through an IV for a while, and very slowly introduced to food. He's not going to live a normal life for some time, but he will. He's four, right?"

"About that, I think. No one is sure since he was a rescue." The words came out husky, the thought of Meatball not living a normal life cutting him in half. That's all they both wanted, to work, eat, sleep, and be free.

"He's got a lot of years ahead," Shane said.

He must have still looked skeptical, because Dr.

Kilcannon took a step closer. "Trust me, Molly's done this surgery before. She saved a Dobie in town not two years ago."

"Oh, yeah," Shane agreed. "That dog was banging on death's door when they brought him in, and I just saw him a few weeks ago running around Bushrod Square. Not the biggest dog in the park, but damn healthy."

That gave him some comfort, but still. "So two surgeries and observation? Like, here? Or somewhere else?" Because how the hell would he get here every day?

"We don't want to transport him," Dr. Kilcannon said. "The days Molly is at the town office, I'm here, and we have a nursing staff prepared to work overnight when we need them to."

Holy crap, overnight nursing. "That...can't be cheap."

Shane and his father shared a look that Trace couldn't begin to interpret, but he definitely got the sense that this had been discussed.

"Trace," Dr. K said, "we are short on trainers at Waterford."

"Really short," Shane interjected, but Trace was riveted on the older man, sensing but not quite believing where this was going.

"My guess is that you don't want a handout for Meatball and you could use a job," Dr. Kilcannon said. "Why don't you work here a few weeks? We'll pay you a fair wage and just deduct the expenses of Meatball's medical care."

Which would be like a dream come true. Except, he was an ex-con. And this place was paradise. "Are you sure? I haven't been to any special school for training." He had to be sure they knew that. "I read books, watched videos, and..." He glanced over his shoulder at the two pups, now playing with each other, oblivious to the conversation. "Did a lot of hands-on work. But I'm not qualified to—"

"I've seen enough to know you're good with dogs," Shane said.

"Meatball is not going to bounce back quickly," Dr. Kilcannon added. "He will bounce back, but he should be under a vet's care for a few weeks. In a special recovery room for at least ten days, minimum. This way, you could see him every day, take him for short walks, and know that he's getting the best possible care."

"I don't have a car, and I'm living at a house"—if you could call the leaky, dilapidated shack that his mother left him a *house*—"on the other side of Bitter Bark."

"How did you get here?" Shane asked.

"Last night, I shelled out for an Uber to get Meatball here. This morning?" He gave an embarrassed smile. "I walked."

Dr. Kilcannon's blue eyes flashed with something that might have been surprise...or he was impressed. "We have living quarters for students who stay for long-term training," he said. "It's not much more than a studio apartment and a communal kitchen, and we provide lunch for the staff. We have a space now. Stay, work, and keep an eye on Meatball."

His jaw loosened as both his shoulders sank a little at the enormity of the offer. "I'm really grateful," he murmured.

Dr. Kilcannon nodded and put a fatherly hand on his shoulder. "We're grateful for the help. Shane will get you started and show you around, and I'm going back to assist on the surgery with Molly."

Molly. He'd completely forgotten *that* problem.

"Look, you don't have to worry about this surgery." The older man added reassuring pressure on Trace's shoulder, obviously misreading his thoughts. "I promise you that Meatball is in the best, most capable and loving hands of a fantastic vet."

But how would that fantastic vet feel about him hanging around to pay off the bills?

Don't leave yet.

Something told him she hadn't meant stick around for weeks. But that was the opportunity life had just handed him, and life didn't hand too many of those to Trace Bancroft. So he was going to take it and hope that, like so many other things, it didn't blow up in his face.

Molly whipped around from the sink, pulling her soapy hands from the scalding water, her whole body still humming from the surgery she'd just performed. Not to mention the bomb her father had just dropped while they both scrubbed down. "He's going to work here and stay in the trainers' housing?"

"It's the perfect solution to many problems," Dad said simply.

Not hers. "He doesn't have to pay for this." She shook off her hands and reached for a paper towel. "I'm just happy Meatball came through okay. We can take care of the dog *gratis*. It wouldn't be the first time."

"That's not what this man wants or needs."

"Dad, we're not running a charity here."

Dad drew back, clearly surprised by her words and tone. "For one thing, in some ways that's exactly what we run, for dogs. Why would we treat a man with any less dignity, Molly, than a dog?"

How much dignity would they treat him with when they found out the truth? "Sorry. Surgery stress," she said quickly, remembering that the only person who knew her as well as Pru did was her father. Too much of this conversation, and he'd figure out the whole damn thing. As it was, he was scrutinizing her expression a little too closely.

"Surgery doesn't normally stress you." Concern darkened his eyes. "You've been so tense, Molly. I don't think you even relaxed at Garrett and Jessie's wedding."

Because it had been New Year's Eve, and she'd promised Pru the truth after the start of the new year. She'd been dreading telling her daughter she was conceived during a one-night stand with the town bad boy in the back of a minivan. And that was before she'd known he was still alive.

And now he was going to be living and working at Waterford? She closed her eyes and let out a little moan.

"Would you please be straight with me?" Her father took her newly washed hand and closed his much bigger one around it. "You promised."

She let out a sigh, knowing the promise he referred to. She'd made it right after her mother had died, when Dad found her sitting at Mom's gravesite on a distant acre of Waterford.

"I can be your mother and father," he'd said that afternoon as she plucked petals from a handful of daisies she brought for Mom. "But you have to share all the things you used to share with Annie. Will you?"

She'd given her word she would, and from that day on, their already close relationship got even closer. Dad had been her sounding board for every veterinarian decision, and many of her parenting problems. And Molly had slipped into her mother's role in so many ways in the family, acting as a hostess for many events they held at Waterford and making sure every birthday and special occasion were remembered and celebrated.

But this new twist in their lives? She wasn't ready to share this with her father.

"It's nothing, Dad," she said, hoping that lie was little and white enough not to come back and haunt her. "Really, it's just been a difficult morning with that surgery."

"Then you agree it's a good idea," he said.

"A good idea? He was in jail for *murder*." It was all she had, and even as she said it, she knew that wouldn't fly with Daniel Kilcannon.

"Now you sound like Pru, and I had to scold her for that last night."

"It worked," she said. "She felt so bad that you reprimanded her that she went over and sat with him during last night's surgery."

"Is that what she told you?"

"We haven't talked about it, but I know her pretty well."

They hadn't talked about anything yet. Shane and

Chloe had taken Pru home last night and Molly had stayed late enough at Waterford to be certain Pru would be asleep when she got home. This morning, Molly had slipped out early. She'd left a note for Pru to have a good day and remember she had choral practice after school and then a history project with a friend to work on until six. With a promise to pick Pru up then, she'd drawn a great big heart and happy face and a row of x's and o's.

Which did nothing to ease her guilt or worry about the pending conversation.

"Good to hear she was concerned about him," Dad said. "I want Pru to learn tolerance and kindness."

Well, she was going to learn something. And soon. "I was supposed to go away with her this weekend," Molly said. "Tomorrow afternoon, actually."

"And you're worried about this dog?" Dad guessed. "I'll be here. I can watch him, and we'll staff with twenty-four-hour nursing if he's still struggling."

She barely heard him. All she could think of was what she'd tell Pru in their much-anticipated truth-telling weekend. *About that man in the waiting room...*

Oh Lord. She needed to talk to Trace. Needed to finish that conversation and make a plan. "Why don't you check on him now, Dad? I want to talk to Trace about the surgery."

A smile flicked over his face.

"What?" she asked.

"I'm glad to hear you use his name. I got the sense you were a bit chilly with him last night, and I would be disappointed if you're passing judgment on a man you don't know."

She gave her dad a grateful smile, then added a quick hug. He couldn't be faulted for his altruism, or his bone-deep belief in human nature, or even for wanting an extra hand at Waterford Farm.

"You're a good man, Dad," she whispered. "And a wonderful example to Pru."

He acknowledged the compliment with a simple nod. "I believe the man got a raw deal, and his dog needs help and so does he. That's all I'm doing here."

"A raw deal?" she asked. "In what way?"

He started to answer, then stopped. "It's not my story to tell. But there's more to Trace Bancroft than meets the eye."

There sure is. Take a real close look at Pru and you might see it.

"I'm sure it will be fine having him here while Meatball convalesces," Molly said, as much to herself as her father.

Clinging to that thought, she stopped at her desk to grab her phone and bag so she could head over to the other Kilcannon vet office in town where she worked most Thursdays. On the way out, she headed toward the kennel to find Trace, but she saw him with Shane as they left the two-story student housing building on the other side of the training pen.

Even from a distance, the sight of him slowed her step. He'd skipped a jacket, as the temperature rose in the middle of the day, giving her a chance to see he held his own and maybe even beat Shane in the muscles department.

Prison gym, of course.

She tamped down the thought, digging for the open mind and good heart that her father had just demonstrated. But she'd opened enough for Trace Bancroft. Her whole body, for starters.

And looking at him across the vast expanse of grass and dogs and trees and time, she could still see why. She wasn't a fan of sleeve tattoos or hair shaved quite that short at the neck or men with prison records and dark pasts, but looking at him objectively? If that was possible, then Cara's assessment this morning had been right.

He's hot.

And that would have to be the last time Molly ever had that thought.

Right then, he spotted her, and she could see the slight shift in his posture, the protectiveness that squared his broad shoulders and made him stand up a little straighter.

He got a raw deal.

Then she remembered how quickly Trace had been ready to let Pru believe her father was dead. Not as a cop-out—at least that wasn't the vibe she got. No, to protect her, to save her the agony of the truth. Maybe to save himself and Molly, too.

She'd never agree to that, of course. As she'd concentrated on every decision, cut, and stitch during surgery today, her mind finally cleared, and the path to what had to be done became obvious.

Lying to Pru wasn't possible. Yes, she'd carefully dodged the truth for thirteen years by avoiding giving her a direct answer, falling back on Pru's youth and innocence. But to tell her he was dead? When in fact he was here, at Waterford, under her very nose?

No, Molly wouldn't consider that. The only questions were when and how, not if. Pru had to know.

She set off toward Trace, hoping that Shane would let them alone long enough to finish that conversation.

Trace met her halfway, crossing the grass with long, determined strides. "How is he?" he called before they even reached each other or Shane caught up with him.

"He's good," she said, happy to have the positive report. "He handled it very well. Slept through every minute and is still snoozing off the drugs."

She saw him exhale with raw relief. "Prognosis?" he asked.

"Excellent. We resectioned his stomach and found a bleeding vessel. It's fixed now and, barring more complications, he's going to head into a long recovery."

His whole expression changed, softening as he closed his eyes. "Thank you."

Shane put a friendly hand on his back. "Told you Molly was the best in the business."

"My dad helped," she said, a little embarrassed by the compliment. Shane had no idea who he was bragging to. Would he be so friendly if he knew this was Pru's father?

"I'm grateful to both of you," Trace said, his voice husky with emotion. "All of you," he added, looking at Shane.

"Yeah, Molly, Trace is going to do some training while Meatball's here, so he'll be close-by for the patient."

And the vet and *their daughter*, who came here after school at least three days a week.

"I heard." She met his gaze, easily seeing the doubt in his eyes as he waited for her reaction to that. She refused to give anything away, especially in front of her brother. "That's really...good."

She caught the most secret glimmer in Trace's eyes, like he knew damn well it wasn't *good* but appreciated her saying so.

"Can I see Meatball now?" he asked.

"Let him rest for a bit," she said. "I don't want him to so much as pick up his head if he saw you."

Shane looked at his watch. "I have a conference call in about five minutes." He turned to Trace and extended his hand. "Thanks again, man. You take today to get settled, and if you need a ride or anything, let me know."

"Thanks, Shane." They shook hands, and Shane took off, leaving Molly and Trace in the middle of the grass, staring at each other.

"So..." she said on a sigh. "You can rest easy for the next few hours as far as Meatball is concerned."

"And as far as you're concerned?"

She gnawed on her lower lip and looked up at him. "I'm at a loss," she admitted. "I'm supposed to drive to the Outer Banks tomorrow afternoon and settle in for a long weekend of telling my daughter everything she's always wanted to know."

He dragged his hand through his hair and looked around for a second, then pinned his dark gaze on her. "That's not why I took the offer to work here for a while. You know that, don't you? I don't want to breathe down your neck or hers. But I have to pay this whole family back for helping my dog."

"That's not necessary."

He didn't answer for a moment, then looked back at her. "I meant it when I said you could tell her I'm dead."

"And I meant it when I said I wouldn't do that. We just have to figure out the best way to break the news." She huffed out a breath, utterly at a loss. "I guess I'll sit her down and tell her today or this weekend when we're off-site."

"I don't want you to do that," he said.

"My dad will be with Meatball."

"No, it's not that, but I have a different idea." He shifted from one foot to the other. "Is there any way you can put this trip off for a while? Let her get to know me as someone who's not a monster or a murderer? Even though..." He swallowed visibly. "Is that possible?"

She considered the request, stepping into his shoes for a moment, the echo of her father's words still in her head. *There's more to him than meets the eye.* Didn't he deserve a chance to show that to Pru, after missing thirteen years of her life?

"Maybe," Molly said. "I could tell her I need to stay with Meatball, which wouldn't be a lie. Let me think about it. I have to go into town now and work at my other office."

"All right." He glanced beyond her at the housing building. "I guess I'll be in there."

"Don't you have to get..." Then she remembered Dad told her he didn't have a car and had walked there that morning, which her father took as some kind of testament to the magnificence of his character. She chalked it up to a man who loved the hell out of his dog, which, to be fair, said a lot about his character, too.

"I'll give you a ride back to your place," she said quickly, half hating the words as they came out, but knowing it was the right thing to offer.

He eyed her for a moment, a hint of a smile tipping the corners of his mouth. "Still got that candy-apple-red Plymouth Voyager?"

She felt the warmth crawl up her cheeks. "It was maroon, and you're kidding, right?"

"Yes. It's called a joke. I seemed to remember you liked them."

"I do, when something is funny."

"Yeah, I guess nothing about this is funny."

She started toward her car, then stopped. "I'm sorry. You're trying to be normal and nice, and I'm terrified, Trace."

All humor evaporated from his expression. "You shouldn't get in a car with me, then. I don't want you to be terrified."

"I'm not scared of you," she assured him. "I'm scared of something changing with Pru. Our relationship is so perfect and real and honest and good."

"Now I show up and threaten to blow that apart."

She shrugged. "It's going to change in some way, and that scares me."

"I'm still willing to get Meatball fixed up and leave. I was going to sell my mother's house, not that it's worth much, but the land is good and real estate has picked up around here. I could go, and we can forget…" His voice trailed off as he looked at her and no doubt read her expression.

"I'm not going to lie to my daughter about who her father is."

He stared at her, then slowly shook his head. "No wonder that kid is so good. The whole damn family are like saints."

"Hardly," she said on a dry laugh. "But even if I were willing to lie to her, which I'm not, could you possibly live knowing you have a daughter and never get to see her? Miss her high school graduation? Her wedding? The birth of her first child?"

He closed his eyes and looked like he was about to reel. "I never dreamed I could do any of that, Molly. I can't put her through having to tell the world what I...that her father..." He ran a hand over his bare arm, flinching a little as if touching his tattoos for the first time.

For a long time, Molly stood in the winter sunshine, the sounds of dogs barking fading into the background as she stared at this broken man.

There's more to him than meets the eye.

And for some reason, some crazy, impulsive, maybe stupid reason, she wanted to know what that was.

"Get in the car, Trace, and while we drive, you can tell me about this 'raw deal' my dad said you got."

He returned her gaze, his ebony eyes rich with gratitude and hope. After a second, he reached up and plucked one of her curls, making it bounce. "Thanks, Irish."

She couldn't help it. She smiled.

Chapter Eight

They drove out of Waterford Farm and onto the highway that led to town in silence. Not the stressful kind that made Trace's arms ache and tightened his throat, but what someone might call a "companionable" silence. A patient, calm, still quiet that gave them a chance to get used to each other.

Even the undersized cobalt-blue hybrid she drove was spacious enough for him to feel like he fit—a sensation Trace didn't have very often.

"I was wrong," he mused, glancing to her.

"About what?"

"Everything." He locked his hands behind his head and let it drop back a bit. "I was wrong about Waterford Farm. Not just what I've seen since I got out, but I bet I was wrong about it all those years ago."

"Well, it was different all those years ago," she said. "It was a family house with a lot of property and some foster dogs. Now it's a thriving business."

"Same family, though," he said. "And from what I knew about Kilcannons..." He shrugged. "I was wrong."

"Simple misjudgment. Happens to everyone."

As a man who lived with misjudgment every day and night, he didn't argue with that. "I didn't expect to be, you know, welcomed."

She shot him a sideways look. "I didn't welcome you," she said softly. "I didn't even treat you with the decency I'd give any dog owner with a very sick animal. I'm sorry."

He forgave with a simple nod. "I shocked you."

"Even before I went to the door last night, I suspected it was you my dad was telling us about, but…"

"He said my name?" For some reason, that hurt. He'd asked Dr. Kilcannon not to use his name, but—

"No, he didn't. He said he'd met someone from around here who seemed to be great with dogs and had been in prison. That's all."

"And you knew it was me just from that?" He let out a choke of a laugh. "I know I had a bad reputation in town when I was young, but to hear 'prison' and jump straight to 'Bancroft' is a pretty damning leap." Although, to anyone who knew his family's truth, it was a very sensible jump to make.

"That's not how I leapt." She shifted in the seat and pulled into the fast lane, accelerating to pass a slower vehicle. "I saw you in town last Saturday when I was shopping with Pru."

"You did?"

"You went into the hardware store, and I convinced myself I was imagining things because I knew the weekend was coming up and I had to tell Pru and I've been pretty stressed about it."

He turned and studied the bare trees in the woods as they cruised by. "You've never ever told anyone?"

"My mother," she said. "I told her it was you the day I told her I was pregnant."

"But not your dad?"

"She and I decided that you had the right to know first."

He laughed softly, getting a questioning look from her. "Sorry, it's just that your family is so...proper. Right. The moral compass points due north in the Kilcannon world."

"I never really thought about that," she said. "But I guess it's true."

She backed off the gas and slid into the right lane when anyone else would have kept flying at a higher speed.

"Must be where Pru gets her rule-following 'cause it sure as hell didn't come from my side of the family," he mused.

"Well, she has a strong moral compass." Molly laughed softly. "That girl never met a rule she wouldn't follow."

Poor kid. Her moral compass would shatter when she found out what her dad was. And her grandfather. A wave of discomfort rolled over Trace, bringing that low-grade sense of internal agony reminding him of what he was and would always be.

Loser. Murderer. Ex-con.

He wiped his hands over his jeans, the comfort he'd felt moments ago disappearing as reality set in.

Molly glanced over, brushing back some of those deep auburn waves to get a better look at him. "You okay?" she asked.

"Yeah, sure. Just, you know, worried about that little girl. New sensation for me."

"My mom's favorite saying was, 'You're only as happy as your least-happy child.' And, until you have one, you can't really understand that."

"I get it," he admitted. "Up until last night, Meatball was my least-happy child."

"Meatball's going to be fine," she promised him. "Give him a couple of weeks and he'll be the dog you knew and loved."

"Pru, on the other hand?"

She sighed. "I can't imagine Pru changing that much. But she'll look at me differently."

"I don't want that, Molly. I really don't want that." He couldn't mean it more. "I've gone all these years not knowing she was alive, and I can—"

"Never forget she is." Molly turned onto the road that led to Bitter Bark. "Where's your house?" she asked.

The last thing on heaven or earth he wanted her to see was where he lived. They had outhouses on Waterford Farm that were nicer. He'd have to tell her to—

Step into the shit and wade through.

He could hear Wally's voice, still, doling out his unwanted but wise advice. *A little discomfort is all,* Wally would say. *Not death.*

"On the other side of Bushrod Square, follow River Run about a mile, then go south on Azalea."

"Oh, back where Kaylie lived." She threw a look at him. "Where we were the night of that party."

"A little farther than that, near Sutton's Mill."

"Oh. That area used to be pretty rough—"

He snorted. "No kidding." There were more trailers than houses out there when he was growing up, though most of them were gone now.

"But that land is on the radar of several developers," she added. "You really might be sitting on more money than you realize."

"I thought I might be," he said. "But right now, it's a hellhole. Brace yourself."

"I'm braced, and ready for more than that," she said as she meandered into town traffic. "I was hoping you'd tell me what happened, Trace. How you ended up in prison." When he didn't answer immediately, she turned, her expression warm. "Knowing the truth can only help me—and you—decide how and what to tell our daughter."

Our daughter. For a moment, he couldn't breathe. He couldn't really look away from her or think straight or comprehend what she'd just said. He tried to look at the red brick buildings and cute little stores and cafés that somehow seemed much more precious than when he lived in this small town. But all he could think about was Pru and how she'd react.

"Please tell me," she said softly.

"Okay." He took a deep, long breath and tried to think of where to start, studying the square named for town founder Thaddeus Ambrose Bushrod. For some reason, he was glad he remembered that. Happy to still have a connection to Bitter Bark, North Carolina, no matter how different and gentrified it looked now.

She drove down a side street of brick brownstones, and as he gathered his thoughts, he studied the polished residences that had never looked quite so upscale when he lived here.

"Swanky," he muttered.

"My brother's wife owns that one on the end," she

said, her voice gentle, as if she somehow knew he needed some time to prepare.

He threw her a grateful smile that she missed, but that was okay.

"I left town a few hours after we were, uh, together," he started, diving in before taking his next breath.

She tapped on the brakes, slowing down at an intersection to look at him. "You didn't go home or pack or anything?"

"I did, but not for long. Bart McQueen had already been to my house and scared the crap out of my mother. My car was at his shop, too. I had to run." He threw her a look. "So, after you dropped me off not far from here, remember?"

She nodded. "I remember dropping you off." She added a sigh and a somewhat shy glance. "I remember everything."

So did he. Which was no surprise, considering what happened next essentially ended his life. "I went home, and my mom was freaking out. Of course, she totally believed Bart."

"She did?"

He exhaled, remembering the words she'd said so often, and each time it was like a razor blade over his heart. *You're just like your father.*

Well, he sure lived up to that high praise.

"I had a little money, so I decided to take a bus to Pittsburgh to stay with my cousin for a week or two. Problem was, I didn't have enough cash to make it all the way there. The next night, I was stuck outside of Charleston, West Virginia."

"So what did you do?"

"Made the biggest mistake of my life and walked up to a bar called Jimmy Square Foot's near the bus station." Why did he go there? Why? He'd asked himself that question a thousand times. "Anyway, there was a line to get in, and the bouncer was having some problems, so I gave him some backup with a troublemaker." Another mistake. He should have found a phone, called his cousin, and waited at the bus station until someone wired him cash. But young Trace had been impulsive and didn't know about bad luck and shitty timing and…parking stoppers.

"Is that when it happened?" she asked.

"No, no. The guy at the door appreciated the help, though, so he let me inside." He closed his eyes for a moment, smelling stale beer and remembering the tinny-sounding speakers blaring Toby Keith. "I almost left." Oh man, if he'd have only left.

"Why didn't you?"

"That bouncer came and got me. He was short-handed and asked if I'd help out. Free drinks, no cover, and they'd let me have a burger at the end of the night. I took that gig…and it turned out to be the worst decision I ever made."

She glanced at him, then back at the road, steering her little car easily onto the old bridge that crossed a narrow section of river next to an old mill, following the directions he'd given her earlier. It was pretty here, he thought, giving his head a break from his story as he took in the quaint North Carolina vista. Pretty anywhere that wasn't Huttonsville.

Freedom washed over him like cold water on a summer afternoon. He had to remember he had that now, and he didn't need to get greedy about a daughter he didn't deserve. He glanced over at Molly right as she looked at him, the sweet softness in her eyes like a sucker punch to his gut.

He didn't need to get greedy about anyone or anything around here. He had his freedom, and that should be enough.

"What happened, Trace?"

"About an hour later, I watched this guy kind of muscle a girl out to the back, giving her a hard time. They went out to a parking lot, and I followed because I smelled trouble." So much trouble. "He was all over her, pissing her—and me—off." He closed his eyes and remembered her face. He could always remember her face. Not the douchebag's, but hers. Not Paul Michael Mosfort, age twenty-three, born in Summersville, West Virginia, second son of Janet and Gary Mosfort.

No, he barely remembered what that guy he killed looked like.

But the girl in trouble? Oh, he could still see the fear in her big blue eyes, the vulnerability when she realized she was drunk, but big Paul Michael was a hell of a lot drunker.

When that prick pushed her against a dumpster and tried to stick his tongue down her throat, Trace could still hear her cry, *Stop!*

Stop! Get him off me! Help me!

"Trace? Trace." He felt the gentle pressure of a woman's hand on his arm, the sensation so unfamiliar that he flinched in surprise. Then he blinked and focused on Molly Kilcannon, pretty, pure, and perfect.

The car was stopped, he realized, and he glanced around, seeing the thick pines in front of his house.

"Are you okay?" she asked.

He took a slow breath and let it out. "Yeah, sorry. I was just…" He wet his lips and forced himself to wade in his shit, as Wally used to say.

"What happened?" she asked. "With the girl and the guy trying to attack her?"

"I…didn't know what to do," he said, locking on the ever-changing green and golden color of her eyes, suddenly feeling…well, not comfortable, but *able*. Able to tell his story to someone who actually seemed to care.

"You helped her?" she suggested.

"I was a bouncer, or at least that's what they told me. And even if I hadn't been, I would have helped her, but maybe I wouldn't have…" He paused. "No. I'd have done the same thing. But my defense was always stressing that I'd been 'hired' to be a bouncer. Except, that didn't really fly with the jury."

"What happened?" she asked again, leaning forward and closing her hand over his arm again. He glanced down at it, at those slender, feminine fingers that saved dogs and fluttered when she talked and probably soothed her sick kid.

His kid.

"I pulled him off her," he said. "I yanked him away, and he was a big guy, bigger than me, and he drew back his hand and sent a fist at my face full force. I stumbled, and in the time it took me to see straight, he smashed her back into the side of the dumpster and ripped her shirt right in half."

His stomach turned as he remembered the sound and her gasp and that bastard's grubby paws slamming onto bare breasts.

"He told me to shut up and I could have some, too, when he was done."

"Oh my God."

He tried to swallow, but his throat was tight, remembering his disgust. "I...reacted. I launched forward and pushed him with all my strength and sent him flying backward."

And that was the end of Paul Michael Mosfort, age twenty-three, of Summersville, West Virginia.

"His head hit a stone parking stopper." He gave a mirthless, dry snort. "Bet you didn't know those things had a name. Well, I know. I heard that six thousand times in court."

"And he died?"

"Right there in the parking lot before an ambulance even got there. I was cuffed and arrested before that girl sobered up and realized what happened." He squeezed his eyes shut. "Turns out Paul was from a wealthy family, that his dad was a lawyer, and Paul himself had started law school that very semester. Lawyers everywhere." He shook his head. "Except for Paul, who never got a chance to go anywhere but six feet under."

"You didn't intend to kill him," she said. "You were protecting that girl. Didn't she testify that you were protecting her?"

"That doesn't matter when the judge is an old law school buddy of the victim's father. The family got to the girl, and she claimed to have no memory in court. I was lucky I didn't have attempted rape thrown at me, too."

"Why? Why would she do that?"

"Because money talks, Irish." He closed his eyes.

"And that family had a lot of it and none of your family's scruples. At least not when their boy was killed."

"But you were doing what the other bouncer hired you to do. You were doing the right thing!"

He almost smiled at the echo of his public defender's arguments. "Except, I wasn't an employee, it was outside the place of business, and whether I intended to or not, I was well aware of the possible consequences of pushing a man that hard, and I did it anyway. I got voluntary manslaughter and fourteen years without possibility of parole."

"Why no parole?"

"Judge. Age of victim. Shitty unfair life." Especially his life.

With the whole thing out, Trace relaxed a little, leaning back, only then realizing she was still holding his arm.

For a long time, she said nothing. Her fingers were still, though, and warm against his skin, making him glad he'd left his jacket back at Waterford. He couldn't remember the last time a woman had touched him so tenderly.

Well, yeah, he could. Because it was the same woman.

"I think I know Pru well enough to say that she'd have been on your side in the courtroom," Molly said.

"Can't change the fact that I did time," he said. "Can't ever change that. And you only heard my side, and if I had any money, I'd bet that girl of yours is the first one to want to see both sides before making a decision. The other side won. Don't forget that."

He felt her intense gaze on him, and the scrutiny

made him want to squirm. But he refused, looking back at her, watching wheels turn and judgments get made and thoughts form. God, he'd love to climb into those heavenly hazel eyes and know what Molly Kilcannon was thinking.

"Why don't we both tell her?" she asked on a soft whisper.

He drew back. "That wouldn't be fair to her. She couldn't react normally. We'd be putting her on the spot." Fact was, he didn't want to tell her. He didn't want to see that disappointment darken her eyes.

She nodded. "Yes, maybe, but it might be easier if we both did it."

Easier for who? He put his other hand over Molly's and pressed firmly, her palm practically burning his forearm now. "Why?"

"Because…you *were* given a raw deal, and that's clear when you hear it coming from you."

"Molly, a 'raw deal' was not how the courts saw it. I was convicted of murder. I will always be a murderer and an ex-con. It's what I am."

She shook her head, a hint of a smile pulling.

"Why is that funny?" he asked.

"It's not. I was thinking of something my mother said the day I told her I was pregnant with Pru."

"You're grounded for life?" he asked on a soft laugh.

"Well, having Pru accomplished the same thing, but no. She said over and over again that Pru wasn't a mistake. That I *made* a mistake, and that mistake doesn't define me. Or her." She inched closer to make her point. "You made a mistake, and it cost a man his life. But that doesn't define you."

If only that were true. "Well, that's a nice way to look at it, Molly, but the fact is, I'm a convicted murderer, and I don't expect a little girl who finds out that's what her daddy is to be okay with that."

Molly shook her head, making those silky waves dance over her shoulders. "You don't know Pru. She's a fighter for the right thing. She might not agree with that jury. Or she might. But she has a right to make that decision, and we have an obligation to tell her."

"Now there's a conversation I'm not looking forward to," he admitted. "This was hard enough."

"In time. We need a little time. I'll definitely tell her that because of Meatball we're not going to the Outer Banks."

"So, see? She'll hate me to start with."

"She won't like it, but she's the daughter and granddaughter of veterinarians. She'll understand. And when the time is right…"

"And when will that be?"

"Sooner rather than later."

"Or later rather than sooner," he suggested.

She dropped her head against the backrest, exhaling again and shuttering her eyes closed. "I never dreamed it would be so complicated."

"Because I came back. I'm still willing to disappear as quickly and easily as I came. Once Meatball is better."

"And I still don't think that's a fair option to you or, really, to Pru."

"What about you?" he asked.

"Me?"

"What do you want?"

He could tell the question surprised her as she

lifted her head, considering it. "I...my...I'm not the issue here."

"How can you say that? You're her mother, you've raised her alone, you call the shots with her. What do you want, Molly?"

She stared at him for a good, long time. "You're only as happy as your least-happy kid," she finally said. "I want her to be happy."

"Then we both want the same thing," he said. "But we have different ideas how to go about it."

"Let's both think about it, okay? Will you be at Waterford tomorrow?"

He rubbed his jaw, already wondering how the hell he'd get there. "I told Shane I could move into the temporary place tonight, but—"

"I'll pick you up around five and take you there. I don't have to get Pru until six thirty tonight. It'll give us the afternoon to think about what we're going to do and we'll decide when I drive you over."

He searched her face, drawing a little closer because she pulled him like a magnet. "You don't owe me any of this," he said gruffly. "Not the help for my dog, not access to Pru, not a ride to a job I didn't even earn."

"Trace." She frowned and reached to him, that gentle hand on his arm again. "You're my daughter's father. Like it or not, that's who you are."

How could he not like it? Right now, it was the best thing he'd ever been.

Chapter Nine

Time flew that afternoon, as it always did when the Bitter Bark Kilcannon vet office was packed with well-pet checks, minor emergencies, and, like that day, the occasional surprise visit from a teacup pig named Chumpy. Molly didn't have a lot of time to mull over the conversation she'd had with Trace, or think about what she, or they, would tell Pru, or when they'd have that conversation.

But still, she was humming with the jitters. It had to be the situation, the anxiety of telling Pru, and the upending of life as she knew it that had her feeling so on edge.

She steadied herself long enough to give a teeth cleaning to Queen Victoria, an old English bulldog she'd been seeing since she'd taken over Dad's practice. After that, she headed into the examination room to remove sutures from a pure-white stray cat adopted by a local woman who had at least a dozen cats in her home, all Molly's patients.

As she turned the corner, she heard a familiar laugh in the reception area, one that never failed to make her heart soar and her lips curl in a smile. She might be a serious straight-A little Dudley Do-Right, but Prudence Anne Kilcannon had a frequent and delightful laugh, and Molly loved that sound more than anything.

Instantly, she detoured from the exam room to pop her head into the lobby.

Pru sat cross-legged on the floor, holding a long, lean tabby cat Molly knew was her next appointment. She looked up, and her whole face lit at the sight of Molly, a reaction that never got old.

"Hi, Mom. Can we get a cat?"

Molly angled her head, not even having to answer a question she'd been asked a hundred times. Considering the number of dogs she brought home from Waterford when one needed special home care, they couldn't have a cat, although looking at her daughter with that sweet baby on her lap, she wished it could be different.

But…*wait a second.* "I thought you had choral practice today," Molly said, flipping through her mental calendar. "And weren't you and Brooke going to work on your history project until six thirty?" Giving her time to pick up Trace and take him to Waterford. Except, now…

"Canceled." Still holding Jack, Pru popped up in one easy move that only thirteen-year-olds and maybe gymnasts could manage. "And Brooke's mom wanted to take her to her brother's orthodontist appointment. Or something." She shrugged, as if this minor adjustment didn't upset a well-ordered apple cart that only a mom, especially a single mom, could balance and make it look easy. "So here I am, the latchkey kid begging for attention."

"You are not a latchkey kid," she said. "You want to do homework in the break room?"

Maybe she could sneak out and run over and tell him—

"Not really."

Molly frowned at the answer. For most kids, that would be the expected response. For Pru, it meant something was wrong. Pru never delayed homework. It was one of her many rules.

"You okay?" Molly asked, only now seeing that there were slight shadows under Pru's eyes. Had she worn mascara to school and rubbed it off...or not slept?

"We never talked last night."

Molly tried to tamp down a tidal wave of mom guilt. "I was late with that dog."

Pru started to respond, but Jack meowed noisily and squirmed to be let down. Like a kid who'd been raised in a vet's office, Pru handled the animal carefully, putting him back into the cat carrier and smiling at the owner, who sat reading a magazine.

"I don't feel like doing homework."

Oh boy. This was serious.

"Can I shadow you for the rest of the day?" Pru asked.

"So...you'd come home with me after work?"

"Yeah. Is that a problem?"

A big, fat problem. "I actually have an errand to run."

"I'll come with you."

Oh *crap*. Now what?

"Oh, Mom, you don't want me to shadow," Pru guessed, completely misreading Molly's horrified expression. "Do you have a...you know? Because I'll go to the library or something."

She didn't have a "you know" this afternoon, but lying about having to put an animal down would ensure that Pru took off in a heartbeat. It was the sad aspect of Molly's job that Pru absolutely hated. But Molly refused to lie to her, even if it was convenient.

Truth was, she couldn't keep Pru and Trace apart forever, especially since he'd be working at Waterford Farm, so why not let her come along to pick him up? It would be weird not to.

Molly reached out an arm and hooked it around Pru's slender waist to pull her closer. "It's all well-baby checks from three o'clock to close. And there's nothing I'd like more than having my very own well-baby with me."

Pru gave her a big blue-banded braces grin. "Okay, then. I'll shadow. But I can't count it."

"Count it?" Molly asked as they headed back to the exam room. "Count it for what?"

"Community service hours for the semester," she said. "I need twenty-five before the end of the year and have to submit my project for approval by tomorrow. But you can't use your parent's job. I have no clue what I can do."

"Twenty-five hours? Last semester it was ten."

"Inflation." She grinned at her, then looked skyward to acknowledge the fib. "Okay, there's a trip to Carowinds if you make twenty-five hours and get them done before the middle of February."

"February? How is that even possible?" Molly asked.

"I don't know, but if I make it, then I'm not only

able to qualify for a trip to the theme park, but I also get to submit to the state competition."

"Don't tell me. Twenty-five *more* hours." Which was wonderful, except for the mother of the overachieving student.

"No, but the state winner goes to..." Pru grabbed her arm and squeezed, dragging out the anticipation.

"The moon?"

"Better. Disney World, Mom. *Dis. Ney. World.* Park fees paid."

"Wow." Molly nudged her into the hall toward the exam room. "Come on, let's ask Mrs. Carpenter if she needs help with her twelve cats."

"Which would be a lame community service project *and* related to your job," Pru said. "Mr. Margolis said it has to be totally 'independent of family,' and we have to find the project on our own. No help from parents. And they're looking for creativity and really helping someone in need."

"You better start looking then, because Mickey Mouse is waiting for you. Also, Lily, one of my favorite kitties. Come on."

With the exception of a standard poodle with a serious case of the runs, the afternoon whizzed by uneventfully. By the time Molly finished making a few calls and reviewing the patient schedule for the rest of the week, it was close to five and time to pick up Trace.

She waited until they were in the car to break that news to Pru.

"So, this errand," Molly said slowly. "It's over near Sutton's Mill."

"'Kay," Pru said, taking out her phone. "Oh my

gosh, Mom, did you see Gramma's blog yet? She did one on Meatball."

"She did?" Her grandmother's blog was a mix of Irish wisdom, country living, child-rearing, dog loving, and more Irish wisdom. The eighty-six-year-old had discovered a passion for blogging a few years earlier when Pru introduced her to the wonders of the Internet. She'd built quite a little following, too, and unexpectedly became one of Waterford's strongest marketing tools, along with Darcy's hilarious Instagram account of dogs being groomed. "She doesn't usually blog about my patients." Or their owners. "Did she mention Trace?" Molly tried to not let her voice rise with low-key panic.

But Pru looked up, eyeing her suspiciously. "Why does it matter so much?"

Of course she'd pick up every nuance. "I don't know," Molly said, trying to sound like she didn't care. "It's just that…"

"I know, Mom." Pru reached over and patted Molly's arm. "He's a murderer. Working at Waterford. It's a little scandalous."

A lot of things were scandalous where Trace Bancroft was concerned. "That's not why I asked," she said. "And you have to let go of that. He's out of prison, and he's going to help train some dogs at Waterford while Meatball is recovering."

"Mom, please. I know he's rehabilitated, and it's quite forward-thinking of us to help him out."

Molly swallowed, taking in her sometimes too mature daughter.

"That's why I went and talked to him last night," Pru said.

"I knew it," she murmured, only a teensy bit satisfied that she understood her daughter better than anyone else.

"Well, Grandpa embarrassed me at dinner," she admitted sheepishly. "I shouldn't be creeped out by the man because he murdered in cold blood."

He didn't murder in cold blood. "Were you? Creeped out, I mean."

"Not at all," she said, pulling her seat belt on. "He was really nice. And so worried about his dog. He even had a nickname for me."

"He did?" There went that voice on high again.

"Umproo," she said with a smile, then waved it off. "Inside joke."

She had an inside joke with Trace now? Molly didn't even begin to understand the emotions that kneaded her chest like kitten paws.

"We just need to be careful around him," Pru said, sounding more like the mom than the daughter, a role reversal they often joked about. Pru was neat, Molly loved clutter. Pru was on time, Molly had to set her watch ahead not to be late. Pru was a rule-follower and Molly…got pregnant in a Plymouth Voyager with a bad boy.

"Why do we have to be careful?" Molly asked, swiping that last thought away as fast as it came.

"He could do it again."

"Honey, you don't even know what happened."

"Do you?"

Molly stared straight ahead and twisted the key in the ignition. "It's not my place to tell you. Let him."

"But you know? Was it cold-blooded? Premeditated? What weapon did he use?"

No, no, and only his two hands to protect a woman being assaulted. But Molly shook her head and knew exactly how to get Pru to stop asking. "He can tell you," she said. "As a matter of fact, we're going to get him now and you can ask him."

As she pulled out of the parking spot, she caught a glimpse of Pru's mouth open in shock. "Right now?"

"Yep, so you can talk to him."

"About committing a murder?" She shifted in her seat and returned her attention to the phone, thumbing so fast Molly doubted she was reading a word. "No, thank you. And you can relax, Gramma doesn't mention he was in the pokey for fourteen years."

Molly didn't laugh, even though Pru's tone was funny, and "in the pokey" would have been something they'd have laughed about...before Trace. Truth was, this was going to upset Pru's world worse than Molly imagined.

"Then you might as well know all the bad news," Molly said softly.

"Oh, don't worry, Mom. I already know you're canceling this weekend."

"How do you know that?"

She held up the phone. "Because Gramma's blog says Meatball had another surgery this morning." She had nothing but disappointment in her voice, which Molly understood. "It's okay."

It wasn't, but Molly didn't fight it. She couldn't make that trip this weekend unless Trace was on board and told Pru ahead of time.

Pru shoved the phone into her backpack and turned to stare out the window. "I hate that guy for ruining our weekend."

Molly sighed. She might hate him for more than that very, very soon.

Trace heard the car pull up outside the house around five thirty and pushed himself out of a noisy, thirty-year-old recliner to answer the door. But before he took two steps, he heard voices...plural. Female voices.

Dipping down to peer between broken plastic blinds, he felt his heart skip when he saw the long, dark hair and waiflike form of...his daughter. It was the first time he'd seen her since he'd known the truth, and if she'd have been sprinkled in sunshine and glitter, she couldn't have looked more beautiful to him.

Along with the woman next to her, who was every bit as beautiful in a completely different way. Molly said nothing as Pru stood stone-still, put her hands on her hips, and took in the run-down eyesore where he'd grown up. Here and Huttonsville Correctional Center—the only two places he could call home.

Shame crawled up his body, pressing against his skin like another tattoo. Conflicting emotions, the two that had been at war in his head and heart for the last three hours, took up their battle positions again and started firing bullets into his brain.

Tell her because she's your daughter and you have a right to know her.

Run away and forget her before you ruin her life and humiliate the poor kid.

Of course, it wasn't entirely his decision, but Molly seemed as hell-bent on taking the high ground as she claimed her daughter was. All he could do now was…answer the door.

One of them tapped lightly, probably because making contact with the door would give them germs. Damn it. He'd stood here debating like an idiot, and now they'd see the inside. He should have been waiting out on the street where he had Molly drop him off earlier.

Taking a steadying breath, he opened the door and looked from one to the other. Blinding, both of them. One delicate, innocent, young, and…good God, she had his mother's little nose, and that tiny cleft in her chin was not unlike the deeper one in his. How had he missed that last night?

Because he'd had no idea he was chatting with *his daughter*.

"Hello, Trace." Molly held his gaze, a challenge and apology and question all at the same time in her eyes. She still looked a little tired and stressed, but she wore it so well, he could have…

No. No kissing. Ever.

"Hey," he said, adding a regretful smile. "Welcome to my humble abode."

"You live here?" Pru asked, trying valiantly to hide her distaste.

"I don't exactly live anywhere," he said. "But my mother owned this house, and when she died, it became mine."

"I didn't know your mother died, Trace," Molly said. "I'm sorry."

"Did you know his mother?" Pru asked.

Oh, nothing was going to get by this one, Trace thought. Not a single thing.

"Actually, no, I never met her." Molly looked beyond him, clearly hoping for a fast change of subject. "Can we come in?"

Holy shit, no. He scratched his jaw, angling his head in invitation. "Yeah, sure. But there's not much to see."

Pru went first, leaving Molly and Trace to look at each other and silently communicate a fast *what the hell?* and *sorry* to each other. If it hadn't been potentially the most emotionally fraught moment of his life since that bastard of a judge handed down sentencing, Trace would have actually gotten a kick out of the fact that he and Molly could silently communicate.

After all, it wasn't like they'd had a relationship. Just sex. Really amazing teenage sex fourteen years ago.

He had to let that go.

"It's actually got decent bones." The unrequested assessment pulled him back to the result of that sex. Pru stood between the kitchen and living room, looking out of place in her sharp jeans and crisp white shirt and navy-blue hoodie with a WF logo that matched the one on the front gate of Waterford Farm.

She looked clean and preppie and all wrong in front of his mother's tie-dyed peace symbol sheet hanging on one wall and a painting of a sun and moon with faces that she bought at a flea market on the other.

"Who has decent bones?" Molly asked, her voice tight enough to tell Trace she was every bit as nervous as he was.

"This house," Pru said. "You could live here."

"Until it rains." He pointed to the ceiling and a huge watermark in the shape of Australia. "Also, the plumbing's a little iffy, and two windows are broken."

"So it's a good thing you're moving to Waterford for a while," Molly said.

"You're going to *live* at Waterford?" Pru asked, her voice catching in disbelief. "In the house?"

"In the training student housing," he said simply, trying not to react to her absolute disgust for the alternative.

"But you're not staying here?" she pressed.

"I don't know yet," he said honestly. Guess a lot depended on how she took the news.

"Pru." Molly's voice had enough of a motherly reprimand to get a reaction from the kid. "I don't know if that's any of your business." The bite left her voice by the last word because, as they both knew, it sure as hell was Pru's business.

She just didn't know that yet.

"I'm thinking," Pru said. "Can I look around? Is that okay?"

A little surprised by the request, Trace nodded. "There's not much to see. One bathroom, two bedrooms, and this. Fair warning, no one has been in this house for a long time. Might see a dead bug or two."

And his mom must have blown out of here in a hurry, because all her old stuff was still in the bedroom, boxes of crap he'd have to throw away at some point.

She shrugged. "Bugs don't scare me." She walked off with a bit of toughness and square shoulders that told him so much about her and made him want to know more.

126

When she left, he looked at Molly, who watched her, too.

"When?" he whispered.

She just closed her eyes.

"Why don't I take my bag to your car?" he suggested, and she nodded, getting the hint that they could talk outside.

"That's all you have?" she asked as he picked up a duffel bag.

"In the whole world."

She sighed at that. "Pru? I'll be right back."

"You need closet doors!" she called back, making Trace bite back a laugh.

"At the very least." He opened the front door to let Molly step out. "She's…something."

That made Molly smile. "Yeah, I'm still trying to figure out what."

"Other than amazing?"

She beamed up at him, the mom pride bringing out a gorgeous green light in her eyes that he hadn't noticed before. "Thanks," she said, her voice still very soft, so the words didn't travel through the door he'd left open. "She is amazing. And this is really hard. I don't know what to do, but I think we have to do something. We have to tell her."

"We?" He gave a slight smile. "You still like that plan."

"I'm honoring your role in this."

The words squeezed his chest. "Wow."

"Wow, what?" she asked as she lifted the small hatchback.

"Wow, I don't think anyone has ever honored anything of mine in my entire life."

She searched his face, her shoulders sinking a bit as the words visibly hit her heart. "That's…sad."

"Don't mean it to be. Molly, what should *we* do?" he asked after a beat.

"Tell her?"

"God, it'll wreck her. It'll hurt her. In one second, with one confession that makes us both feel better, you'll take her perfect little life and turn it upside down and inside out."

For a long time, she stared at him. "I can't believe you."

"What?" He drew back. "Do you want to tell her that badly?"

"No, I mean I can't believe you…you *get* that. It takes a parent to get something like that."

He smiled. "I am a parent. Now."

"Well, I appreciate the way you're approaching this. So, what do you want to do? What would be your number one choice?"

The fact that she was giving him a choice practically clamped his throat with gratitude. "I'd still like to wait a little," he admitted. "I'd really like her to know me first. Not, you know, like best pals, but to see that I'm not a killer who lives in a hovel. Well, I am, but…"

"There's more than meets the eye."

More gratitude strangled. "Yeah."

She let out a slow sigh. "That's fair. I don't know how long I can put her off, but—"

"I have it! I got it!" Pru came tearing out of the house, both hands extended in victory like she'd just crossed the finish line and broken the ribbon. "I know what my community service project is going to be!"

Her what?

"What is it, Pru?" Molly asked.

"Oh, please say yes," she replied, directing the request to Trace. "Please, please say yes, because if I can do this and take pictures and get an interview with you, I might not only get the trip to Carowinds, I could win the state competition for best community service project. Heck, I could go national!"

Nothing made sense, not a thing. But he couldn't help smiling because her enthusiasm was infectious.

"Pru, what would the project be?" Molly asked, clearly a little more in the know than he was.

"This house!" she exclaimed with a loud clap. "I can help you fix up this house. I mean, not the roof and plumbing, but I can paint and clean and fix it all up so you can live here again or sell it or whatever, and *can you even imagine?*"

"Imagine the house fixed up?" he asked. "Yeah, I could. It would be a lot of work."

"Can you imagine how I would blow everyone else out of the community service water if I did a house renovation for a mur...a guy...a con...a person who was in prison?" Color rose on her cheeks, diminishing some of her excitement and turning into embarrassment.

As he knew it would.

"I mean, as community service projects go, this one would beat even those overachiever Eagle Scouts who like to collect canned goods or give used books to libraries. This would *rock*. So would you be okay with that?" Pru asked him. "How would it make you feel?"

Other than humiliated and confused and maybe a little bit excited to help her? "Uh, great. Yeah. I mean, I'd be impressed if I were judging."

"You can't judge if you're part of the project," Pru said, as if the rules mattered as much as the project itself. "And you're not immediate family, so it's perfect and valid."

It took everything in him not to exchange a look with Molly. A look that might have given away the truth that he most certainly *was* immediate family.

Molly stepped forward. "Pru, are you sure you want to take on something this big? It'll be much more than twenty-five hours."

"I don't think so," she said, glancing over her shoulder. "I could work evenings and weekends and enlist some friends who want hours but aren't going to compete for the state prize. Oh, please say yes." She looked from one to the other, a classic kid pleading with her parents.

Only this one had no idea these *were* her parents.

"Twenty-five hours?" Trace asked.

"That's all. Twenty-five hours." Pru beamed at him. "Please, Mr. Bancroft. Pretty, pretty please with lots of paint and curtains and nice stuff on top." She put her hands up in a prayer position. "Please."

He laughed in spite of himself, in spite of the fact that it was crazy, in spite of the fact that nothing was funny. But deep inside, all he could think was that after twenty-five hours, she'd know him well enough to maybe not have the truth wreck her. Maybe.

"If your mom says it's okay."

They both looked at Molly, who was a little pale, but she nodded.

"Oh, thank you, Mommy!" She threw her arms around Molly and looked up at Trace. "And thank you. It's just twenty-five hours, I promise."

When she pulled away, he shared a look with Molly, and they both said the same thing at the same time. "Twenty-five hours."

That's how much time he had to make his kid like him. Until then, he was her personal community service project. *Great.*

Actually, it kind of was.

Chapter Ten

The twenty-five hours wouldn't kick in until Pru's project got approved by her teacher, but in the days that followed, it was all she talked about. She shopped for supplies, came up with a work plan, and enlisted friends to help. Molly spent even more time at Waterford than usual because Meatball's convalescence was steady, but slow.

Through it all, there was Trace.

Sometimes, it seemed he was everywhere. In Meatball's recovery room every morning when she arrived, in the office on his breaks to take him out and visit. Of course Molly, as the vet, accompanied him on quick strolls close to the vet office, monitoring Meatball's strength and celebrating each milestone, like moving him off IVs to solid foods and taking him out of intensive care into a more laid-back recovery room.

It seemed like Trace was constantly on the edge of Molly's awareness, hovering close enough to make Molly tense and in a constant state of anticipation as to when she'd see him next.

Late Wednesday afternoon, Molly was locking up

the office, already hungry for the family dinner, when she took a glance over her shoulder to the kennels and saw Trace walking out. He moved with a touch more confidence than when he'd arrived, wearing a Waterford Farm fleece vest like Shane did, to make sure his arms were free for training but he was warm enough. It accentuated his shoulders, the thermal shirt underneath pushed up to show the tattoos, hair, and muscles of his forearms, making him look strong, sexy, and like he belonged there.

And all of those things made Molly's stomach do an unexpected flip. In fact, having him around had her constantly humming with a low-key sense of anticipation. Followed by that weird sensation of something warm every time she saw him. Too weird. Too warm.

As much as she tried to get used to it, she couldn't.

"Did Meatball have his dinner?" he asked, coming closer.

"I'm trying to stretch out the meals, so I thought I'd come back over in a few hours and feed him."

"I can take care of that," he said.

"It's okay. I'll be here for Wednesday night dinner."

His brows rose. "You're the third person I've heard mention that today. It's a thing?"

She laughed. "It's a Kilcannon thing. If you're in town on Wednesdays, you eat here. Crystal cooks, and we catch up on life and business. We do it on Sundays after church, too, and that's way more fun because there are Bloody Marys and Jameson's. You should join us tonight."

The invitation was out before she really thought

about it, because including guests was so normal for the family. And suddenly, she realized how much she wanted him there.

But he stepped from one foot to the other. "Well, it's been a long day of training."

A little twinge of disappointment pricked her chest. "Yeah, when the weather's good like this, Shane pushes the dogs and the trainers." She took a breath and dove a little deeper. "You sure? You'd be welcome."

"That's okay. I actually promised the trainers I'd help cook a group dinner." He glanced at the office. "But I haven't seen much of Meatball. Not since this morning."

"Oh, of course. Let's go see him." She stuck the key back in the lock.

"Do you have time?" he asked, always sensitive to her schedule.

"I do. My sister-in-law Andi is picking up Pru at home, which is only about ten minutes from here, and bringing her for me. I was on my way over to the house to hang out with Gramma Finnie."

He grinned. "That lady is a trip."

"And a half," Molly agreed as she opened the door.

"She brought me a pillow for my room."

Molly sighed with a burst of love for her thoughtful grandmother. "Don't tell me. It was embroidered with an old Irish saying."

"It's in the shape of a shamrock and says something like, 'A good laugh and a long sleep cure all.'"

"That would be Gramma Finnie." She gave him a playful look. "You know she only gives pillows to people she likes."

He waved off the compliment. "I think it's the

puppies I'm training she likes. We ran into her on a walk, and she was pretty taken with both of them. Told me about how she and her husband came here with a dog who barked at the name of the town and they knew it was home."

"It's her favorite of many stories. Did it take very long to tell it?"

He considered that. "A few minutes, maybe more."

"Because she only tells the long version if she *really* likes you. See, there's Corky, the setter who barked his way to a new home." She pointed to the beloved sepia-toned photo on the wall. "There's been a family setter ever since, and they're all up there, from Corky to Rusty."

He shook his head, scanning the wall of Kilcannon Irish setters over the generations. "You've got a great family, Molly."

"Don't think I don't know it. That's my mom." She walked closer and touched the picture of Mom with Buddy, the setter Molly grew up with before Rusty. "Annie Kilcannon."

"You look just like her," he said, inching closer. "She's beautiful."

Another sigh, this one a little sad, of course. "She was that, inside and out. Best mother in the world."

"Second best." He gave her a sly grin. "Don't think I don't see how fantastic you are with Pru."

Warmth curled through her. "It's my greatest goal to be half the mother she was."

"I think you're twice the mother of anyone I've ever seen."

"Trace." His name caught in her throat, thick with emotion, as she remembered her mother making that same prediction long, long ago. "Thank you for saying that."

"It's true."

The compliment settled on her heart as she led him into the hallway. Halfway to the room where Meatball was, Trace paused, listening to the quiet. "Is that other dog that was staying overnight in the room gone now?"

"The Aussie terrier, Pepper? Oh, yes, she's fine and home now. But she was a barker."

"Then Meatball's all alone."

"Don't worry about him. He still needs rest, and I'm afraid the other dogs would excite him if we put him in the kennels."

He gave a little grunt. "Solitary's still solitary," he muttered.

She didn't respond, which was what she often did when he made even remote references to prison. He never talked about it, or his childhood, and Molly was never sure what she could or should ask him about.

"How are the pain meds? Could you take him off them today?"

"Not completely," she said as she opened the door to Meatball's recovery room. "As you know, he doesn't do well with pain."

That made Trace laugh. "Dog's a total baby."

There was only one large cage, up on a sturdy table so the patient was always eye level, with two very soft lights on either side. Meatball slept peacefully on a fleece bed, covered with a light blanket. He lifted his head when they walked in.

"Hey, Meatball," Molly whispered as she approached the cage. "How's my best patient doing?"

The dog scooted closer, his intense green eyes on Molly.

"Hey, bud," Trace said.

Meatball didn't even look at him, but gave a huge dog sigh and dropped his head back down.

"Uh oh," Trace said. "He's pissed."

Molly opened the crate, not bothering to disagree. "Give him a second. He'll respond to you."

Sure enough, when Trace reached into the crate and placed both hands gently on Meatball's head, the dog looked up at him with the most pathetic expression Molly had ever seen. He all but screamed, "How can you do this to me?" Then he turned away, looking toward the wall instead of Trace.

"He's a little dramatic," Trace said, making her chuckle, but she heard the hurt in his voice.

"It's not unusual for a dog to pull away from their owner after this kind of trauma," she said. "He's got to blame somebody."

Trace stroked the honey-colored fur slowly and steadily until Meatball lifted his head. "He's the best dog, right, Meatman? You're the best."

Meatman responded by pushing up a little, getting on his haunches, but he stared at Molly, making Trace choke softly at the insult.

"He's looking at you the way he used to look at me," Trace noted.

"I'm the one who doles out the meds." Molly stepped back, trying to give them a chance to rebond. "And you have been gone all day."

As Meatball worked his way closer, getting his head out of the cage, Trace responded in kind, wrapping his arms around the dog as if he'd climb right into the crate with him if he could. Trace kissed his head, closing his eyes, so affectionate with the animal that Molly could literally feel the love.

She watched, a little mesmerized, a little moved. She often judged people by how they dealt with their animals, whether that was right or wrong. It said a lot about a person to her. And this moment reminded her how wrong she'd been about Trace. He was strong, quiet, gentle, and not anything like the troubled teenager she remembered.

Molly wasn't sure quite how long she watched, but it was long enough to feel her heart slide into a place it had no right going. But there it was, headed where it had threatened to go for a week now. *Attraction*. Pure, simple, and as real as the affection she was witnessing.

"I take it you don't know his breed or who his parents were," she said, trying so hard to be a vet in the room, and not...a woman watching a man do something sweet and sexy.

"Does it matter? I mean, obviously there's pit."

"It matters medically, to some degree. Some breeds heal faster than others. He's definitely a Staffy, which is a very strong dog. And Lab, I'd guess. But there could be other breeds in his line."

He inched away from Meatball, but kept one hand on his head. "I imagine his dad was a big bad pit bull who was constantly in trouble, and his mom was a fluffy, flighty Lab who couldn't get serious about anything." He shot her a look with a half smile. "My shrink would say I'm transferring my own parents' story to poor Meatball."

She drew back, not sure what surprised her more—

138

the revelation about his parents or that he had a shrink.

"Most inmates have therapists," he said, no doubt in answer to her questioning look. "Many have psychiatrists 'cause they dole out the drugs. But I had a therapist."

"That's...good."

"Actually, it's great. Wally—his name is Jim Wallace—not only became my best friend in prison, he fought like hell for me to keep this dog when I got out. It's unusual for dog trainers to get to do that, but he went before the warden and made the case. Not sure what he said, but it worked. I left with Meatball and my head on straight."

While he talked, he never took his hands off Meatball, and Molly could see both man and dog changing before her eyes with the touch. That low-grade buzz of tension that seemed to vibrate around Trace evaporated. His broad shoulders relaxed. His jaw loosened. Even his dark eyes seemed less sharp and wary.

And Meatball's body changed, too. His lips pulled back in an attempt at a smile, and the stiff tendons around his paws softened.

"You never mention your father," she said.

Trace lifted a shoulder as if that didn't matter at all. Or his father didn't matter. Instead, he loved some more on Meatball, who accepted the affection but didn't exactly return it.

"I can see why they let you take him," Molly said, placing her hand on his forearm to make her point, but always struck by how strong and warm his ink-covered skin was. "He's truly therapy for you."

He looked down at her hand as if he felt that same

heat, too, staring at her fingers on the red and blue swirls and curls and words that she suddenly wanted to read. Slowly, he lifted his gaze and met hers, narrowing thick lashes, saying nothing.

But she still couldn't take her hand off his arm. It was like a magnetic connection that caused a sensation of pure pleasure somewhere deep in her belly.

"You know what you're doing, Irish?"

And another jolt of pleasure, this one from the sexy softness of his low voice and that ancient nickname that did crazy things to her heart. "Where the dog's health is concerned, I do."

He put his hand over hers, his fingers completely covering her hand, hiding it, sandwiching it between his forearm and palm. "What about where I'm concerned?"

A pulse jumped in her neck as her heart rate picked up speed. "I'm just reassuring you."

"You're touching me."

She swallowed. "Is that not allowed?"

He leaned an inch, maybe less, closer to her. "It's fine. It's…powerful."

"Oh." The sound slipped out, more moan than word. "Sorry."

"Don't be." He held her gaze, his eyes dark and dizzyingly intent. "But I want you to know I feel it."

"That's kind of the point of a touch, isn't it?"

He exhaled slowly. "The last time I was with a woman was the back of a minivan squeezed next to a dog kennel," he admitted in a husky voice.

"The…last…" That couldn't be. But if he was arrested the next day, she supposed it very well could be.

"I want you to know that," he added. "I want you to know that you weren't forgotten. And wouldn't have been, even if I hadn't gotten arrested the next day. I just want you to know it wasn't, you know, a meaningless one-night stand."

For some reason, the words touched her with the same force as his hand on hers. "I see." Although the only thing she could see were the deep, dark, bottomless eyes of a man making a confession that scared and thrilled and mystified her. "I'm glad it wasn't meaningless. But not glad that you've been alone. I'm sorry you've been alone."

He finally lifted his hand. "I've learned how to deal with it."

"That's good."

"But I do remember. Frequently."

Heat whirled through her, tugging at her insides, twisting things in knots that suddenly ached to be unraveled, making her cheeks burn.

"I'm sorry if that embarrasses you. I'm blunt sometimes. My therapist taught me that was the best way to get through things that make me uncomfortable."

"Embarrassment isn't what's making me blush, Trace."

He laughed, low and sexy in his chest. "Gotcha."

She studied him, seeing the way the laugh made his face less angular but no less handsome. "You looked like him just then," she whispered.

"Him? Who?"

"The Trace Bancroft I remember."

"Oh, really?" His brows rose in amusement. "Not sure I want to hear who that guy was."

He was the senior in high school she'd tutored in chemistry and crushed on. The risky youth who'd barely graduated. The local boy who drifted in and out of town long enough to get in trouble and sneak off to have sex in a van, then disappear.

"He was intimidating," she confessed. "Attractive, intriguing, and a little scary."

"That's funny. You just described everything you were to me." He leaned a little closer. "And still are."

"I'm not scary."

He burned her with a look. "What's scary is how hard it is to stand this close and not kiss the holy hell out of you."

Kiss the holy hell out of you. The words from their one night together drifted through her memory banks and caused a reaction not unlike the one she'd felt that night. A jump of her heart, a tightness in her chest, a crazy excitement way down in her belly.

"Don't worry, Irish. I won't." But she could have sworn he moved ever so slightly closer. She could smell the bit of cool air that clung to him, and she could remember that night, too. The heat of his mouth against her skin, the smoothness of his hands as he took off her clothes, the way he filled her...

She felt her eyes shutter closed as she tried to push the thought away. "I'm not worried."

"You sure? 'Cause you look kind of worried."

"I'm not. I trust you. And..." She opened her eyes and met his gaze. "I remember, too."

For a long time, they looked at each other, both of them *remembering.*

"Then you won't be surprised..." He put a finger under her chin, tipping her face up, searing her skin.

"That I had every intention of coming back after that night."

"For more?"

"For you." He lifted her face one more centimeter, lowering his face a bit, ready to—

"Mom!" They both whipped around at the word, uttered with nothing but shock and that undertone of a reprimand that only General Pru could deliver. "What are you *doing*?"

She knew it. She totally *knew* it. Pru wasn't imagining that Mom acted a little too weird every time this guy's name got mentioned.

Pru stayed frozen in the doorway, completely forgetting the real reason she'd run over here. Not to witness *that*. Were they going to kiss? Was Mom out of her freaking mind?

He was a *murderer*.

"Hi, honey." Even Mom's voice sounded tight and weird. "You got here fast."

"No, I've been at the house for like ten minutes waiting for you." She finally looked at Trace, who nodded a silent hello and suddenly was really interested in Meatball, while Mom turned to the workstation like some monitoring device needed attention.

"Everyone's here for dinner," Pru added with a tiny bit more insistence.

"I'll be over in a minute, Pru."

"I'll wait here with you." Otherwise, Mom and Mr. Shawshank Redemption might start looking all hot for each other again.

"Then maybe you can help me ask your mom a big favor," Trace said.

What? He wanted to *kiss* her? 'Cause that was kind of obvious. "Maybe. What is it?"

He gave a sideways look to Molly. "Any chance Meatball can sleep in my room tonight? I really think he's forgotten who I am."

Mom considered the request, but Pru knew that narrowed-eyed look too well. That would be a no. "I know you want him to, Trace, but he's really better off here. He needs a good, soft bed, and any excitement, like a new environment, could be bad for him."

"I understand. Thanks." He glanced at Pru, something really strange in his look. Probably guilt, because it was so obvious he had the hots for Mom. "And thanks, Pru."

"For what?" she asked, hating that the question came out sharply and really hating the look Mom gave her. "I didn't help you."

He took a moment to close the crate door, which made Meatball whimper and cry. "For keeping your mom in good spirits while she takes care of the world's whiniest dog," he said. "I better get going. See you tomorrow then."

He nodded to both of them and hustled out, leaving Pru staring at her mother, who was now focused on getting the lighting right in the recovery room. And not looking at Pru.

"Mom, what were you doing with him?"

"Talking. Let's go." She sailed right past Pru, jingling office keys as she marched to the lobby, gesturing for Pru to go outside, and then locking up with efficiency. "I'm starved, Pru. Aren't you? I hope Crystal made something with pasta. I have a total carb craving. Did you have a nice ride over with Andi? I guess it's Aunt Andi now, so—"

"You were not talking," Pru said through clenched teeth. "He was touching your face."

Mom's eyes fluttered for a moment, then she pulled off some kind of look that said she hadn't even noticed how close they were. "Really? Maybe I had something on my chin. Or—"

"Something *on your chin*?" Pru practically choked. "He was going to kiss you."

She gave a light laugh. "Oh, Pru. Your imagination is a thing of beauty."

Pru grabbed her arm and stopped her mother as she strode toward the house. "This was the real reason you skipped the Outer Banks, isn't it?" Pru demanded. "Not because of a dog that Grandpa could have handled. But because you like him."

She blinked. "Like...like *like* like?"

Normally, that would have been funny to both of them, but this wasn't funny at all. "Mom, he's an *ex-con.*"

Her mother's eyes flashed with fury. "Which makes him good enough for you to use for a community service project but not good enough for me to talk to?"

"And flirt with."

Mom's eyes tapered to angry slits. "Watch it."

Pru swallowed and corralled her thoughts, knowing she was pushing hard across an unspoken line of respect she rarely crossed. "Look, I understand Grandpa wants us to be nice to him and treat him with respect even though he killed a man, but you don't have to kiss him! When I said you should date someone, I didn't mean...*him*."

The minute she said it, she knew it was wrong. She braced for Mom's expected shot of discipline, but her mother took a step backward instead. Her eyes filled a little as she looked at Pru, clearly upset but weirdly silent.

"You're right, Pru," she said softly.

Oh God. "About what? That you like him, or that he's an ex-con?"

"There is...another reason I didn't want to go to the Outer Banks this past weekend, and don't want to go for a while."

Pru stared at her, waiting.

"I'm not ready to tell you yet."

"Really?" Frustration pressed on Pru's heart. It was all she wanted, really. The truth about who her father was. And Mom had promised to tell her right after the start of the new year. In January. She'd *promised*. "You're not?"

"I need some more time."

"How much?"

"Whatever you'll give me."

Well, she couldn't really go out of town until the service project was done, anyway. "I forgot to tell you my big news," Pru said, remembering why she'd come tearing over to her mother's office in the first place. "Mr. Margolis approved the project. Said it sounded 'ambitious and outstanding.'"

"Oh, wow." Mom pulled her a little closer and planted a kiss on her head. "Just like you."

"I can't be alone there with him, so I have some friends lined up to work with me. And you, I hope."

"Of course."

"So I guess it's okay if we wait to take our trip until after that's done."

Pru could feel her mother's whole body relax a little. "Yes, that's perfect." She added another head kiss. "And, honey, I...I don't want you to misjudge Trace."

"Mom, he's already been judged," she whispered. "And spent the equivalent of my life in prison."

Mom flinched a little. "There are two sides to every story. You should get his."

She gave a slight shrug. "Maybe I'll ask him when we work on the project."

Mom nodded and suddenly got that gooey sad look that usually preceded a hug, kiss, and *I love you.*

Right on cue, she slid both arms around Pru and pulled her closer, kissing her hair. "I love you, Pru."

Pru laughed softly.

"What? You don't love me back?"

"Yeah, I do. You're so predictable."

"Beats confusing."

Pru slipped her arm around her mother's waist, and they walked together to the house. "You're confusing, too. I mean, do you like that guy?"

"I don't *dis*like him."

"Were you really going to kiss him?"

Mom just squeezed her really hard and didn't say a word as they walked up to the porch. She didn't have to.

Chapter Eleven

S he was the kind of female who wrapped around a man's heart and owned it from the very first featherlight kiss. Trace was enamored of everything she did.

Natasha—whom he'd started to call Tashie from the moment they met, knowing it was important he have a name that only he used in training—was born to be a service dog. She was responsive to every touch, easily connected, and obeyed basic commands even as a tiny puppy.

"C'mere, Tashie." Trace curled his fingers under her tiny puppy snout and watched her eyes shutter with pleasure, then she looked up at him, still and patient. Ready for anything. Alert, loving, and crazy smart.

On the other hand, Boris, or Bo, as Trace dubbed the boy, might never rise to that level. He'd be a helluva therapy dog, born to bring comfort to the masses. But Natasha? She was a one-man dog, and that made her ripe for service training.

"You want to bring them outside for a while?" Shane Kilcannon approached the kennel where Trace had been with the puppies for almost an hour on a warm Friday afternoon.

"I think they're bone-tired," he said, pushing up to a stand, aware that Tashie watched his every move. "But if I told that one she had to climb a mountain, I'm pretty sure she would."

Shane grinned. "She's definitely a special dog. Think she's our first official Waterford Farm service dog?"

"I do," Trace said, rubbing his jawline and remembering he hadn't even thought about shaving that morning because he'd been so anxious to see Meatball. And Molly.

"I need to find the perfect trainer," Shane said as they walked outside together.

Not for the first time, Trace's gut tightened at the thought of handing Tashie and Bo over to another trainer. But surely the Kilcannons would want someone with a record. A *training* record, not a *prison* record.

"You ready for distraction training?" Shane asked as they stepped into the sunshine to see the seven trainees and dogs already at work in the pen.

"Always ready." It wasn't a lie. Every time he stepped out to this grassy pen, drank in the gorgeous farmhouse and vista of North Carolina hills, Trace wanted to be right where he was. He could feel himself falling in love with this business, these dogs, this life.

The whole place charmed him...as well as some of the people in it. Every once in a while, he could forget who he was and what kind of life he'd lived. Every once in a while, he could pretend that this was where he belonged. During those scant moments, he felt the closest thing to heaven he'd ever known.

Then he'd see Molly and get even closer.

He shouldn't be falling for Molly or Waterford. He knew that. But he couldn't stop himself.

For the next few hours, Trace worked with Shane and the student trainers on doggie distraction training, which was as entertaining as it was exhausting. Some of the animals were far more distracted than others. A few never missed a beat, ignoring treats and toys as they went about their work. Some couldn't stay focused for more than a minute, and those trainers were the most frustrated. It reminded Trace of the guys in prison who desperately wanted to get in the Puppies Behind Bars program but didn't have the touch with the dogs.

Trace had it, in spades. And every time Shane noted that, Trace felt that intense shot of pride that was so unfamiliar, he wasn't even sure what to make of it. He'd spent his life being told he was a carbon copy of his loser father, then made that prediction come true. Then he'd spent fourteen years on the inside, being reminded that he was no better than an animal. Way worse, actually.

Then life had thrust him here, where he felt worth and purpose and contentment. It was going to hurt like a mother to leave this place. To leave Molly...and Pru.

He tried not to think about it, focusing on Shane's teaching, admiring the man's concentration and patience. But in the middle of a sentence, Shane suddenly seemed as distracted as some of the dogs, looking to the driveway, his words fading to nothing.

Everyone, including Trace, followed his gaze to a brunette woman dressed in jeans and a stylish jacket walking toward the training pen, a stocky brown Staffordshire terrier on a leash next to her. Trace immediately recognized the woman as Chloe Somerset, Shane's fiancée.

"'Scuze me," Shane murmured as a smile pulled at his strong features. "Take five, team."

The trainers seemed relieved for the break, and so did the dogs, who sensed they could romp, sniff, and pee with abandon. Shane walked toward the five-foot chain fence that surrounded the pen, leaning over to get a kiss from the woman.

Trace held back, of course, splitting his attention between the dogs in the pen and the new arrival. After they'd talked for a few minutes, Shane turned and gestured to Trace.

"Can you c'mere for a sec?" he called.

Trace went immediately, saying hello to Chloe, whom he'd met once in the past week, bending down to greet the dog through the fence.

"This is Ruby," Chloe said, giving her pupper a rub on the head. But Ruby was on her haunches, paws on the fence, barking noisily at Shane. "Who is dying to slobber on her daddy right now."

Shane reached his fingers through and tickled Ruby's fur. "So, Trace, Chloe has a favor to ask you."

"A favor?"

She gave him a smile he imagined most people—especially Shane—would be incapable of saying no to. "The Puppy Parade needs a representative from Waterford, and Shane told me that little dachshund we were counting on has been adopted."

Trace nodded, remembering the fanfare he'd been told was tradition when a dog was adopted. The whole staff had gathered to say goodbye, Garrett Kilcannon wearing some beat-up old cowboy hat he called his "doggone hat" while he and his wife, Jessie, drove off to deliver the dog to a new home.

"And Shane tells me there are two more, but they're young."

"Boris and Natasha? You want to take them to a parade?"

"I want you to take them," she said, biting her lip as if she was a little embarrassed to ask. "I need you to walk them down the street in the Better Bark Puppy Parade."

Frowning, Trace took a step closer. "Excuse me?"

At his look of abject confusion, Chloe laughed. "You're not from around Better Bark?"

"Used to be," he said. "Back when we called it Bitter Bark, but I heard you changed that."

"Only for this calendar year," she said. "Part of my campaign is to have at least one major dog-oriented event a month. Tomorrow night is the Puppy Parade, and I've already been told every hotel and bed-and-breakfast within ten miles is sold out. At least, the ones that accept pets. If not, bet they're sorry now."

Shane grinned, pride in his eyes. "My fiancée, the tourism genius."

She waved off the compliment, her attention on Trace now. "It's really not a big deal for the dogs if they're people-friendly. They're leashed, with owners, and they walk through town with the Bitter Bark, er, *Better* Bark High School band, cheerleaders, and some dancers. Trust me, it's not going to be the Macy's

Thanksgiving Day Parade, but I have fifty puppies signed up. Companies and businesses get promotional benefits, and I think it's important for Waterford to be represented."

"There is no shortage of dogs here," Trace said as a low-grade sense of dread bubbled in his gut. A parade in town? No, people hadn't recognized him so far, or had any idea where he'd been for fourteen years, but still. With Trace's shitty luck? Anything was possible.

"But it's a *Puppy* Parade," Chloe said. "The cute factor is off the charts. They have to be under one to qualify. The younger the better."

"That's your Natasha and Boris," Shane said. "And it would be a great test of their skills, if they're ready."

His Boris and Natasha. In his dreams. "I think they're ready." But was *he*?

"I'd take them, but I'm leading the parade with Ruby," Shane said, giving a little eye roll. "I made that promise in a moment of weakness."

Chloe tapped the chain link playfully. "You said you wanted to lead the parade."

"Honey, no man wants to be *in* a parade, trust me." He grinned at Trace. "Which is why I'm asking, not telling, you, Trace. It's your call."

Well, he sure as hell didn't want to seem like he wouldn't do anything for the dogs, and he honestly didn't want anyone else taking them. "Sure. I'll do it."

Chloe beamed a thousand-watt smile at him. "Awesome! Now if I can get Molly and Pru to work the Waterford table, I'll be all set." She gave a tug on Ruby's leash and backed away. "Is she in her office?"

"Yeah," Shane said. "Molly's working here today.

And we're going to be done in ten minutes, so don't go far." He threw her a kiss, getting rewarded with a wink and a sweet smile as she and the dog took off toward the vet office. Shane never took his eyes off of Chloe until she walked into the building.

Shane put his hand on Trace's shoulder. "I owe you one, dude. Let me know if you ever need a favor."

"I might need someone to help me navigate the white water of a puppy parade," he said on a dry laugh.

"Get Molly," he said. "She'd rather do that than run the table."

"You think?"

"Can't hurt to ask," he said. "Come on, let's get these dogs in shape. That golden doodle is a lunatic."

Trace laughed, walking back to the dogs and trainers, but the idea of a Puppy Parade just took on a whole new level of possibilities. It wouldn't be a burden with Molly. It would be…fun.

At the tap on her office door, Molly looked up from the patient notes she was typing into her laptop and silently cursed the deep, feminine reaction she had to the sight of Trace Bancroft standing in her door. Messed hair, dark whiskers, well-decorated muscles on display in a clean Waterford Farm T-shirt all managed to tilt her a little bit off-balance.

When was she going to get used to that?

"Am I interrupting?" he asked.

Yes. All her concentration was shot to hell at the sight, sound, and smell of the man. "Oh, no. I'm

154

finishing for the day. And week. You came to see Meatball?"

"I actually came to see you."

"Me?" And that tilted her world some more. But of course he wanted to see her. She was Meatball's vet. *To get a report.* "I can tell you he's a little antsy today." *Like the rest of us.*

"Is that bad?"

"Actually, it's good. He's ready for a proper walk, I think, which might be why he's whining and crying at a whole different level now."

He laughed, shaking his head with a little embarrassment. "I've been able to train him to do just about anything except man up."

"Most of them are babies when they get cooped up for so long."

"You make a lot of excuses for him, have you noticed?"

She shrugged. "He's won me over."

"Oh, I'll have to get him to tell me the secret."

As if you don't already know. "Would you like to take him for a walk?"

"If you'll come with us."

She couldn't help laughing at the flirt as she pushed up from her seat, aware of his gaze dropping over her and how that millisecond of a glance made her feel so...attractive. How did he do that? He'd always done it.

"Come on," she said, ushering him down the hall, insanely aware of how close they were, how strong he felt when their bodies accidentally brushed when she showed him into the recovery room.

Meatball was pacing the confines of his crate, but

barked and raised up on his front paws at the sight of Molly, as he always did.

"Someone is feeling good today," she said, going straight to open his latch. "Hey, Meatball. Want to take a walk?"

He barked several times at the word *walk*, padding his paws as if he couldn't wait to get out.

Trace lifted the dog out of the crate, and quite easily, considering he weighed in at just under sixty pounds since surgery. As he lowered Meatball to the ground, Trace turned his face to offer a cheek, but Meatball went straight to Molly and nuzzled her leg.

"Whoa." Trace, still crouched on the ground, turned to watch the exchange. "Color me forgotten."

Meatball looked up at her and panted with a look of adoration it didn't take a trained professional to recognize.

"He's in love with you." Trace sounded more than a little bewildered. And maybe jealous.

"He's spent a lot of time with me." Laughing, Molly snagged a leash and collar from a hook. "Take him on a walk, and he'll forget I exist."

He gave a little scoffing choke, pushing up slowly. "Molly, he doesn't *need* a leash. Have you ever seen him try to run off?"

"This is the best he's felt in a week. It's exactly when he'll run." She held the leash out to him.

Looking up at her, he closed his fingers over her hand and gave the slightest squeeze, which she, of course, felt right down to her toes. "You never said if you'd come with us or not."

She should say no. She should not encourage evening strolls and casual contact and long conversations with him. She should realize that he caused a string of electrical sparks that made her remember things like how he—

"Don't think too hard, Irish. Life's more fun when you're spontaneous."

"Fun? Maybe you forgot what happened the last time we were spontaneous."

A slow smile pulled at his lips. "That was fun."

She bit back a laugh. "There's no winning with you."

"There's no losing, either. Just take a walk, okay? I want to ask you a favor."

"All right." It wasn't like she seriously considered *not* going with him.

He didn't say what his favor was, but a few minutes later, they both retrieved jackets from a coatrack in the lobby, stepping outside. There, Molly inhaled deeply and lifted her face to the sky, willing herself to calm down around him.

"God, it's beautiful here," Trace said, buttoning his jacket and looking around.

She took in the view with him, looking out to the horizon where the sun would soon disappear behind distant mountains. That left the foothills of Waterford bathed in the silver tones of a midwinter evening with a hushed quiet falling over the bare trees and patches of frozen grass.

"This is one of my favorite times of day," she said. "I love those few minutes of transition between day and night. It always feels peaceful and familiar, with the day ending and life beginning."

She turned to watch Trace adjust Meatball's leash then stand tall, that fading sun sharpening the angles of his face and highlighting a five o'clock shadow that made him look dark, sexy, and strong.

"Life?" He gave a soft snort. "I'd call it my least-favorite time of day, but maybe that will change."

"Why?"

He studied her for a moment, his brows drawn as if he considered how to answer the question. "Because daytime in a prison, if you're smart and play the system, can be endured. There's work to do, purpose, and people. Nighttime means an eight-by-eight cell with snoring, swearing, fighting, farting, and the occasional wail of remorse."

She tried—and failed—to imagine the dark and desolate loneliness of that situation.

He came down the step to join her. "When I'd catch a glimpse out a window, which was rare, this time of day meant that was what was ahead."

"I'm sorry."

"Don't be. You didn't kill anyone."

The statement silenced her, compelling her to stick her hands deep into her pockets and make a fist of frustration. He didn't actually kill anyone...but he did. What a miserable thing to have to live with.

"So why do you like this time of day?" he asked, adjusting his pace so that he and the dog walked in time with her.

"Well, I guess because the start of evening always signaled something good. When I was a kid, it meant the far-flung pack would be gathering soon, around a dinner table." For her, that meant laughter and teasing and family and security. "When I became a mother, it meant school and work and all that distraction was over, and all that lay ahead were hours with Pru."

"What did you do during those hours with Pru?"

So much, she couldn't begin to list. "We played games and took baths in the early years, then homework and projects, like volunteering at shelters or baking something fun."

Suddenly, it all sounded so light and bright and normal when viewed through the lens of a man who'd been in prison. And that made her heart ache for him and what he'd missed.

"I know you were gone and I had no way of knowing where you were," she said, "but honestly, I'm sorry I didn't do a better job of trying to find you. Of telling you."

"No, don't be. I'm glad I didn't know."

"You're glad?" She found that hard to believe. "Why?"

"Because it would have made every one of those five thousand one hundred days even longer."

Ouch. "You counted days?"

"Hours seemed like overkill."

Molly's shoulders fell as she imagined the weight of all those days.

"Bet you never realized you'd had five thousand-plus days with Pru."

"No," she admitted. "And every one has been amazing." Looking up, she held his gaze. "I'm really, really sorry, Trace."

"I mean it when I say don't be sorry, Molly. I don't want you delivering constant apologies. There will be five thousand more days, and five thousand days after that, and a lot more five thousands beyond. But right now? We have to get through the next *five*."

"We will," she promised, though she wasn't quite

sure how. The impending revelation to Pru still hung out there like a dark cloud, threatening stormy weather they both didn't want to face.

He exhaled, burying whatever thought accompanied that sound, then nodded to Meatball, who was keeping pace but pulled his head to the left to let his displeasure with the leash be known loud and clear. "Not my fault, Meatman," Trace said. "Doctor's orders. Blame her. Oh, wait, I forgot. She's your new best friend."

Molly laughed, but didn't relent. She'd seen a few dogs, when unleashed for the first time during convalescence, take off and set themselves back days in recovery.

"I know somewhere we can take him," she said, suddenly wanting very much to bring Trace to a place that was so deeply special to her. "It's a perfect walk for him, and by the time we get there, he'll be tired enough that I'll trust him off leash." She paused for a moment. "It's near where my mom is buried, and there's a beautiful sunset over the mountains visible from there."

"I'd like to see that." They walked in silence for a few minutes, both of them watching each step Meatball took as he navigated the path. Most of the snow that had fallen last month had melted, but there were still patches where drifts had been, and the dirt was hard and cold. Meatball was moving slowly, but he finally seemed to be out of pain as he stopped, sniffed, and watered a few trees along the way. Mostly, he kept a perfect rhythm and pace with Trace.

"He's back in tune with you," she noted.

"We *have* been together for well over a year, and you've had him for less than two weeks," he said, that little bit of jealousy in his voice again. "But this dog and me? I don't think I've ever been that in tune with another creature."

So he'd never been in love, Molly mused. And the last person he'd been with...was her. "I'm like that with Pru," she said. "It's a pretty wonderful place to be with another person. Or dog," she added.

He waited a beat, then asked, "Why Pru?"

"Because we've been together constantly for thirteen years."

"No, I mean why'd you pick that name? Is Prudence a family name?"

"No, not really. I liked the sound of it, kind of old-school Irish. Plus, the irony amuses me."

"Irony?"

"Let's just say I didn't demonstrate any 'prudence' in my behavior the night she was conceived." She leaned into him to make the confession more playful, but that only made her realize how solid his shoulder was. And how much she wanted to slip her arm through his and hang on to that muscular arm.

"Maybe I don't know what prudence means, then," Trace said. "Because you didn't do anything wrong."

"Prudence means good judgment and discretion. It's a perfect name for her."

"Yes, it is. And maybe your judgment was off that night, but it seems you were discreet. Only telling your mother all these years."

"Speaking of my mother," she said softly, leading him to the crest of a hill. "See down there in the valley, that oak tree? She's there."

He followed her gaze, squinting. "I see three markers from here."

"My grandfather Seamus and my uncle Liam, who died as a child. And my mother."

"So you brought me to the family burial grounds?" he noted with a soft laugh.

"It's one of the prettiest valleys at Waterford. We don't have to go down there, although I often do when I want to talk to my mom. Grandpa Seamus put a bench up here for Gramma Finnie after Liam died. We all use it now. Come on."

"This is beautiful," he said as they continued along a worn path between more oaks and pine trees.

"Yeah. I come out here frequently, especially since my mother died."

He eyed her, quiet for a moment. "Must have hurt to lose her so young," he said as they made their way around the last grouping of trees. There, a wooden bench had been strategically placed to take in the vista beyond the hills to the horizon and also look down on the valley where some precious people rested in peace.

"It was agonizing for all of us," she told him. "Especially my dad, but...it did result in Waterford Farm in its current iteration."

"How's that?"

When they sat, she told him the story of how losing her mother had inspired her father to bring all of his kids back to Waterford to start an elite canine training and rescue facility. Three of her brothers had been living in Seattle at the time, along with Darcy, but they'd come back.

"And the youngest one? Aidan? Shane said he's a helicopter pilot in Afghanistan."

"A Night Stalker, actually. So badass it hurts. He

was home for a really short visit at Christmas. We're all hoping he's home for good soon."

"He'll leave the military?"

"Maybe. Probably." She looked to the distance remembering the pain that crossed in her little brother's eyes when he'd been home for that short visit. "He enlisted with his best friend, Charlie, and they went through boot camp and then Ranger training and something called Green Platoon to train on specialized helicopters. They've done multiple tours together, too. We don't always know where Aidan is, but he's been in Afghanistan for the last year or so, with Charlie until…" She took a deep inhale. "Charlie was Aidan's door gunner on the Black Hawks he flies, but he was killed about six months ago."

"Oh, man."

"Yeah, Aidan's really struggling and he told my dad when he was here in December that he might not re-up this spring. He enlisted at eighteen, and we were sure he'd stay in until retirement, but Charlie's death hit him hard."

Trace thought about that, nodding. "I didn't know your family well, obviously, but every once in a while, I'd see some Kilcannons in town, and I remember a wild little blond boy always being carried on some big kid's shoulders."

"Big kid was Liam, no doubt. They're the youngest and oldest, but surprisingly close. Liam was a Marine and I'm sure that's why Aidan enlisted so young. So no doubt that you saw our Golden Boy, Aidan."

He reached down to Meatball's collar. "Now?"

"I guess I can trust him not to run."

"You guess?" He snorted softly. "You underestimate

my dog…and me. Watch." He removed the leash and stood, snapping his fingers twice, exactly as she'd seen Shane do with a trainee a thousand times. Instantly, Meatball stood at attention, his usually floppy ears perking a bit, haunches down, his haunting green eyes pinned on his master in perfect stillness, waiting for a command.

"Meatball, walk four steps to your right."

He turned like a soldier and walked four paces.

"Three to your left."

When he followed that command, Molly gave a soft whistle. "That's good."

"Meatball." When the dog looked up, Trace pointed toward the open area behind the dog. "Fifteen steps."

Molly counted them and laughed when he stopped at fifteen, turn around, and looked expectantly at Trace for another command.

"At ease, Meatman."

He flopped onto the hard, cold grass and put his head down.

"Well, I stand corrected about the leash." Rubbing her bare hands together, she blew into them as she scooted to one side to make more room for Trace on the bench. "Is he being trained for a specific service?"

He shrugged. "I didn't have him long enough to focus on one service, and once I knew I was about to keep him, I decided to, well, keep him. If I train him for service, he'd have to go to someone else. Not sure I could part with him now."

"I understand." She waited a beat, then asked, "So what was that favor you wanted?"

"Ah, yeah. My favor." A smile pulled at his lips, a

little shy, a little sly. "Something called the Puppy Parade."

"Chloe's event tomorrow night?"

He nodded. "I got roped into walking Natasha and Boris. Would you..." He hesitated long enough for Molly to know he wasn't sure he should finish the question. "Be my puppy partner?"

"You want me to walk them in the parade with you?"

"I really don't want to march through Bushrod Square all by myself with two crazy puppies that do nothing but draw attention."

She laughed, imagining that, and maybe to cover up just how much she wanted to join him for that experience. "Well, I was going to help run the Waterford desk, but Pru could cover for me if I bribe her with dinner afterward. Let's ask her when we're at your house tomorrow afternoon. You can tell her how much you want a Puppy Parade partner, that is if it fits into her workflow chart, assignments, and a timeline."

He grinned like a proud parent, which hit her in the gut. "That kid."

"Welcome to the world of General Pru trying to win a state competition."

His smile faded a little, then. "Speaking of irony, has it dawned on you yet that Pru has the same person for a community service project that her mother had?"

It hadn't, actually. "Pretty sure we signed up for different reasons."

"What were yours?" he asked.

She bit her lip, knowing it didn't matter now, but she sure wouldn't have wanted him to know then. "I didn't need any more hours. I had my quota well met that year."

A spark of humor danced in his dark eyes. "Yet you signed up to tutor me anyway."

"Yeah."

He leaned a little closer. "Crush?"

"Kinda."

"Aw, Irish." He reached for her hand, covering her fingers with his. "Why'd you wait two years to make a move?"

"I didn't make..." Then she remembered her request in the car that night.

Kiss me.

Thought you'd never ask, Irish.

"I was scared," she admitted. "Terrified of you."

"What'd you think would happen?"

She laughed and turned her hand to hold his, loving the comforting touch of his rough skin. "I thought exactly what happened would happen. You'd take my virginity in the back of a van with a dog crate smashed against my backside."

He laughed, then he stopped suddenly, pulling his hand away and holding it frozen in midair. "You were a *virgin?*"

"Of course I was a virgin."

He grunted and closed his eyes. "I had no idea. You faked it well."

"I didn't fake anything." The confession sent some heat through her and, by the look in his eyes, through him, too.

"One time and you got pregnant." He choked softly. "What are the odds?"

"Apparently, good. My mother reminded me that I come from fertile stock. And you should probably check the dates on your condoms."

166

His soft snort reminded her that he'd been in prison and not with a woman all this time. He searched her face, his gaze intense and direct. "You know, Irish, I got a confession myself to make about those hours in the study hall and library, too."

She could feel herself drawing closer, imperceptibly so, she hoped, but he was magnetic and she couldn't resist. "Yeah?"

"You got to me."

Lifting both brows, she didn't understand the admission.

"You had that...that *thing*. I never really could put into words what it was about you, but it got to me."

She flicked her fingers, scoffing at the compliment. "It got you one night in a minivan after a few beers and a brush with danger. Otherwise, don't try to pretend I was much more than a diversion during your study hall when you were forced to be tutored in chemistry."

For a long time, he looked at her, silent. Then he lifted his hand and stroked her cheek with a featherlight touch she barely felt. "You are so wrong, Molly Kilcannon," he said huskily. "I never made a move, because you were so completely out of reach for me. Then you walked up that driveway one night. You and that other girl...I don't even remember her name."

"Isabella Henderson. Dizzie Izzie, as I dubbed her."

"She didn't exist."

"Then you were blind, Trace, because that girl was gorgeous, and she still is."

"You're friends with her?"

"I'm the vet to her dog, and our daughters are in the same class."

He frowned. "She had a kid the same year you did?"

"Stepdaughter," she corrected. "She married Allen Phillips. Do you remember him?"

He thought for a minute. "Lawyer? Loaded? Has to be in his fifties now."

"That's him. Criminal defense and family law, richer than God, and has every imaginable trophy, including Izzie."

"Well, she had nothing on you. None of those girls did."

Molly laughed softly. "You know, that's funny you would say that, and even that you'd think it, because that night? I was feeling so down about myself. So not pretty, so not…worthy. That's probably why I fell into your arms so easily."

"And here I thought it was my good looks and great kissing."

"That, too."

He smiled, studying her again. "By the way, Irish, you don't even belong in the same sentence as the words 'not worthy.'"

"Tell that to a nineteen-year-old girl with a few pimples and curly hair."

"I *love* your hair." He reached for it, taking a handful and sliding his fingers through the curls. "It's so…rich. And your skin is gorgeous."

"Thanks. I guess I'll be looking for wrinkles soon instead of blemishes."

"You're flawless." The words were sweet, and his touch was even sweeter, making her tilt her head into

168

his hand for the sheer delight of his fingers and this moment and...and...how close he was. A foot away, maybe, but close enough to count every eyelash and get lost in the depths of his dark, dark eyes.

"You're flirting with me," she said on a sigh.

"Not exactly."

"Yes, you are."

"Am I not allowed to do that? To make you laugh or talk to you or...touch your hair? What are the rules? Where are my boundaries?" Still holding a strand of her hair, he twirled it around his finger, sending chills up the back of her neck.

"The rules?" Probably that he shouldn't give her chills. But was that so wrong? Being with him felt...exciting. "Just use common sense," she whispered. "That's the only boundary." And she needed to remember that. She needed the same boundary.

"Got it." He leaned a little closer and planted a kiss on her forehead. "Sensible enough for you?"

Much, much too sensible. "Yeah."

"Then we'll stop right there."

No, no. Don't stop.

But he stood, took her hand, and snapped his fingers for Meatball, who meandered over, happy to have had fresh air. "We better go," he said. "It's dark out here."

Exactly. Dark and quiet and the perfect place for a kiss. She looked at him, long enough to let him know exactly what she wanted, but he smiled. "You still get to me, though."

On a soft sigh, she nodded. No kiss. Only a compliment. A very nice compliment. "Nice to know."

As they walked together, hand-in-hand, Molly knew what she should do.

She should let go. She should keep things platonic and forget parades and projects and the past. She should practice common sense.

But at that moment, in the deepening twilight, with frost and uncertainty in the air, Molly held his hand and loved it.

Chapter Twelve

I t made no sense—common or otherwise—but the only way Trace could describe how he felt on Saturday morning was *nervous*. For the tenth time, he wiped his damp palms on his jeans and looked around the little house, seeing it through his daughter's eyes. That had to be what had him uptight.

He wasn't nervous about seeing Molly. On the contrary, the time he'd spent with her had one effect on him—the desire to spend more time with her. She didn't make him tense, unless he counted the low-grade and constant need to lean closer and kiss her.

Which he damn near did last night.

But today wasn't about Molly—this was about Pru. And the more time he spent at Waterford Farm, the more he realized why Pru saw his home as a "service" project. Molly had told him he couldn't contribute anything major to help unless he was "given" a job— that was against the rules. Pru was bringing cleaning supplies, tools, paint, and, he hoped, a strong stomach, since the house was old, unlived in, and…weird.

His gaze fell on the giant purple tie-dyed sheet with a peace sign in the middle that had hung on the living room wall since he was a child, then moved to a bookshelf full of self-help and new-age titles, not to mention at least twenty books on astrology. And don't forget the crystals in every room.

When did his mother decide to become a hippie astrologist? He couldn't remember exactly, but it wasn't long after they moved here, and he was really young. She liked being weird, because it kept people from getting close and asking questions, he guessed. Maybe she just liked being weird.

But sometime, someday, probably soon, Prudence Kilcannon would learn that this weird woman was her other grandmother, and that was one more thing that would shame the poor kid.

He marched over to rip down the peace-sign sheet just as he heard tires on the gravel drive. He yanked hard, but the sheet didn't budge. Of course not. He'd hung it himself for his mother, in an effort to prove to her that he wasn't like his old man, no matter how frequently she muttered that he was. And, of course, he'd done an over-the-top job. There were probably a hundred tacks holding that sheet up.

For a fleeting second, he thought of Pru. Maybe some of her determination to do the right thing *was* from him. Holding that nice little thought, he headed to the front door and opened it as Molly reached the other side, making her draw back a little and let out one of her sassy, easy laughs.

"Good morning," she said, smiling up at him. "The work crew has arrived."

He peeked past her to where Pru was climbing out of the backseat of an SUV, carrying a huge cardboard box.

"How many?" he asked.

"Just Pru, her best friend Brooke, and her other best friend Gramma Finnie, for today."

He lifted his brows. He liked the old woman, but for eightysomething, she was as sharp as one of those hundred tacks in the wall. Could she put two and two together and came up with...Pru?

"Okay, that's cool," he said, shifting his gaze back to Molly. Her face was fresh and clean with barely a drop of makeup. Had she ever had a blemish on that creamy complexion? He didn't remember any. Her reddish-brown curls were pulled up into a loose ponytail that cascaded down from the top of her head, and she wore jeans with holes in the knees, sneakers, and a Waterford Farm sweat shirt.

Without trying—maybe actually trying not to— Molly Kilcannon was the sexiest woman he'd ever known.

Of course, he hadn't been around many women in the last fourteen years, unless you counted Wally's admin and the ladies in the laundry. Still, he didn't have to have had his face in *People* magazine for more than a decade to know there wasn't a movie star as pretty as the woman standing in front of him.

"Oh, and one other member of the crew," she added.

Again, he glanced beyond her to see Pru opening the back of the vehicle and reaching in, and then a honey-colored paw poked out. One still wrapped where an IV had been.

"Meatball!" As he stepped forward, Molly moved to the side to let him practically run to his dog. But he slowed himself and turned to her. "Thank you," he said to her.

There was nothing but warmth in her eyes. "I thought that would make you happy."

He didn't know how to respond to that, taking a halting step toward the dog as an unexpected emotion rocked him. She cared about him being happy. She really did.

He couldn't remember the last time someone had cared about that. His mom, once in a blue moon, when she wasn't harping about his many flaws. Sometimes Wally. But no one else. No one had cared about his happiness since the day that judge dropped the gavel and Trace officially became a "murderer." Even before.

He wasn't sure he was worthy of it, but now wasn't the time to wonder. Meatball was here, and Meatball sure as hell loved him.

"Take it easy with him," Molly called. "No running or playing. He'll have to be crated if he moves too much."

"Same with me." The little old grandma popped out of the passenger seat, sporting a black-and-white checked sweater and a camera hanging around her neck. "I'm kidding. I'm only here for the pictures and color commentary."

He threw a smile at her, but Meatball was the center of Trace's attention right then. Kneeling down, he got face-to-face with his mutt, closing his hands around his tawny head and meeting his gaze.

"There's my big boy," Trace murmured into a kiss against fur.

Meatball lowered his head, then turned to sniff the

ground, trotting off without so much as a bark, heading straight to Molly. Oh, *come on.*

"I got a treat, Meatman," Trace called.

He glanced over his shoulder with the most disinterested look Trace had ever seen, then continued to his target, looking up at her like she was the queen of his world.

"Sorry," Molly said with a self-conscious laugh. "We're still bonding." She reached down and gave Meatball a nudge to go back to Trace. "Go see your master. Go say hello."

He dropped his head and started sniffing the gravel around Molly's sneakers.

"Hey, bro," Trace said, trying to keep it light. "I wasn't the one that ate a bag of dog food and ended up in the ER."

Molly came up next to him, putting a light hand on Trace's arm, probably totally unaware that he felt that contact right down to his toes. "He'll come around and love you again," she assured him. "He's understandably disoriented. How long were you here at this house before he got sick?"

"Couple of days."

"So this place is still new to him, and he's used to me right now."

He looked down at her, smiling. "Dog shrink, too?"

"They're not that complicated," she said. "Not like people."

Pru marched by carrying another huge carton, talking into a headset with earbuds under her hair. "I know that—"

She veered away as Trace automatically reached to help her with the box.

"Uh uh," she said to him. "You can't help unless assigned."

He did a playful salute. "Ready to join the Umproo Crew," he said, making her laugh heartily.

"The Umproo Crew! Did you hear that?" she said into the microphone as she headed to the house. "We have a name."

Her friend carried some mops and a bucket, but gave him a shy smile. "Mr. Bancroft?" When he nodded, she offered a smile full of the same orthodontics as Pru's. "Hi. I'm the best friend, Brooke, second-in-command of the Umproo Crew."

"Hello, Brooke."

Molly headed to the SUV, Meatball hot on her heels. "I have permission to take some supplies in, and I transfer that permission to you," she said to Trace. "Can you get that box of brushes and trays and grab the paint can? Pru selected a lovely neutral shade of white. Plain as Day White, I think it's called. Maybe Boring as Hell White. Certainly Uninspired White."

"Any kind of white will be an improvement over Decades-Old Dull." He came up next to her, peering into the back where the big cage they'd used for Meatball stood open. A rush of memories almost knocked him over.

"That looks...familiar."

Molly sucked in a little breath and elbowed him. "Hush. Gramma Finnie is right there."

But her grandmother was already walking through the open door to the house, leaving Trace and Molly alone. "Tell me that doesn't remind you of..." He leaned down to whisper in her ear, but she slipped away.

"You can't do that," she said softly. "You can't make casual references to…that."

"Nothing casual about it, Irish, but I get what you're saying. Still…" He put his hand on the wire rim of the crate and gave it a noisy shake. "Brings back fond memories."

She closed her eyes and shook her head.

"Not fond?"

"Not yet," she said.

"Then there's hope." He scooped up the paint tray and hooked a paint can handle on his finger.

"Hope for what?" Molly asked.

"That I can make you laugh about it. Remember it with anything but regret."

"I don't regret that night," she said quickly. "I got Pru."

He turned, arms full, and looked at her. "Would you do it again?"

"Are you asking me to?"

He laughed at that. "Let's see how the Puppy Parade goes tonight."

Her jaw dropped, and if he'd had a free hand, he'd have tapped it back in place. Instead, he winked at her and went inside, where he was bombarded with plans, a schedule, assignments, and something called a Project Management Workflow Coordination Map.

"She's taking a business class," Gramma Finnie explained as she snapped a picture of Pru lining up her paperwork on the crappy Formica counter. "I think she's going to be a CEO."

Pru turned to them all, hands on narrow hips, her thick, dark hair—precisely the color and texture of Trace's—in two long braids over her shoulders. She talked, and he tried to listen, tried to process the sequence of events she had planned not only for today but for at least a few weekends into the future, but her words were muffled and lost in the thumping pulse in his head.

That's my daughter. That's my girl. That's my offspring, flesh and blood, DNA, child of my loin. I made *her.*

Most fathers had years to look at their kids and get used to the thrill of that, but it was so new to Trace. And all he wanted to do was throw his arms around her, lift her off the ground, twirl her, and tell her and…and…

And watch her face fall in horror when she realized her father was an ex-con with a murder rap and she was the granddaughter of an ex-con with a felony sheet longer than her to-do list.

"Don't you think that's a good idea, Mr. Bancroft?"

No, he knew it was a very, very bad idea. "Let's start by not calling me that," he said, grabbing the first thing that came to mind, since he had no idea what she'd asked.

"Okay, Trace," she said, shrugging off the request like she had so many more important concerns than his name. "But can we split up and each take an assignment in a different room? It might mean you live in more of a mess than if we did it room by room."

"I'm not living here," he reminded her. "Mess it up to your heart's content."

She grinned at him, showing braces and a shocking similarity to…his mother. Good Lord, she did look like his mother. In the high cheekbones and delicate chin especially. The eyes were Molly's, but everything else was his, even that cleft.

Without thinking, he rubbed his chin, aware that in his determination to be clean-shaven, he'd left a telltale clue right out in the open.

He glanced at Molly, but she was tracking Meatball, who was making his way around the room, sniffing everything at nose level and below.

"Remember, you can't do anything that's not part of an assignment I've given you," Pru continued. "Gramma Finnie will monitor the workflow and document to be sure we meet all contest rules. Mom will start emptying things and Mr....uh, Trace, you can give your permission as to what to throw away and what to keep."

"Throw away everything."

Pru lifted her brows. "Oookay. We'll use discretion. Brooke and I will start with the back bedroom. That first one? With the, uh, cannabis décor bedspread?"

Trace looked skyward. "My mother was...eccentric. This was her house. I only slept here. Sometimes."

"You don't have to explain, sir," Brooke said. "We know where you've been."

"Brooke!" Pru shot her a warning look. "I told you not to talk about it."

"It's okay," he said, holding up two hands. "I'm pretty sure it wouldn't be such a great service project if I'd been traveling around Europe for the past fourteen years."

Pru gave him a shaky smile. "I don't want to be rude."

"It's not rude," he assured her. "And it's not the

first time my shortcomings had me in line to be someone's service project."

As soon as he said it, he realized his mistake, mostly because of the nearly inaudible and sudden intake of Molly's breath. Damn it! What was he doing, saying things like that? He tried to cover by making a move toward Meatball, who was eyeing the sofa for a jump.

"No, no, boy. You can't do that." He caught the dog's collar and glanced up at Molly, seeing the wild warning in her eyes, exactly as expected.

"That's right," she said sternly, coming over to where he was. "You *can't* do that."

She made it sound like she was talking to the dog, but he knew better. Pru had no idea they'd even known each other in high school. She wasn't dumb. Good God, she was the smartest person who ever swam in his gene pool.

"We'll be careful, right, Meatball?"

The dog barked, looked at Molly, and curled up at her feet.

Oh, this could be a long day.

Molly wasn't alone with Trace again for at least an hour, when they were assigned to the kitchen to empty cabinets into cartons divided for donations and trash.

"You're starting to make me nervous," Molly whispered when they were alone.

"Starting?" He whipped open a cabinet and eyed the contents, then shot her a smile. "Kidding. I'll be careful. I'll be quiet."

"No, but if you're not ready for her to know, then you have to be careful."

"She's very intelligent and perceptive," he agreed. "She's also beautiful, funny, sweet, and respectful. God, you've done an amazing job with her, Molly. I can't..." He swallowed noisily, as if finishing the sentence was difficult. "I can't get used to it."

"Shhh. You will." She pulled out a stack of chipped dishes. "Keep or throw?"

"Throw. Did you tell her about the Puppy Parade?"

"Uh, not yet."

"Chicken."

"You should talk." Molly pushed up on the counter, then got to her knees to start pulling out glasses one by one. "Wow, there's not a match in the set."

"She liked flea markets," he said with a dry laugh.

"You don't have to apologize for her, Trace. Being a single mother isn't easy. I don't know how she did it. I had a whole giant family behind me."

"And went to vet school."

"The family is *how* I went to vet school." She gingerly pulled out a cracked martini glass that had seen better days. "Do not underestimate the power of a big family. I'm not raising Pru alone." She stretched for something in the back, but couldn't quite get it. "And I can't reach the top shelves. You're up."

He reached for her hand, but she wobbled a little, and he grabbed her waist to assist her down, holding her tight so she wouldn't slip off the counter. For a long beat of time, probably too long, he kept his hands there, setting her down and holding her gaze.

"But you're her mother. You get the gold star for amazing work."

She looked up at him, at his whisper of a smile that she longed to see more of. "A gold star?"

"Unless you want something else."

Like…a kiss. She could read the word in his eyes, feel it in the way his grip tightened.

What were they talking about? Oh, Pru. "I don't deserve a gold star for raising her."

"I get at least *some* of the credit."

At Gramma Finnie's voice, they jerked apart, as guilty as two people could possibly be.

"That's true," Molly said, nervously clearing her throat. "Gramma and Pru are like…salt and pepper, next to each other at every family dinner."

"I'd be the salt," Gramma said, giving her wispy white hair a pat.

Molly didn't answer as she mentally recapped the conversation and wondered if her grandmother had been listening. Not that she'd eavesdrop, but they'd been talking all morning about family and life and her school. They hadn't said anything revealing, she was certain. They'd talked like two adults about her life and child, not like he was Pru's *father*.

"The love goes both ways," Gramma said. "After all, she taught me how to blog, and I've taught her everything an old woman can know in eighty-six years."

"That must be quite a bit," Trace said with that same note of jealousy when he joked about how attached Meatball was to Molly. Maybe he was jealous of any and all who helped raise Pru.

"Aye, but I fear I might be gettin' into sticky territory that only a mother can handle," Gramma said. She leaned in, cupped her hands, and stage-whispered, "Heads-up for someone named Cody Noonan."

"Cody Noonan?" Molly nodded. "I've heard the name from the front seat of the car. I think he's new at the middle school, and the very thought of him elicits some giggles. Why is that sticky territory?"

Gramma gave a one-shouldered shrug. "Apparently, the lad recently moved here from *Texas*." She said the word as though it were equal with Hades. "He should be in ninth grade but is in eighth, allegedly because the 'school calendars' didn't line up or something, but he's nearly *fourteen*, drums in a band, and looks like Harry Styles."

For all her youthfulness and social media savvy, Gramma Finnie was still an octogenarian. The kid was probably in a drumline, not a rock band, and anyone with a mop of hair and a pretty smile looked like Harry Styles to Pru and her friends.

"It's okay, Gram—"

"Is it?" Trace asked sharply. "I'm not sure I like this."

Was he serious? Molly and Gramma both turned to look at him, but probably for entirely different reasons. Her grandmother might be surprised by Trace's opinion, but Molly just wanted him to be quiet. If anyone could figure this out, it would be Gramma Finnie. Who was staring at Trace a little too hard right then.

"I mean, she's obviously a sweet and innocent girl, and I don't know who Harry Styles is…" He stumbled, knowing exactly what his mistake had been. "But a fourteen-year-old drummer? Molly, that's…"

She narrowed her eyes at him. "I got this," she said. "She tells me everything, and you two don't have to worry."

Trace's dark brows flicked enough for Molly to read his silent question. *Didn't you tell your mother everything, too?*

Gramma Finnie's eyes showed the same wariness. "You sure about that, lass?"

Her subtext—the same as Trace's—was clear, too, despite the Irish brogue. "Don't you have pictures to take, Gramma?"

"Actually, I do have to go outside." She pulled out a phone. "I want to check my blog comments, and there's no wireless in here. I'll have to find some cell service." She gave a little wave goodbye. Trace and Molly stood stone-still until she was gone.

"Sorry," he murmured after a second. "I shouldn't have reacted like a...you know."

Like a father. "We should tell her," she said, the urgency pressing on her. "You aren't going to keep this secret for long," she said in a soft whisper. "It's all over your face when you look at her and talk about her. Gramma can do math, too, you know, and she's one of the wisest people I know."

"And how do you think she's going to take it when you tell her?" he shot back.

"Better than if she figures it out on her own." Either way, it could change everything, and Molly simply wanted that over with.

"She won't figure it out," he said. "I swear, I promise, I give you my word I won't slip up again. But, Molly, not yet. Please. I want her to know me as a person before she has to accept me as a—"

She put her finger over his lips before he said it. "Shh. Don't say it."

"Please," he repeated. "You might be ready, but I'm not."

The honest pain in his eyes did something to her deep inside, and so did the warmth of his breath on her fingertips. "Okay," she relented. "We can wait. But be careful."

"I will be." He reached up and closed his hand over hers, pressing that finger against his lips and kissing it lightly. Just then, a sudden burst of giddy laughter came from the back of the house, and once again, they shot apart before getting caught.

As Molly moved back to the cabinet, Pru came into the kitchen, holding a shoe box. "Excuse me, Trace? I don't think you want to throw this away."

"What is it?" he asked.

"It looks like journals. You know, diaries? I opened the top one, but it had an entry, and I swear I closed it immediately. I would never read another person's journal."

Molly fought a smile at Pru's sincerity, peering around Trace's shoulder at the box. It held cloth-covered books, and the sides were stuffed with loose papers and envelopes.

"That's my mother's," he said. "You can toss it."

Pru sucked in a breath, her jaw loose. "Throw away journals?"

"They're junk."

"Junk?" Pru seemed horrified. "Don't you care what she wrote?"

Molly saw his shoulders rise and fall with a breath as she checked out the box, her gaze moving to the papers jammed into the side. Papers, receipts, and pictures. Well, one picture. The corner of one that showed the edge of something yellow. A yellow...house.

"She took the time to write something," Pru continued. "Her thoughts and feelings are in there, I'd guess. Don't you care?"

He answered, but Molly didn't hear because of the sudden rush of blood in her head. That wasn't any yellow house. That was Waterford Farm.

"Well, here you go." Pru handed the box to him. "I sure as heck wouldn't throw something away my mother wrote." She grinned past him at Molly. "I swear, Mom."

Molly struggled to smile, but her head felt light and dizzy and weird.

"Back to work, you two," Pru said with a playful snap of her fingers. She pivoted and went bounding to the back of the house.

Trace tossed the box on the counter, which caused a journal to move, revealing more of the photo. A photo Molly remembered instantly. Clearly. Vividly. And hadn't noticed it was missing.

"Trace." His name was little more than air.

"What's wrong?" he asked, putting his hands on her shoulders as if he suddenly realized she was reeling. "What's—"

She reached to the box, plucking the picture with two fingers, sliding it out of where it was wedged between the side of the box and the stack of hardcover journals.

"This...is what's wrong."

Very slowly, she turned it over, already knowing

the image. It was Pru, on her first birthday, standing on the porch at Waterford with her arm around Buddy, the setter they had when Pru was born.

He stared at it, silent, then he looked up at her, his face as bloodless as hers probably was.

"She knew," he whispered. "My mother knew about Pru."

And they'd just come *that* close to Pru knowing, too.

Chapter Thirteen

T race had managed to make it through the afternoon. After the crew went home for dinner, he'd stared at the diaries for a long time before opening one.

He had no desire to read her ramblings, astrological garbage, and bad poetry. He flipped through the journal that had the latest date and found a single piece of paper slipped inside with the name Annie Kilcannon written in blue ink, a phone number, and some cryptic notes.

Trace had tucked that into his jeans pocket, but since he'd met up with Molly in town, there were so many people and two completely crazy golden retriever puppies on leashes, so they hadn't talked at all about what they'd discovered today.

By silent agreement, they were waiting for the right time, which seemed to be the theme for their entire relationship.

"I don't remember Bitter Bark being quite this festive," Trace said as he and Molly walked toward Bushrod Square, which was so lit up with white lights on the trees that it felt like daylight as they got closer.

Tashie and Bo tugged at their leashes and scampered ahead, both of them wearing sparkling rhinestone collars that Molly explained were given to all the puppies in the parade. They weaved back and forth, getting tangled, barking so hard they both jumped on their hind legs like toy dogs.

And everyone who passed oohed, awwed, and stopped to pet them.

"First of all, this is *Better* Bark," she reminded him. "At least for this calendar year, and we've always put white lights on the trees in the square all year long."

"Never noticed." Trace squinted into the crowds that filled the square, as many dogs as people, it seemed, and there were many, many people. The night was clear, and the temperature had cooperated to make for a picture-perfect setting for the town's first Puppy Parade. "Guess we'll see some familiar faces."

"Some." Molly wrapped Natasha's leash around her hand with the expertise of a person who'd handled dogs since birth, easily guiding the puppy around a stroller. Of course, everything was easier with Natasha. Boris was borderline bat-shit crazy, darting back and forth on the sidewalk, peeing on the grass every ten steps, greeting every other dog with a noisy, high-pitched bark. "But a lot of these people are tourists, too. Which was the whole idea of the Better Bark name change. You are walking through the Most Dog Friendly Town in America."

"Brilliant idea," he mused, smiling as a few little girls stopped to squee over the puppies.

"Chloe is gifted at the whole tourism thing." She added a laugh. "She won over the whole town and my brother Shane, too."

"So, once they get married, all three of your brothers will have met their wives and gotten married within, what, the same twelve months?" When she nodded, he added, "Shane credits your father for that, you know. He told me that one day in the kennels."

"Oh, I know. Dad's a bit of a matchmaker, it turns out."

"But he hasn't matched you."

She looked up at him, a playful smile tipping her pretty lips. "That's 'cause I'm his favorite."

"Oh?" Somehow, he doubted Daniel Kilcannon had a favorite, but he played along. "And you know this how?"

"I just do. I remind him of my mom, for one thing, and I'm the only one who went to veterinary school, for another."

He nodded, thinking of all she'd told him about those early years of being a young mother trying to get her degree. "I can see that that would impress your father."

"And we're close, my dad and I. He talks to the boys, of course, but with me? He tells me the emotional stuff. I know how much he's grieving, how much he misses my mother. My brothers and Darcy know, too, but I've actually talked to him about it."

He considered that, racked it up as another thing he liked about Molly Kilcannon. "And that's how you know he won't matchmake you?"

"I don't think he could find a man he considered good enough for me."

Trace's heart dropped with a thud. Yes, they were walking so close they had to touch, but that was because the sidewalk was crowded and she was probably cold. Yes, they flirted with each other, but only because they'd had an old attraction years ago. And yes, they shared a child, but the only thing they *truly* shared was the burden of how to break the news.

He had no business thinking anyone in her family would think Trace was good enough to date Molly. Not Pru, not her sweet Gramma Finnie, not her brothers, especially not the patriarch they called the Dogfather. It was plain stupid to think that.

"Ooh. Look, Take a Paws for Chocolate. How cute is that?" Molly tugged his arm in the direction of one of the many stands set up in and around the square. "Let's get some hot chocolate before we line up for the parade."

Just then, a blinding blue Porsche zoomed into a rare open parking spot in front of the stand, making more than a few people stop, turn, and tug their leashes closer.

"Jeez, fellow, there are pedestrians and dogs everywhere."

"That's Allen Phillips," Molly said softly. "Remember I told you Isabella Henderson married him?"

A man climbed out from the driver's side, looking around with that air of a person who expected to draw a crowd. He might be deep into his fifties, but he carried himself like someone who lived at the gym, and he had the looks of one of those handsome corporate dudes from a Viagra commercial.

Only then did Trace notice the passenger door open—no thanks to the driver of the car—and a woman he recognized climbed out. Isabella had aged well, if you liked the rich doctor's wife type, which he didn't. But she oozed money, style, and threw a zillion-watt smile in their direction.

"Hello, Molly," she called, waving as they came closer.

"Hey, Izzie," Molly replied as Tashie pulled her a little closer to inspect the new arrival. "Good to see you."

The women gave each other quick, friendly hugs on the sidewalk while the husband came closer. But Isabella's blue-eyed gaze was pinned on Trace.

"Oh my God! Is that who I think it is?"

"You remember Trace?" Molly said, her voice tight.

"Remember him?" Isabella let out a laugh that was a little too loud. "Of course I do. What are you doing back in Bitter Bark?" she asked as her husband joined them.

"And who's this, Isabella?" he said, also looking at Trace.

"Well, you know Molly, Titan's brilliant vet, and this is a boy I went to high school with."

Trace gave half-smile at the term *boy* and extended his hand to the other man. "Trace Bancroft."

"Allen Phillips," he said, scrutinizing Trace's face like he was searching for clues to a crime. "Bancroft, did you say?"

"Where have you been all these years?" Isabella asked, getting a little closer.

He didn't answer right away, feeling the man's gaze locked on him, judging him, finding him wanting.

"Oh...here and there," he said. Here being *here*. There being *Huttonsville*.

"And he's working at Waterford Farm now," Molly interjected, scooping up Tashie and trying to divert their attention with the dog.

"Are you?" Isabella petted Tashie's head but stared at Trace. Then Molly. "Well, that's...convenient."

"What do you do now, Trace?" the husband asked with that serious look that super-executive types seemed to have with other men. That *let's bond over our manly jobs* kind of thing that made Trace recoil.

When Trace didn't answer immediately, Molly lifted the pup higher. "He's training some of our service dogs, like this one."

"Oooh, how interesting," Isabella said as if Molly had announced he was running for the Senate unopposed. "I've been thinking about having Titan certified as a therapy dog. Would you help me, Trace?"

"*Service* dog," Molly corrected.

"Titan doesn't need to be a special-needs dog." Her husband shot down the idea before Trace could take a breath to answer. "Or a show dog. Or whatever..." He flicked his hand dismissively toward Trace and Molly. "Whatever kind of dogs you do. Titan is a *family* dog, and that's all he needs to be, Isabella."

She plastered on a smile in response. "Well, of course he is, hon."

"There you guys are!" A teenage girl came bounding up to them, long, honey-colored hair swinging over her jacket. "I thought you'd never get here."

"We were at dinner," Isabella said. "You know your father doesn't like to rush dessert."

"Okay, but guess what?" the girl asked, sliding between Allen and Isabella with a familiarity that made Trace suppose she was the stepdaughter Molly had mentioned. "I'm going to walk in the parade!" she announced. "Lauren and Madison both have puppies, and they want me to come with them. Okay?" She directed the question to Isabella, but it was her father who scowled in response.

"I don't think that's a good idea, Corinne." Whoa, the guy was a killjoy, evidenced by his daughter's crestfallen face. "We're here to *see* the event, not *be* the event. You'd do well to remember that, young lady."

"But they—"

"Corinne."

She tipped her head in resignation, but then she noticed Molly and brightened again. "Oh, hi, Dr. Kilcannon. Is Pru here?"

"She's working the Waterford Farm information table, which I think is way at the end of the parade route," Molly replied. "I'm sure she'd love company." She stopped and glanced at the girl's father. "If that's okay with your parents."

"Pru Kilcannon?" the man said, as if he were putting two and two together and realized Molly was Pru's mother. "She's a good girl," he said, nodding his consent.

Trace felt his fingers tighten over the leash and his jaw clench. Who the hell was this guy to pass judgment on *his* daughter?

Oh, yeah. A *lawyer*.

"Oh, look at this little guy!" Seeing the puppy Molly held, Corinne cooed, then noticed Bo bouncing around at the end of his leash. "Two of them! I could die from the cuteness!"

The distraction lasted for a moment, but Trace still felt Isabella's gaze on him. He turned and met it, bracing for some questions he really didn't want to answer. Where had he been? What had he done? Where was he living now?

But Molly leaned closer to the other woman before any questions were asked. "Izzie, you know it's almost time to sell wrapping paper, don't you?"

Another deflection, which he could have kissed her for.

"Oh sweet Lord, I was hoping I could get off that school fundraising committee this year." She smiled up at Trace. "It seems all I do is volunteer these days."

"That's what you're supposed to do," the husband interjected. "That and be a mother to your stepdaughter."

Isabella gave him a smile that never got anywhere near her blue eyes. "I know that, honey."

The one-second exchange felt awkward, and again, Molly shifted the course by putting Tashie on the ground and tugging leashes. "Well, we need to be in that parade, and I'm not going without hot chocolate. Come on, Trace, let's go before the line gets long."

"It's nice to see you back in town," Isabella called to Trace as they walked away, and he nodded his goodbye to walk with Molly and the dogs.

"Thanks for the save," he muttered.

She looked up at him, her eyes wide. "I wasn't really saving you, but I'm sure you're dreading the questions from locals."

He shrugged. "You were saving me, and I appreciate it."

"Actually…" She slowed her step as Tashie sniffed some grass. "I was saving both of us."

"How's that?"

"Well, when we were talking, it dawned on me that Izzie is the only person who knew I was with you. That night," she added, as if it needed to be said.

"You told her?"

"No, of course not. But remember she left us out on the lawn right before Bart McQueen showed up? I never went back to that party, and neither did you."

He nodded slowly. "So she could do some math, same as I did."

"She could, although it's generally understood by my high school friends that I got pregnant in college and that's why I quit UNC after a year. It's ancient history, really."

"Until I show up."

"No." She squeezed his arm. "Don't think of it that way. I wanted to get out of there. Plus, her husband is a butthead."

"That's being kind."

She smiled up at him, her eyes bright with their shared opinion, the whole exchange somehow bringing them closer as they got their hot chocolate and sipped it on the way to the start of the parade. They talked easily about some other people they'd both known in high school, and the tension of the conversation melted away as he walked with Molly like it was the most normal thing in the world.

If only this could be his life. If only he were good enough to take Molly Kilcannon on parade dates with hot chocolate and have conversations like couples had.

The ache for that was so strong he felt it in his head, his chest, and right down to his toes. And all he could do, after tossing their empty cups, was hold her hand and be grateful she didn't let go except to wave at the crowds down Ambrose Avenue and around Bushrod Square. The whole time, Trace was as happy as the two puppies who twirled and pranced and trotted in front of them.

But then they reached the end, and there was Pru, surrounded by friends and family, talking and laughing and looking like a dream.

Did he really want to turn the girl's little world into a nightmare? There was only one way to find out, and he was dreading it.

"Who's that with your mom, Pru?"

At Shelby's question, Pru turned to look over her shoulder in time to catch her mother scoop one of the retriever puppies into her arms and hand it to Trace. And she got that kick in her stomach again. She thought she'd handled it really well that afternoon when Mom casually dropped the *I'm going to help Trace out with the puppies in the parade* bomb. Pru had agreed it was a great idea. Not enthusiastically, but she'd agreed because it wasn't a *date*.

But they looked pretty couple-ish, if you asked her. Of course, no one had *asked* her. Not even Mom.

"It's just some guy."

No way was she telling any of this crowd she hung out with what her community service project was. She couldn't trust these overachieving nerds. Some might be her true friends, but some might snatch that trip to Carowinds right out of her hot little hands.

"She likes him," Teagan said.

"He's kind of cute, in that old guy sort of way," Shelby added.

For a second, Pru didn't know what to say, blinking at them, then sliding a look over her shoulder to see Mom and Trace face-to-face, laughing at some shared, secret joke.

"He's working at Waterford," she told her friends. "And my mom is taking care of his sick dog."

"That doesn't mean they aren't hooking up," Shelby said.

"Well, they're not," Pru spat. Because he was a *murderer*. Even the thought made a little guilt crawl up her spine. She knew she wasn't supposed to judge, but still. It was sure to come out eventually, and the next thing she knew, her friends would be making *Orange Is the New Black* jokes about her mom.

Plus, if they were dating, it would probably be against the project rules, though she wasn't sure about that.

"And your mom tutored him in high school," Corinne said. "My stepmother just told me—"

"Whoa, code red." Brooke's eyes widened as she hid a pointing finger with a cupped hand. "Girls, we have a code red. Or should I say a 'Cody' red?"

That cracked everyone up, but Pru didn't laugh or care that Cody Noonan had arrive. Mom and Trace had known each other before? She'd *tutored* him? What the—

"Pru!" Brooke nudged her. "Two o'clock. Moving in fast with Zach Stowe right next to him."

"Oh my God, he's so cute," Corinne said under her breath, lifting brochures from the table and tapping them like the last thing in the world she cared about was the new kid.

"He can drum me anytime," Teagan deadpanned.

"Like you've ever drummed anything, Teagan." Shelby's joke made them all explode with laughter. Except Pru, because her head was spinning. Why wouldn't her mother tell her she had *tutored* Trace?

"Oh, please," Teagan shot back. "Like you'd know what to do after a kiss."

"I wouldn't," Shelby admitted. "But I'd like to find out."

That got another squeal of hilarity, and a lot of people turned to look at them.

"Sounds like the natives are getting restless," Uncle Shane teased from where he and Chloe were talking to some people a few feet away.

"He's walking the other way!" Teagan said, elbowing Shelby. "Let's go."

"Wait, Pru can't leave the table yet," Brooke said.

"Sucks to be you," Shelby said. "Come on, Corinne."

Corinne shook her head and looked in the other direction. "I told my parents I'd find them after the parade. I have to go. Good luck with all that drumming," she joked. She started to walk in the other direction, but Pru couldn't stop herself from snagging Corinne's jacket sleeve.

"Are you sure about what your stepmother said? About the tutoring?"

"Yeah, why?"

Because then Mom essentially lied to me. "I didn't think they knew each other before, that's all."

Corinne looked over Pru's shoulder. "Well, they know each other now." She grinned. "You better check your facts about this not being a date."

Pru whipped around to see Mom's head tilting back in her easy laugh, so familiar that Pru could imagine exactly what it sounded like, even though she was too far away to hear it. Mom put her hand on Trace's shoulder, and whatever she said cracked him up, too, then the dog between them started squirming, and they put it down at the same time, giggling like that was all kinds of hilarious, too. But if they knew each other, then—

"Hey, Pru."

The boy's voice yanked her back around as effectively as if he'd put his hand on her shoulder and turned her. Then she was staring straight at the unusually large Adam's apple of Cody Noonan, watching it bob once before she had the nerve to look up and meet his gaze.

"Oh, hi, Cody. Are you here for information on Waterford Farm?" Where did that come from? She didn't know, but she thanked God she managed to stay so cool. "We are the largest canine training and rescue facility on the East Coast. Are you a dog lover?"

His lips curled up. "I'm into cats."

"Cats are cool."

He narrowed his eyes in a way that might have been an attempted smolder, or maybe one of those long lashes got under his eyelid. Either way, it was kind of cute. "Want to come over and meet mine?"

She almost choked. "Excuse me?"

Zach came a little closer, looking at Brooke.

"We're jamming at Cody's house tonight," he said. "You guys can be the first to hear Salvation's Fury."

"What's that?" Brooke asked.

"Our band," Cody said. "Some other kids are coming over, too."

Right then, Teagan and Shelby closed in on the circle, acting like they were so cool and not absolute Cody stalkers.

"Can you make it?" Cody asked, looking right at Pru with those insane eyes that were cuter than Harry Styles's, to be honest.

"I, uh…" She glanced at her mom again, who was now headed in this direction with the guy she *tutored in high school.* How could she not tell Pru? "Let me ask my mom."

Cody's eyes flickered like that might have been the lamest thing he'd ever heard, but too bad. She had to ask.

She slipped past him and walked toward her mom and Trace, who didn't look quite so close now that they knew she was watching. But they *knew each other* from before. Why hadn't Mom told her that? It was key information.

"Pru, what's wrong?" her mother asked as she got closer and searched Pru's face.

"Is that kid bothering you?" Trace asked.

She shot him a look and shook her head, grabbing Mom's arm to pull her aside for privacy.

"Why didn't you tell me?" she demanded.

Mom literally paled. She could see the blood drain from her face. "Tell you…"

"That you tutored him in high school!"

"How'd you find out?"

Find out? Why would she use that expression unless she'd been hiding it? "Why'd you lie?" Pru shot back. "Better question." She heard the hiss in her voice and knew it was wrong, hated that she was doing this, but *come on.* "Don't you realize, Mom? Don't you know? It could ruin everything."

Mom just stared at her, as speechless as Pru had ever seen her.

"Don't you see?" Pru insisted. "It looks like you got me the project!"

"Oh…is that all?"

"Is that all?" Pru's head almost exploded. "I can't break the rules, Mom."

Mom started nodding, fast and furious. "I get that. I understand. You didn't. You didn't do anything to break the rules."

Not yet, anyway. "But if you're, like, with him."

"I'm not with him."

"Or you knew him before."

"We went to the same high school, Pru. The only one in town. I was a year behind him. It was fifteen years ago. More."

Pru sighed, realizing she was probably overreacting. "Yeah, you're right. Everybody went to Bitter Bark High."

"Exactly. Is that all you're upset about?"

Wasn't it enough? "Well." She looked over her shoulder at the kids, knowing the next request wasn't going to be that easy. "I was wondering if I can go out with friends after this thing is over?"

"With Brooke?" Mom glanced at the group around the Waterford information table. "And…is that Shelby and Teagan?"

"Yes."

"And those boys?"

Pru closed her eyes and weighed her options. She could lie. After all, Mom had. She didn't want Pru to *find out* that she'd already known this Trace guy. So it would be easy…but wrong.

"That's Cody Noonan and his friend Zach. A bunch of kids are going to his house to hear them play. They formed a band."

"Cody Noonan." She bit her lip, thinking.

"Don't look at him, Mom," Pru warned. "Please don't embarrass me."

Mom blinked at that, but then she nodded. "I won't embarrass you. But I don't know his parents, Pru."

"Mom." She sighed. "I'm thirteen. I'm not going to do anything wrong. I'll be with three of my girlfriends you've known since I was little. He lives about ten minutes from our house, and I'll have my phone on with Find My Friends, so you'll know where I am every minute. Please?"

Her mother glanced over her shoulder, and Pru turned to follow her gaze. Trace had walked the puppies to the table and was talking to Shane. And… "Is he giving Cody the evil eye? What the heck?"

"He's just…" Mom didn't finish, but took Pru's arm and got her attention back. "Yes. You can go."

"Really?"

"Keep your phone on and text me every hour or so, and I'll pick you up at ten."

"Ten?"

"Thirty," Molly added. "What about dinner?"

"What about it?"

"We were all going to go out."

All? Like Trace and Mom and Pru? She puffed out a breath. "I shouldn't go out with my community service project. It might be—"

"Against the rules, I know." Frustration tightened her mother's voice. "Pru, he's a human being first and a community service project second. Get your priorities straight."

"Okay," she said, burning a little because most kids would have shot back with *Get yours straight!* But she wasn't most kids and never would be. "But I'll grab something with Brooke. I have some money." She leaned forward to give her a quick kiss. "Thanks, Mom."

"Pru, wait." Mom grabbed her jacket. "Do you like him?"

Pru lifted a brow in response. "Do you?"

Her eyes widened, and she knew exactly what Pru was talking about. "Pru, I—"

"Please don't mess up my project, Mom. If Mr. Margolis thinks I'm working on my mom's boyfriend's house, I'll never win."

She could have sworn her mother's eyes flashed with fear.

"Didn't think of that, did you?" Pru asked.

"He's not," she said simply. "He works for Waterford, and I'm his dog's vet."

Exactly what she'd told her friends, but then Corinne's words came back. "And you tutored him in high school," she added, then made a face. "In what?"

"Chemistry." Mom gave her a little nudge. "You go now. Have fun."

She wanted to say, *You, too*, but couldn't. So Pru gave a little wave and ran off to her friends, not even looking at Trace Bancroft.

But something told her that Mom wasn't telling the truth about him. She *did* like him.

Chapter Fourteen

Shane took the puppies back to Waterford for Trace, freeing him and Molly up for a long, quiet dinner. Molly suggested Ricardo's because the wait wouldn't be too long. The wait for a table, that was. The wait to finally have a quiet, private time to talk about what they'd discovered that afternoon seemed interminable.

That wait wasn't over until they'd settled into a booth and each had a glass of wine and, finally, complete privacy.

Trace lifted his to toast. "To secrets."

"And how hard they are to keep."

The glasses clinked, and she took a taste of merlot, but the real kick came from the way he held her gaze over the rim of his glass. A steady, still gaze that felt intimate and honest and nice.

"I found this in one of her journals." He shifted so he could pull out a wallet, then slid a small piece of paper across the table for Molly to read.

Annie Kilcannon
555-492-8749
2:00 PM B.S.

"Mean anything to you?" he asked.

"That's our old Waterford Farm house number, which was disconnected years ago. We all use cell phones, and there's a business line now. That's not my mother's handwriting."

"It's my mother's," he said. "After skimming her diaries, I know that without a doubt. What's BS? What Annie told her?"

"My guess is Bushrod Square. A meeting at two o'clock."

He inched back. "Nice work, Sherlock."

"My mother always met people there. She liked to get coffee, take one of her dogs, and walk the paths in the square." Molly took another sip of wine. "So your mother must have been the 'good authority' who told my mother you were dead."

He flinched a little, and Molly immediately regretted that theory, putting her hand over his. "I'm sure she thought she was protecting you."

His look said otherwise. "Probably transferring her wishful thinking."

Molly's jaw dropped. "That you were dead?"

He averted his eyes on an exhale, quiet for a moment. "My father died in prison," he said, the simple statement nearly taking her breath away.

"What?" She'd had no idea his father had been in jail, no idea about his father at all.

"He went in for armed robbery when I was really little, three years old. My mom moved around a lot, but finally settled in Bitter Bark and became…whatever the hell she was. A fake." He lifted his wine and looked at it, deep in thought. "My dad had a heart attack, or so they say, when I was ten, and my mother started proudly calling herself a widow, which I guess was better than 'married to a cell warrior.' But she had a lot of bitterness and resentment, and I guess I look a lot like my old man. Every time she looked at me, it reminded her of the loser she married, and she constantly told me I was like him. Exactly like him."

Molly tried—really tried—to imagine being raised like that and simply couldn't. It also made sense why he never talked about his childhood.

From across the table, he gave a sly smile. "You look like you're in literal pain, Irish."

"I am. For you. It's so wrong to have that put on your shoulders as a child. So unfair to you." She realized she still had her hand over his and turned her fingers to thread them together. "You are not the sum total of that woman's opinion."

He looked doubtful.

"She stole your self-worth." Molly spat out the words, and when he didn't agree, she leaned closer. "Didn't your therapist tell you that?"

"Yeah, but do you have any idea the percentage of prisoners who are second-generation? Third? It's a legacy, Molly, handed down from loser to loser."

She pushed back, breaking the contact to cross her arms. "I refuse to believe that, and if it's true, it's not nature, it's nurture. *Your* daughter wouldn't know how to break a law if she had to."

He conceded that with a tip of his head. "Thanks to her mother."

She looked at him for a long time, her heart softening for this handsome, strong, honest man who'd been given such a raw deal. Uncrossing her arms, she leaned closer again. "She's half yours, Trace Bancroft."

His smile was slow, and so real it reached his eyes and then climbed right into Molly's heart to take residence there. "I couldn't have picked a better mother for my child." Reaching across the table with both hands, he took hers and added a light squeeze. "Look, can we change the subject? Can we not talk about my parents or our child or the past or the future or anything like that?"

She lifted a brow. "What's left?"

"Life. Food. Current events. Dogs. Work. The way my heart feels like it might stop whenever I touch you. There's so much to talk about on our dinner date."

She stared at him, the admission about his heart doing the same thing to hers. "So, it's a dinner date?"

He didn't answer, because the waiter showed up with an appetizer to share and chatted with them about the specials like they were any couple on a date during a busy Saturday night in Bitter Bark. When they were alone again, Molly answered his question as she picked up her fork.

"Yes, Trace, we can talk about anything you like. Will you tell me how you train service dogs? I really don't know that much about the process."

That smile lit his face again, and for the next two hours, they did exactly as he'd wanted. With the exception of the casual reference to Pru or prison as part of the stories they shared, fourteen years fell away as they talked openly, ate heartily, and finally shared tiramisu for dessert.

By the time they left, Molly felt a glow that had as much to do with the company as the one glass of wine she'd had. They didn't hold hands as they walked through the square toward Molly's car, but their fingers brushed, and each time, a little electricity shot through her.

"Feel that, Irish?" he whispered as they meandered down a path.

"Yeah." Why lie?

"That's what I was talking about."

She looked up at him. "Pretty strong stuff."

"Always was with you." They wandered past the statue of Thaddeus Ambrose Bushrod and past the wrought-iron fence around the Bitter Bark tree.

"Did you know that's really a hickory?" she said, nodding to the massive tree. "Talk about dark secrets that this town kept for years."

He laughed softly. "This town has really changed," he noted. "So many tourists. So many more businesses and shops."

She looked around, thinking about a meeting that might have taken place in this very square between two grandmothers at two o'clock one day. "When did your mother leave Bitter Bark? And not sell her house?" she asked.

He thought about it for a minute. "My best guess? Ten minutes after she found out about Pru. The house never sold and when she died, I signed some paper to take it off the market."

For some reason, that hurt. "Why would she leave after finding out about Pru?"

"I don't know." He looked down at her and slid his arm around her. "I thought we weren't going to talk about it."

"Pru will want to know when we tell her."

"Or that. We weren't going to talk about that, either."

"Trace, we have to—"

"I know, I *know*." He added a squeeze. "Don't ruin my first date in fourteen years by making me worry about stuff I can't change tonight."

"Your first..." She slowed her step and looked up at him, the white lights on the trees behind him blurring in her vision. "I hadn't thought about it like that."

"I did," he whispered. "All through dinner, I kept thinking, whoa, this is what I missed. Dinner with a pretty girl in a nice restaurant with great conversation. And thanks to your brother, I could actually pay for it."

She smiled up at him. "Was it all you'd hoped it would be?"

"No." He slid his arms around her waist, very slowly and deliberately, easing her closer. Their jackets were bulky enough to add a barrier, but he was warm and close. "It was more."

"Yeah," she agreed. "A good date. Our first."

"And you know that no good date is complete without..."

"A kiss," she finished for him.

He inhaled softly, holding her gaze, inches apart, the anticipation almost as thrilling as what she knew was about to happen. She felt suspended in his arms, floating closer, a little dizzy and achy.

But he didn't move.

She bit her lip with a sly smile. "You think you forgot how?"

"I might need a lesson."

She put her cold hands on his face, feeling the angles of his bones and the very first hint of nighttime whisker growth. "First, you get really steady."

"I'm steady." He tightened his grip on her waist.

"You feel a little wobbly, though."

"You do that to me," she whispered, letting her gaze drop to his mouth, which was still as beautiful as the first time she'd kissed it.

"Then what?" he asked.

She lifted on her toes to get to the right height. "Then you line up."

He angled his head one way, then the other, as if finding the right spot. "And?"

"And then you close your eyes."

"But I can't see you."

"Use your imagination." She closed hers. "See the person in your heart."

"Molly."

She dropped back on her heels and opened her eyes at the way he said her name, almost as if his voice cracked. "What?"

"I'm afraid."

"Of what?"

"That our first kiss will be our last."

His tender admission folded her heart in half. This rough, tough, tattooed former inmate was nothing but the kindest, sweetest, most humble man she'd ever met. She could hardly look at him her heart was pounding so much, filled with something she didn't quite recognize. Affection. Attraction. Desire.

But something else, too.

"It won't be," she promised. "It will not be our last, Trace Bancroft."

To seal that promise, she closed the space between them and pressed her mouth to his. She felt him sigh at first, then find that perfect amount of pressure, warm and delicious, against her lips.

Lost, Molly forgot about tiptoes and closed eyes and secrets and years and decisions they'd yet to make. All she could do was feel the smooth, sexy, sultry mouth over hers and taste the tip of his tongue as he deepened the kiss. She clung to his cheeks, then dragged her hands over his neck, melting into him, letting a whimper escape her throat.

No, it would not be their last kiss. She honestly wondered how she'd be able to stop at one. Or why she should.

How had he lived without this? How had he dragged his sorry ass through fourteen years of prison and punishment and abject loneliness? Trace had no idea how he'd survived without this kind of contact, but he knew one thing: He couldn't survive without it now.

She tasted so good, so right and real and womanly that he honestly thought if he had to go another fourteen years without kissing Molly Kilcannon, he'd rather die.

At the warning of trouble in his head, he managed to break the contact, but she instantly tilted her head back and invited his mouth to taste her sweet jaw, her soft throat, her delicate skin. In the distance—or at least it sounded that way with the pulse thumping in his head—he heard a dog bark and voices, laughter and chatter.

It broke the spell and made him lift his head, looking from one side to the other, to realize the square was definitely not empty. And he shouldn't be seen making out with Molly like a crazed teenager with no concern for the fact that she was well-known and loved in town.

"C'mon," he said, wrapping an arm around her and pulling her into the shadows, away from the strings of white lights.

"My car's on the other side of the square, parked behind my sister-in-law's town house. You came with Shane, right? I can drive you back to Waterford."

And come into his studio apartment? No, he couldn't let her do that.

"How else are you going to get home?" she asked when he didn't accept the offer.

"Don't you have to pick up Pru?"

"I have half an hour. I can get you there and back."

He nodded, refusing to let go of her until they reached her little blue car, parked in a quiet, empty alley behind that row of brick town houses. He kept a hand on her shoulder as she fished out her keys and unlocked the passenger side. He took the keys from her hands.

"Let me drive."

"I'm fine."

"It'll keep me from leaning over and kissing you while you're driving."

"What'll keep me from doing that?"

He gave her a good long look, caressing her lower lip with his thumb. "Common sense, remember?"

"I think you just kissed it out of me."

Oh man. Why did she say things like that? It gave him hope, and if there was one thing Trace Bancroft had learned to live without, it was hope. "Get in the car, Irish."

She didn't move, looking up at him for a long time, silent, searching, her lips parted like she longed for one more kiss.

"You won't get to Waterford and back in time to pick up Pru."

"I have a better idea," she said softly, and the way the words slipped out made his chest tight and his whole body hard. "Why don't we pick up Pru together? Then we'll drive you home."

And that would be safe, no chance of begging her to come inside, no long good-night kisses that made him want to die of need.

"Yeah, okay."

"Good." She curled a hand around his neck and pulled him closer. "Time for more of this."

The kiss shocked him, not only because he wasn't expecting it, but the heat index had somehow risen in the ten-minute walk between there and here. Her kiss was openmouthed and hungry, holding nothing back as she let him taste the vanilla and coffee lingering on her tongue.

"Irish," he whispered into the kiss. "Do you always have to kiss me first?"

"Looks that way." She inched back. "Unless you want to try to beat me to it."

He felt his lips curl up in a smile as he leaned her whole body against the car and braced himself in front of her. "This one's mine." He put his hands on her cheeks and cradled her sweet face against his palms. "Let me take my time."

Her eyes shuttered closed as she drew closer. "Not too much time, please."

He looked at her, eyes closed, lips parted, that

mane of curls swirling around her precious face.

"Waiting," she whispered, making him laugh.

"I'm memorizing you," he admitted.

She opened one eye. "Excuse me?"

"So I can dream about you."

"Where'd you learn the smooth lines, Bancroft?"

"Oh, I read romance novels in prison."

That made her laugh, which changed her whole face, taking it from pretty to spectacular. The sound of her musical giggle echoed in the alley, her delicious body moving against him as she tipped her head back to laugh. She was the most beautiful creature he'd ever seen, this dog-saving, perfect-child-raising, first-kissing woman whom he thought of every single time he thought about sex, which was a whole helluva lot.

"Molly." He whispered her name because it sounded as pretty as she was, moving closer to her mouth, holding her tight, and initiating a kiss for once. She kissed back with all her passion, with the spark that made her so unusual and bright, and enough desire to send all his blood thrumming south to make his jeans so tight, he wanted to scream.

His hands ached to get under the jacket to get closer, one touch. One single touch of her skin was all he needed. He ran his hands up and down her back, pulling her into him, aware of her fingers sliding into his hair, over his neck, and along his shoulders, like she was seeking a way under clothes, too. He vibrated with need, humming, pulsing, and he could feel her doing exactly the same—

"Wait, wait."

He jerked away at her request.

"My phone is going crazy."

"That's your phone vibrating?"

"Among other things." Pulling it out of the handbag, she sucked in a soft breath.

"What's wrong?"

"Pru."

He stepped away, a little stunned at the shot, like a hypodermic full of adrenaline had been stuck in this gut. "What's wrong?"

"I don't know. But she texted me about ten times, and I didn't even notice. She needs me to get her, now."

He was already moving her aside, opening the door, nudging Molly into the passenger seat. "Let's go."

Closing her door, he jogged around to the other side, yanking the car door open, and moving on an instinct he hadn't even known he possessed: protection.

He blew out a breath, the thought making him a little light-headed. "What happened, Molly? Is she okay?"

"She's fine. She wants me to pick her up sooner."

"She texted ten times. She must be in trouble."

"Or impatient." Molly clicked through the texts on her phone as Trace left the alley, then read him the address. "It's not far from here."

Even still, he accelerated hard out of the alley and onto the main street.

"Slow down, Trace," she said. "There's no reason to go back to prison."

He shot her a look. "If that little prick put a hand on her, I will."

"Wow."

As he headed down the main drag, he glanced at Molly. "What, wow?"

217

"You really are her father."

He started to argue, then stopped, tapping on the brakes when he came up to another car at the light. "Yeah, I guess I am."

As he turned, Molly reached over and put her hand on his arm. "Which is almost as attractive as the way you kiss."

"Almost," he said, keeping things light, even though he felt anything but light.

Ten minutes later, when Pru came running down the driveway of a darkened house as they pulled up, any chance of lightness disappeared at the sight of her.

"Has she been crying?" Trace asked, hearing the tautness in his voice.

Molly didn't answer, but the very moment the car stopped, she threw the door open and hopped out.

"Are you okay?"

It was all he heard, because she pushed the door closed as she took off to reach Pru, leaving Trace to sit at the wheel and watch the two of them carry on a conversation. He couldn't make out the words, but he could read the body language of a young girl spewing a story, a mother listening, hushing, touching with comfort, nodding with understanding.

His fingers curled around the door handle, ready to jump, to fight, to defend, to do whatever was necessary to make that kid feel good again. He'd do anything for her. *Anything.*

The realization slammed his chest and literally took his breath away.

When did this happen? How? Were genes that strong? Was it real? This...this...love? How was that even possible, and what did it mean? If he'd do anything for her, would he leave if he had to? If that's what she wanted?

The questions beat at his head, blurring his vision and squeezing his brain as Molly and Pru walked to the car.

"Hey," Pru said, climbing into the backseat.

"Hi." He studied her face in the rearview mirror. No sign of tears was visible, but her expression was pinched and unhappy. "You okay?"

"Fine." She dropped her jaw into her palm and turned to look out the window.

But clearly she wasn't. And he was not going to be fine with whoever put that sadness on her face.

Molly climbed in, silent, pulling her seat belt on. "It's okay, Trace," she said softly. "Just, you know, teenage girls arguing."

Really? That's what this was about? "Oh," he said, glancing again at Pru, who closed her eyes as if she simply couldn't bear to be where she was at that moment. "Well, that's a new one for me," he admitted.

Molly put a hand on his arm. "Let's get back to Waterford Farm."

In other words, his help, advice, and support weren't wanted. Would it be different if she knew he was her father?

He didn't know, and deep inside, he almost didn't want to find out.

Chapter Fifteen

Looking down at her last patient's chart, Molly walked out of the examination room and smack into her father as he came around the corner.

"Oh, Dad. Sorry, I wasn't expecting you."

He frowned a little, searching her face. "Distracted, Molly?"

"No, why?"

His eyes narrowed. "We had a conference call with the NVA at ten."

"Shoot! I totally forgot."

"It wasn't on your calendar?"

She swallowed, knowing full well that the call with the National Veterinary Association was right there on her desk calendar and on her phone. But at nine thirty, the trainers had had a break and Trace had come over to walk Meatball. He'd been so happy because the dog was being released tonight and...she let out a sigh. Yeah, distracted.

They'd dallied a little longer than necessary on a long walk. She tried not to blush remembering those stolen kisses while Meatball ran around for the first time in a few weeks. The last thing Molly had on her mind was the NVA chapter phone call.

"I was with a patient." It wasn't technically a lie.

But Dad's brow, still dark despite the generous amount of silver in his thick hair, lifted enough to know she was busted. "Can we talk?"

"Sure, in my office." For a split second, she was twelve again and had forgotten to feed her dog. Why did her growing attraction for Trace feel like she was doing something wrong? Because they hadn't come clean with the secret? How could they? Pru was still ticked off about Saturday night, when her friend Corinne texted with the news that she and her parents had seen Molly "making out" with that guy in Bushrod Square.

And Molly had yet to tell Trace any details about why Pru had texted ten times, because she knew he'd want everything to stop. She'd let him think it was girl problems. If he even slightly suspected that Pru wasn't happy about them being together, he'd put the brakes on everything. All the kisses. All the laughing. All the, well, kisses.

And Molly didn't want any of it to stop.

"So, I guess since I missed the call, I got roped into coordinating next year's seminar," she said lightly, slipping around her desk to slide into her chair.

"I'm going to do it," he said, taking the guest chair. "I suspect you have too much on your plate."

She eyed her father, still trying to figure out if he was ticked about her missing the call...or had something else on his brain. "That was very nice of you, but I'll help, I promise."

"Do you?" he asked.

"Do I...promise?"

"Have too much on your plate?"

"No, not at all," she assured him. "Everything's fine."

"I mean, it's a lot, Molls. Being a single mother, running two vet offices, having a…social life."

And *that's* where they were going. "All under control, Dad."

He leaned forward, putting his elbows on the desk, his crystal-blue eyes intent. "You know you can tell me if it's not."

"I know." She waited a beat. "And you know you can come right out with whatever is *really* on your mind."

He smiled a little, his strong jaw loosening as if he was relieved. "So how *is* your social life?"

"Well, it's fine, thank you very much." Did she actually have a social life? "I haven't exactly been a butterfly lately, but I'm going shopping this weekend with my growing group of sisters for Chloe's bridesmaid dresses. And I was invited to a party for the owner of one of my patients, and oh, I walked in the Puppy Parade on Saturday."

"I heard."

She bit back a laugh. "Which version? The 'they were holding hands,' or 'gee, they seem really friendly,' or 'Molly Kilcannon was kissing someone in Bushrod Square.' That one seems to be making the rounds."

"The one that upset Pru."

Molly closed her eyes on an exhale. "The last one." When she looked up at him, Dad was shaking his head slowly. "What? I can't? I shouldn't? I'm too young? Too old? He's not good enough? Which is it?"

Dad's eyes flashed. "I didn't say any of those things, and you know it. Nor did I think them," he added before she could argue. "But Pru made a few comments on Sunday I couldn't help noticing, and she was looking a little sullen. When I asked her—"

"You asked her?"

He looked hard at her. "You've never had a problem with me, or your mother, or your grandmother, talking to Pru about anything at any time."

"Of course not," she said quickly. "But why didn't you ask me?"

"Because you weren't the one mumbling about her mother embarrassing her when she was loading the dishwasher after dinner on Sunday."

That was because Annie Kilcannon had never once done anything embarrassing. But Molly was not Annie Kilcannon. "I'm sorry she feels that way."

He scanned her face, almost as if he was looking for more than she was saying. The truth? An admission? "What?" she asked.

"You need to be honest with her, Molly."

For a moment, blood drained from her cheeks. "Honest?"

"If you are seeing Trace as more than the owner of a patient, if there's a...a relationship brewing, you need to include her."

"In everything?"

"Everything that matters, like your feelings for him. If you know what they are."

She knew what they were, and they were nothing she wanted to discuss with her father or her daughter. "I like him. Is that a problem?"

He didn't answer, but held her gaze.

"Dad? Is it a problem?" She heard her voice rise, suddenly aware that she might face more than Pru's disapproval. She might face her father's, too.

"I'm not sure."

She dropped onto her elbows on her desk and huffed out a breath. "Why?"

"Shane really likes him."

She grinned at him. "I found him first."

Dad laughed. "Shane likes him as a trainer. Possibly a long-term trainer."

"Ahh." Now she caught his drift. "And you think if I start dating him and things go south, he'll leave Waterford Farm, and I'll be responsible for us losing a good service dog trainer."

He gave her that look he used to give her when he would help her solve an algebra problem in eighth grade. That *now you get it* look that he was so good at.

"Well, I certainly don't want to get in the way of the training programs, but..." She wet her lips and carefully chose her words. "I'm not going to let that stop me if I decide he's..."

"He's what?" Dad asked, his voice tight, like he really cared what she was going to say.

"He's...special. Different."

His smile was slow and kind of screamed, *I told you so*. "More than meets the eye?"

"Yes, Dad. You were..." She narrowed her eyes at him and leaned back, scrutinizing him this time. "Was this an act of the Dogfather?"

"What? Molly, please. That whole matchmaking thing is overblown by all you kids. I have more things on my mind than who you're dating, believe me."

"But you came all the way over here to talk to me about it."

"To talk to you about *Pru*," he corrected. "She won't be embarrassed or upset with you if you include her, talk to her, and are one hundred percent honest with her."

She sighed. "I really want to be."

"Then what's stopping you?"

She looked down, actually considering for one crazy minute the possibility of confiding in her father. But she had no idea how he'd take it. Maybe he'd march out and send Trace away. Maybe he'd insist she tell Pru that very minute. Maybe he'd be...disappointed.

Honestly, that was the possibility that scared her the most.

"Nothing, Dad. I'll talk to her tonight. I'll tell her Trace and I are..."

"Are what?"

She smiled at him. "A thing?"

He laughed and pushed up. "Happy to say I don't even know what that means."

She leaned forward and snagged his wrist. "Dad, no matter what happens, if Trace is being considered for that job, please don't let this stop you. He really wants it, and I think he'd be amazing. And what an opportunity for him. I would never want to get in the way of that."

For a long time, he looked at her, the shadow of his smile deepening.

"What?" she asked, again unable to read the expression.

He shook his head. "Nothing. You reminded me of your mother right then."

"Thanks. There's no higher compliment."

He winked and left the office, and Molly sat at her desk for a good ten minutes, wondering exactly what she was going to tell her daughter about Trace. Something between "I like him" and "he's your father."

Chapter Sixteen

Trace finished work early, took a long hot shower, and made his little home as close to perfect as a furnished studio apartment with no real kitchen could be. For some reason, he felt like Meatball's homecoming was a test he had to pass.

A brand-new comfy dog bed and a fleece blanket rested in the corner of the living room, with two shiny new bowls for food and water, a few chew toys, and yes, a leash.

Now all he had to do was go get his boy. Molly had told him to come to her office around six for a formal patient checkout, so in the few minutes he had left, he washed up, brushed his teeth, and pulled on clean jeans.

But before he put on a T-shirt, he heard a knock at the door and hoped to God it wasn't one of the new trainees who had arrived and checked in for a month of dog training certification. Shane had told them that if they needed anything, Trace was living in student housing to offer assistance.

The mini-promotion had felt great at the time, but right now he didn't want to help out a newbie. He wanted to go get Meatball. And see Molly. Both held equally strong appeal.

He went to the door, not bothering with a shirt or the top button of his jeans, hoping the nonattire would send the message that he didn't really want to shoot the shit about day one of "basic training" with anyone right now.

But he yanked the door open to see Molly and Meatball. Instantly, his dog barked and lifted his two front legs at the sight of Trace as if he might jump. Molly just stared. After a split second, her brows rose and her gaze dropped over his torso, a flush deepening in her cheeks as she checked him out for a few seconds past a casual glance.

"I wasn't expecting you," he said.

"Yeah, I see that." She laughed, a little breathless. "I wanted to surprise you, but I guess"—she swallowed noisily—"the surprise is on me."

There was enough admiration in the comment that he shot her a quick smile as he crouched down to greet Meatball.

"Welcome home, Meatman." He snuggled the dog's neck and fur and looked up at Molly, who was still staring down at him. Well, at his back and ass. "I thought you wanted me to come over to the office."

"I did. I do. I want you, I mean, I wanted you to fill out...jeans." She laughed, shaking her head in apology. "Sorry. You, uh...wow."

He stood slowly, seeing the heat in her expression. That look in her eyes was starting to get familiar to him, one he'd seen frequently after a long, intimate kiss. Or six. "Should I put a shirt on?"

"Not on my account," she joked, poking his bare

chest to back him into the apartment with Meatball, who nosed his way in, barking and sniffing. "Meatball might be a little distracted, though."

"Meatball, huh?" He let her in and closed the door, that low-grade rumble of anticipation and tension he always felt around her settling down in his belly. He didn't know if he'd ever get used to it, or if he wanted to.

"This looks homey," she said, glancing around and sliding off her jacket and tossing it on the sofa armrest.

"It looks like the other ten studios in this building, not that I'm complaining."

The room was six times the size of a cell, with a double bed, a sitting area with a TV, and a coffee bar and mini-fridge for sodas and snacks. The walls were painted a comforting blue-gray, with carefully chosen art and a gorgeous view of the Blue Ridge Mountains through a picture window. Plus, the building had a fully equipped kitchen and a gathering room for trainees to socialize, eat, or hold meetings. It was luxury living, even if he hadn't spent the last fourteen years at Huttonsville, which, for once, he wasn't even going to remind her. "It was really smart to build this as part of the facility," he said.

"My dad had such a vision. He and my mother had talked about a canine training and rescue business for years, and he was following the plan of a hundred hours they shared on the porch imagining how it would be. Having a housing facility really encourages the longer class sessions, so trainees don't have to find a hotel."

"A group started that'll be here for four weeks," he said. "That's a commitment."

"But they're certified dog trainers at the end of that four weeks, and they'll all start businesses. Look at him." She pointed to Meatball, who was trotting between his bed and the sofa, like Goldilocks trying to make the right sleep decision. "Go to the bed, Meatball," she said, walking to guide him back. "I don't love the idea of him jumping up and down from a sofa yet."

"Oh, sure." He snapped his fingers and pointed to the bed. "Sleep, Meatball."

He trotted right back and gingerly stepped into the fleece and then started rooting around the blanket, making them both laugh at his enthusiasm.

"You want something to drink, Molly?" he asked, heading toward the wet bar.

When she didn't reply, he looked over his shoulder and saw her staring at him again, a funny smile on her face. "What is it?"

"That tattoo on your shoulder. Is that a shamrock? I didn't know you were..." Her voice trailed off as she finished with a whisper. "Irish."

"I'm not," he said, confirming what he knew she was thinking. He turned back to get them both cold waters from the fridge, waiting for her response, but she was silent. "They all mean something," he finally said softly. "I tried to use the ink to commemorate good moments in my life."

"Oh."

He could hear the wonder, maybe a little shock, in the single syllable. "Yes, you were one of the good moments, *Irish*."

"And you didn't even know about Pru."

He turned slowly. "It was a good moment even without knowing the unexpected outcome."

She stood stone-still, her arms wrapped around herself. "I'm flattered. And a little sad."

"Sad?" He nodded to the sofa in invitation. "That I remembered you with a tattoo?"

"That you remembered me. That I…" On a sigh, she sat and he did, too, giving her some space and time to gather her thoughts. "I didn't have any fond memories of that night," she said softly. "I remember you and the maroon Plymouth Voyager and the…"

Sex. Hot, wild, incredibly satisfying sex.

"The dog crate," he supplied for her, opening her bottle and handing it to her. "Noisy as it was."

She laughed but her smile disappeared quickly. "I so misjudged you."

"I don't know about that. You thought I was a bad guy, a loser, a troublemaker, and that I died in a bar fight, which, you could argue, I did for fourteen years. No *mis*judgment at all."

She stared at him for a long time. "My dad knew."

"What? About us? Pru?" He jerked back with each question as the possibility hit him.

"No, no, he knew about *you*. Your character. Right away, after meeting you in town a few weeks ago. He told me, 'There's more to him than meets the eye.'" She lifted her brows and wiggled her finger in the direction of his torso. "And he hadn't even seen this."

He smiled at the compliment, thinking about the conversation he'd had with Daniel Kilcannon in the Bitter Bark Bakery. "It was Meatball that got us talking, of course. And your dad was so engaging and honest, I came right out and told him my story."

"Have you told anyone else in town?"

"No." He picked up his bottle of water, running his

thumb over the condensation that dampened the label. "I mean, your brothers know, obviously. But no one else in Bitter Bark." He looked at her. "There are some people I'd like to talk to. Bart McQueen, for one, but he moved away."

"I guess you blame him, in a roundabout way."

"I don't blame anyone." That was something Wally had drummed out of him. "My hands pushed Paul Mosfort to his death." He stared at his hands, dredging up that old hate for his *deadly weapons*.

"You paid the price," she said quietly. "You're... reformed."

He gave a sharp laugh at the word. "That's what they call it."

She closed her hand around his wrist, her fingers landing on the edge of the image of a metal pipe that twisted around most of his forearm.

"Another good moment?" she asked.

"Yes. I enjoyed the welding trade and would have been good at it. I actually got really good at metal sculpting in prison. I made little animals, dogs mostly, and some more esoteric art."

"You can sculpt little metal dogs? We could sell those at Waterford."

"I'd make them for you."

She smiled at the offer and gently twisted his arm to see the underside, trailing her fingers along his skin lightly enough to make him crazy. "What's this?" She tapped on a red flower that spiraled up his bicep.

"My mom went through a gardening phase," he said. "I helped her plant all these bushes in the backyard one summer when I was about twelve or thirteen. They're still there, all overgrown and messy.

I liked gardening, I'm not ashamed to say. That's not a prison tattoo, obviously."

"Why is that obvious?"

"Prison tats are blue ink only. That's why my shamrock isn't green. Prison ink isn't like the sweet tattoos you get at the mall. There's an element of danger involved."

"How so?"

He made a face, not wanting to tell her too much about the dark, ugly, dangerous side of prison. About making tattoo guns out of the motors of CD players or running a needle through a ballpoint pen. Didn't want to tell her about seeing gang members get teardrops for each kill or burn Bible pages to get ink from the soot. The ugly words and ruined men and vile things that happened behind bars. He'd never put a single one of those images in her head.

"Let's just say the guards frown upon it," he finally said, the understatement damn near laughable.

"How many of these did you get in prison? I know you had some when you were in high school."

"Anything blue came from Huttonsville Correctional Center."

"Mmm." She worked up to his pec, each air-light touch of her fingertips sending pulses from his arm through his gut and lower. "Who's this handsome bull terrier?"

"Bogie." He grinned. "My first dog. Got that ink when I was seventeen and he died. I loved the hell out of that dog. He was a total badass who hated everyone but me."

"Terriers definitely have their favorites," she said, walking her fingers over his shoulder. To the shamrock tattoo. It was very simple, just three leaves and a curved line for the stem, deep blue. It wasn't the best of shamrocks, no shape or nuance. In fact, each leaf wasn't much more than, well, three hearts. Three very exaggerated hearts.

"Trace, have you ever really looked at this?"

Turning his head and lifting his arm a bit, he could see it well enough, even though Fat Eddie had put it a little off-center and more toward his back. "Yeah, why?"

"You're looking at it upside down."

"Not in the mirror." Not that he spent a lot of time looking at his reflection, but he occasionally did an ink inventory as a little trip down memory lane.

"The leaves are three perfect hearts."

"Fat Eddie wasn't exactly Michelangelo," he joked. But maybe Fat Eddie had known what he was doing after all. "That's...interesting."

She leaned forward and pressed the softest kiss on the tattoo, burning him.

He put his hand on her head, holding her lips against the shamrock, closing his eyes to enjoy the moment of woman and warmth. She stayed there, not moving, letting him tangle his fingers into her waves so the strands slid over his skin like silk.

Need started to build. Not just sexual need, which burned like a welding torch constantly around her. This was a different kind of need. The need for touch. The need for connection. The hot, achy, miserable need to fill a hole in his heart.

But mostly, it was a need for Molly.

When she lifted her head to look at him, he saw the same need in her burnished green-gold eyes that he felt in his chest. And that possibility stole his ability to get through the next breath.

Her lips parted as she inhaled with the same ragged effort. She dragged her hand from his shoulder, back over Bogie on his chest, and splayed her fingers right over his hammering heart.

"You know what I think those three hearts are?"

"Bad art?" He tried for a light note and failed.

"Symbolic." She tapped on his chest, matching the rhythm of his pulse. "Two hearts connected by the one they made together."

"Are you sure you aren't a greeting card writer on the side?" he teased.

She smiled. "You know I'm right."

"I know you're…" Beautiful. Perfect. Sweet. And still so far out of his league, it hurt. But looking at her, holding her, and being this close to her only made him want to forget that and take what it appeared she was offering.

"I'm what?"

"Killing me," he whispered, coming closer. "You're making me lose my mind, Irish. All I want to do is…"

She leaned into him and finished his thought for him. Her lips were soft and still parted, kissing him with that same pent-up passion she'd had that very night he'd commemorated with a shamrock tattoo.

"Always, always, I have to kiss first," she joked as he tipped her head back and pressed his lips on her jaw and throat. "Why is that?"

Slowly, he pulled back to look at her. "You don't know?"

"You're a gentleman? You're cautious? You like to be pursued?"

"I'm not good enough to kiss you," he admitted gruffly.

She eased farther back, narrowing her eyes. "You were good enough for me to have sex with in a minivan. You were good enough to give me the greatest gift I've ever known. You are good enough to work in this place, to own up to your fatherhood, and to kiss me."

Pulling her closer, he clung to her words as much as her body, feeling her soften as he grew harder, hearing her breath matching his, and kissing her like he actually believed all that she said. He felt the moment she completely relaxed, melting under him, drawing him closer and closer, until there was nowhere to go but horizontal.

Blood thrummed as he lost the fight not to touch more of her, caressing her hair, her back, and up and down her waist. She did the same, her fingers exploring every inch of his exposed skin, adding pressure on his muscles, moaning in sweet appreciation.

"Irish." He murmured the nickname as he lowered her onto the tiny leather sofa, way too undersized for what their bodies wanted to do.

She didn't seem to care, wrapping her hands around his neck, dropping back enough so that he could cover her whole body with his. She rocked under him, sucking in a breath at the first moment their bodies met and fire licked through both of them.

When she arched her back, he took the invitation, slowly sliding his hand up her side to close over her ribs and thumb the rise of her breast. She hissed in a breath and whispered his name, which sounded like poetry on her lips.

She clung to his back, her hands coasting over his painted skin like the art was Braille and she wanted to read it. His head throbbed, every nerve burning and screaming and aching for more.

Until a low, angry growl right in his ear, followed by a loud, sharp bark had them both startling in surprise. Meatball was three inches from their faces, his hot breath coming out faster than theirs, his jade eyes judgmental and jealous.

Under him, Molly laughed. "Meatball doesn't approve."

"Go back to bed, Meatman," Trace ordered. "There's nothing to see here."

He barked in response, his dog disagreement loud and clear.

"Meatball!" Trace channeled some of his frustration into the name. "Back to bed."

That just got a low, under-the-breath growl of aggression. Trace started to sit up so he could point to the bed, a command that dog would never ignore, but Molly reached out a hand to the dog. "Go sit down, baby," she said.

Meatball licked her hand, then turned to meander back to his bed.

"What the hell?" Trace pushed up, astounded at the exchange. "He never ignores me. He answers only to me, and who calls him baby?"

That made her chuckle. "When are you going to realize that people—and dogs—can change, Trace Bancroft? And, at risk of being called a dog shrink, in my professional opinion, he thought you were hurting me."

Trace hadn't even considered that. "Am I?"

237

"If you stop, you will."

But he didn't lay back down. Instead, he rose up some more and brought her with him, looking right into her sweet eyes. "Not on the sofa," he finally said. "And not on the bed in here, either," he added before she could drag him there with one little touch.

"Minivan?"

He laughed softly. "You want to do this again, Irish?"

"I'm starting to think so, yeah."

"Then we're going to do it right the next time."

"Right?"

He nodded, pushing them all the way up and gently straightening her T-shirt. His knuckles grazed her skin, and just that touch made him want more. But not so badly that he'd sacrifice what she deserved.

"Then give me a little time," he said.

She lifted a brow, silent. He couldn't quite read her question, but it didn't matter. He knew why he needed time, and he knew that he risked her changing her mind by taking it.

"You will be my first lover in fourteen years. And you also happen to be the mother of my daughter."

Her eyes shuttered at the last whispered word.

"Everything has to be right."

She searched his face, reaching to cup his chin and stroke the cheek he'd shaved a few minutes ago. "Don't you think we should tell Pru first?"

"That we're going to sleep together?" He choked on the idea.

"The truth. I don't like duplicity, Trace. It's weighing me down. In fact, I had a long talk with my father, and he wants me to be honest with her."

"He *knows*?"

"He knows we have something going on here. He knows I'm seeing you as more than Meatball's owner. And he knows that Pru deserves the truth. He means be honest about our relationship, but I am taking that to the next step."

He stared at her. "That will ruin everything."

"How?"

"For one thing, her project, which is going so well, will no longer qualify for the competition."

She rolled her eyes. "In the scheme of things, I don't think that's important."

"It is to her."

Molly closed her mouth on the next argument, leaning back. "Okay, you have me there. And color me ashamed for putting my needs above hers."

"You're not seeing it through her eyes."

"I'm not seeing it through your eyes," she replied. "You're scared she's going to reject you. You're terrified you'll somehow shame her. And I'm scared, too, Trace. Don't you think I'm petrified that this will change the relationship I've spent thirteen years building? She's my life, my heart, my whole world. But because of that, I owe her the truth, no matter how much it changes everything."

He blew out a breath, studying her carefully, weighing the pros and cons and everything in between. "You can tell her if you want."

"Not without you."

He closed his eyes.

"What? You don't think that's right?"

"I think it's so right that...that..." He bit back a smile, knowing his eyes might be a little damp, but he didn't care. "That I was right when I said I'm not worthy of you, Molly Kilcannon. You are one of the most exceptional women I've ever known."

"You haven't known that many," she reminded him.

He put both hands on her cheeks and held her face. "I don't need to," he whispered. "Everyone else is downhill after you."

"When?" she asked softly.

"She only has to work sixteen more hours this weekend," he said. "The rest of the time will be spent putting her presentation to the school together, and she'll have her hours. Can we please wait until after that? This matters to her."

"You know what, Trace?"

He wasn't sure he wanted to, but he nodded. "What?"

"I'm afraid everyone else is downhill after you, too."

He closed his eyes and pulled her closer, unable to find the words to thank her for saying that.

Chapter Seventeen

P ru peered through the missing ceiling, the wood planks of the rafters, and through a hole in the roof Trace had created by pulling off the shingles. "If you fall through, I better have my camera."

"I won't fall," he assured her. "But if I can finish this roof when you finish the inside, I can live here again."

"That's kind of the idea of the project," she said, stirring the paint before pouring it into a tray. "And I'm definitely finishing today, even if my loser friends don't show since they got their paltry ten hours and I need at least seven more."

To get those hours, Mom had picked Trace and Meatball up at Waterford and brought them all to the house to work today, but then she got an emergency call from the vet office in town. Ever since she took off to see to a very sick pug, Trace had moved up to the roof to work, even though fixing the roof wasn't part of the official project.

Pru strongly suspected he went up there because he didn't want to break any rules by being in the house alone with her. She wouldn't have minded, but gave him points for following project regulations to the letter.

Plus they could still talk through the hole, which was kind of cool.

"Just don't fall through the roof," she said. "I'm sure Mr. Margolis will take points off if the beneficiary of the community service project ends up in the ER."

He laughed and started hammering at something again, still visible as she finished painting the last wall in the living room.

"Would you really live here?" she asked when the hammering ceased for a minute.

"Sure."

"I thought you hated this place."

"Not anymore."

Wow, she'd really done that great a job fixing it up? Pride warmed her. "That's really good, Mr. Bancroft."

She heard him snort at the name. "Thanks to you, Umproo."

"You always have nicknames," she said. "I noticed that."

"Usually only with dogs. You know, it's part of how I train a service dog. If I have a special casual name, they know I only use that for playtime."

"Like Meatman."

"Yep." He tapped the hammer.

"And Irish."

The hammer stopped. "Well, I'm not exactly training your mom," he said softly, but she still heard it through the rafters. "But you're right. I do like a nickname for people I..."

"Make out with in the square."

He was silent for a moment, then his face filled the hole in the roof. "Can I ask you a question, Pru?"

"Yeah?"

"Is that what you were upset about on Saturday when we picked you up? 'Cause your mom told me it was trouble with your friends."

It was her turn to hesitate, not really sure how to answer. "It's complicated."

"Try me." He stayed in the spot, staring down at her, only his head visible. The weird setup made her more comfortable for some reason, able to talk to him with a barrier.

"Well, okay." She dipped the brush, wiped it off, and started painting again. "Yeah, I was a little ticked off to have heard that about you and Mom from someone from school."

"I can understand that."

She looked up. "Can you?"

"Sure. You don't want to be surprised about things involving people you love and trust. Plus, she's your mom, and I guess that made you feel embarrassed because…" She heard the hesitation in his voice and what sounded like a deep sigh. "Of who I am."

Shame shot through her, making her step back from the wall and look up. "Oh, no, Mr. Bancroft. Trace. That's not…" Well, it was true. And if she said it wasn't, she'd be lying. "I'm not used to my mom seeing someone, though." That was true, too.

"And that's why you were upset?"

She started painting again, slathering the brush over and over the same spot as she replayed what happened last Saturday. And how Cody treated her in school all week. "It was a bad night. I was moody, and a whole bunch of stuff ticked me off."

"Like?"

"Like how I didn't know my mom tutored you in high school. Why didn't she tell me?"

He didn't answer right away, silent long enough for Pru to step back and look up, waiting for a response.

"Probably because it was so meaningless, she forgot," he finally suggested.

Or because it wasn't meaningless at all. And she didn't want to talk about it, because that wasn't the real problem on Saturday night. "I was mostly upset about a kid," she admitted.

"Cody?" She heard him shift overhead and imagined he was staring down through that hole again.

"Yeah."

"Oh. Want to tell me?"

"No."

"Okay, but I know a little bit about boys. What did he do to upset you?"

"Nothing," she said. "And that was the problem. He acted like he was so dying to have me come over, and then he barely talked to me all night. There were like nine different girls there, and we all thought the same thing—that we were special."

"You were there for his ego."

"Right?" She stabbed the brush in the paint, the embarrassment and anger rising again. "I felt like an idiot for falling for it."

"Well, now you know what he's made of."

She snorted. "Except at school this week, he was all attentive again, at my locker, flirting with me in the

244

cafeteria, then wham. Five of my friends are convinced he likes them, too."

"So he's a player."

"Totally."

"Unless he likes you, and he's trying to make you like him more by making you jealous."

The brush froze as he put into words her exact thoughts. "Yes! But I don't know which it is."

"Either way, it's kind of a crappy move," he said. "If a guy won't come straight out and tell you how he feels about you, then he's a game player. And a lot of them will do that because the thrill of the chase is more fun than the catch."

She sighed, knowing he was right.

"Anyway, you're too young for boys."

She laughed. "Now you sound like my grandfather. Girls my age have boyfriends, you know."

"Boys who are friends. I've met some of yours, and I like them. But that boy?"

"Well, I invited 'that boy' to help today and be part of the Umproo Crew, but I guess he's not coming." Not that she really expected him to.

"If he comes and wants to climb up here and show off his roofing prowess, I'll give him a chance," Trace said. "Otherwise, I don't like him."

She laughed, leaning back to look up at him. "You don't get an opinion."

"Too bad, I have one."

"Do I get one about you and Mom? 'Cause I know you two are, like, a thing."

He didn't answer for a long time. She heard the hammer hit a few times, then after a second of silence, he cleared his throat. "Yes, Pru, you get an opinion, and I am very much interested in what it is."

"Well, I think…" She stopped talking at the sound of tires on the drive, followed by Meatball's bark as he walked to the door to check it out.

"It's a red truck," Trace said from the roof. "Is that your boy?"

Yes! She squeezed her eyes shut to try to slow her pounding heart. "His older brother's truck. He can't drive yet." She heard her voice rise in excitement as she laid down the paint brush in the tray and looked out the window, which gave an unbroken view of the front now that she'd taken down those wretched blinds.

And there was Cody Noonan climbing out of the passenger side in jeans and a beat-up Black Sabbath T-shirt, looking so darn fine.

"Okay," she whispered. "Be cool."

Wiping her paint- and sweat-covered hands on her jeans, she opened the door and stepped out, followed by Meatball, who quieted with one touch but stayed completely alert at the arrival of a stranger.

"S'up, Pru?" Cody asked.

"Nothing. What's up with you?"

"Who's this?" Cody looked at Meatball and took a few steps back. "That a pit bull?"

"It's Meatball, and yes, he's part Staffy." *Please don't be one of those people.*

"Looks like a pit to me. He fight?"

She made a face at him. "You're kidding, right?"

He kept a wary eye on Meatball. "Yeah, yeah. I remember your family is all about dogs. You sure he won't bite?"

"He won't bite. Unless…" She turned to look up at

the roof, but couldn't see Trace from here. "Unless I tell him to."

Cody didn't laugh, which made her think, not for the first time, that he had no sense of humor. "So," she said. "You here to get some hours?"

He snorted. "Nah. I don't do that community service crap."

Disappointment squeezed her stomach. "I thought that's why you were here."

"No, I'm jamming today. I want you to come and hear us play."

That's what he was here for? "Don't tell me, you're rounding up groupies."

He gave a self-conscious laugh. "Only pretty ones, Pru."

She felt her face warm at the compliment...even though she knew he was playing her. "Well, this pretty one has to get her hours and finish a big project."

He squinted at the house. "What are you doing here again?" he asked.

She'd already told him in great detail. "Fixing up a house for the guy who lives here."

"Oh, so ditch it for today."

Ditch? To be a groupie? "No."

His brother honked the horn. Hard and long.

"Hang the eff on for a sec, loser!" Cody called, making Pru cringe and Meatball bark sharply.

"I can't leave," she said. "Sorry."

"Why not? It's some stupid service project, and it's Saturday afternoon, Pru."

Which is when you do service projects. "I know, but I have to get it done. None of my friends are here today." *Including you.*

"So nobody would even know you left. You can fake that hours shit. Everybody does that, you know."

"I'm not everybody."

He narrowed his eyes at her, and something deep inside made her want him to say something sweet, like *I've noticed*, but he was silent. Then his gaze moved up and over her head. "Who is that?" he asked, as much fear in his voice as when he'd asked about Meatball.

Pru didn't have to look. "He owns the home."

"Holy crap," he muttered under his breath. "Looks badass."

"Bad enough to ask you to either help or take off, son." Trace's words rolled down from the roof, giving Pru an unexpected jolt of joy. She stepped out a little farther to stare up at Trace, ridiculously grateful for the backup.

"It's cool, man." Cody immediately backed away, scowling. "No need to get all bat-shit crazy."

"I'm not bat-shit crazy. Yet."

Pru bit back a laugh, but Cody mumbled, "What the hell?" under his breath.

"You're welcome to stay and help," Trace said. "Otherwise, you're gumming up the project by standing there and taking up air."

"Yeah." Cody choked softly, obviously nervous. "Not today, man. But thanks." He turned back to Pru. "You think you're safe here alone with that scary dude?"

Pru stared at him, silently measuring Trace Bancroft against Cody Noonan. One of them was a fine person. The other, a piece of dog poo.

"I'm completely safe with him," she said. "But if

you don't get out of here, I can't be responsible for what he or his guard dog will do."

He paled visibly, glancing to Meatball, who took a step closer and growled like Trace had secretly made the command from the roof. For all she knew, he had.

"'kay. See ya." He jutted his chin to Pru, glanced up at Trace, then turned away and walked a little too fast to be cool to the truck. His brother took off, spitting gravel and making Meatball run after the car with a nasty warning bark.

Pru stood there for a good thirty seconds, weirdly thrilled with what just happened. She turned and looked up at the roof, shielding her eyes from the morning sun, getting a good look at the man who didn't look so badass to her. But maybe if you didn't know him…you'd misjudge him.

Like she had. "Hey, all you need is a cape, Superman."

He took a few steps closer to the edge of the roof. "So you're not furious at me?"

"Not in the least. Kind of wish I had the whole thing on video so I could put it in my presentation."

"He's a jerk," Trace said simply.

"Seriously." A slow smile broke as she stared up at him. "And you were pretty cool."

"You think?"

"Yeah." She scooped her fingers around Meatball's collar to lead him back into the house. There, she took up her paint brush again, replaying the whole conversation and so damn proud of how it unfolded. She was so much better than Cody Noonan.

"Hey, you never answered my question," Trace said, back in place over the hole in the roof.

"What question?"

"What do you think about your mom and me?"

She didn't say anything, painting a long, thick line along the door casing instead. "I think…" She bent back down and refilled the brush. "That you and Mom…" She painted over the line again, stalling as she tried to come up with the right thing to say. "Are really good together."

She stepped back and looked up, seeing the expression on his face. It was pretty much the happiest she'd ever seen him. Beaming from ear to ear. "So you really like her," she concluded, making him laugh. "Then I guess it's time I know the truth."

His jaw dropped. "The truth?" She could have sworn his voice cracked.

"I want to know," she said. "What happened that night when you killed someone?"

She could see his broad shoulders fall as if she'd hit him hard, and that made her feel a little bad, but if he was going to date her mom, she had to know.

"I had to leave town one night," he said after a few silent seconds.

"Why?" She peered up at him. "Don't leave out important details. How else can I make a decision about whether you're guilty or not?"

"I've already been found guilty, Pru. There's no decision to make."

"Then let me hear your side." She squinted hard. "You have a side, right?"

He nodded. "But they still found me guilty."

"I know, but I want to hear for myself. Start at the beginning."

He didn't answer right away, then, "I had to leave

Bitter Bark one night because my boss thought I did something I didn't do."

"What was that?"

He sighed heavily. "It had to do with his wife."

"Oh."

"It's not what you think, Pru."

"Then enlighten me."

She heard him shift around on his roof perch. "You sure you want to hear this?"

"Yes, and don't leave anything out 'cause you think I'm a kid."

"Okay. Here we go."

Pru stopped painting and listened, closing her eyes to picture a bus and a bar and a bad, bad man. With each imaginary image painted by the man sitting on a roof, her eyes stung and her chest pounded with the total and complete unfairness of it all.

"Wow," she said softly when he told her what the judge sentenced. "That *sucks*."

"It's the law."

"Yeah?" She choked her disgust. "Then we need better lawyers. Maybe *that's* what I'll be."

"Don't, it'll break my heart."

The way he said that was so...so honest. Like he cared what she'd be when she grew up.

"But you did everything right, and I absolutely hate unfairness. You were Superman again, defending a girl. You made one mistake." Yes, it was a big one, but still.

When he didn't answer for a few minutes, didn't laugh or say a word, she inched back and looked up, and at that very second, she caught him bunching up his T-shirt to use it to wipe his eyes.

And that just about broke her heart.

She was going to have to tell Mom tonight that he was a good guy. But then, maybe Mom already knew that.

Chapter Eighteen

The first thing Molly heard as she climbed out of her car was laughter coming from the side of the house. Lots of laughter. That familiar squeal of Pru's giggle and Trace's low, from-the-chest chuckle. And Meatball's happy bark.

She started to open her mouth to call out to them, but stopped, taking a minute to listen to the sound again, because it was so darn beautiful.

"Oh, look at him!" Pru's voice rose an excited octave. "He looks like an old Englishman wearing a monocle."

"How do you know what a monocle is?" she heard Trace ask.

"I read Charles Dickens!" she announced.

"You're so stinkin' smart, Umproo."

Pru laughed, but Molly's heart swelled with an emotion she couldn't begin to name.

"Maybe you should do the other side, too," Pru suggested. "Give him glasses."

Curiosity beat out Molly's need to stand there and soak up the sounds of this happy family. Curiosity and fear. How long would there be laughter? She swallowed, determined to stick to the plan. She and Trace would sit down today and quietly tell Pru the story of her conception.

As it was, it would take some power rationalization to get Pru to understand why they hadn't told her sooner. Especially when the truth was: *we were scared*.

"What's with all the frivolity?" Molly asked as she came around the side of the house.

Trace was kneeling in front of Meatball, a paint can next to him, a brush in hand. The dog turned the instant he heard Molly, barking and trying to pull away to get to her.

"We're giving Meatball tattoos!" Pru said. "Not real ones, though."

Trace let go of Meatball, who trotted over to greet Molly with a quick lick of her hand and a nuzzle. And Molly cracked up at the big black circle that had been painted around his left eye.

"You've been inked, Meatball."

"We came out to clean brushes, and things got a little out of hand," Trace said, sharing a secret look with Pru. "*Someone* dared me."

"Someone took the dare," she shot back, her eyes dancing as she looked at him.

Well, well. What was going on here? Molly bent over to love Meatball a little more, but kept her gaze on Trace. "Well, that's...good."

"Is it against vet rules?" Trace asked, probably sensing her uncertainty.

"Not unless there's something toxic in the paint."

"Mom!" Pru gasped. "You know I wouldn't use anything but environmentally-friendly paint. How's the pug?"

"Responding to medication, I'm happy to say. How's the project?"

"Finished!" Trace and Pru answered in remarkable unison.

"Really? Wow, that's great. I thought you'd need me to paint the kitchen."

"Trace did the whole thing."

"All under the project manager's close supervision."

Molly glanced around, looking to see if the rest of the Umproo Crew were still here, but there were no signs of her friends. "Didn't you get any other help today?"

And...another shared secret look.

"Almost," Pru said, biting her lip in a way that reminded Molly of herself. "But we got rid of them, right, Superman?"

Superman?

Molly angled her head in a silent question.

"Mom, *he* showed up here."

Oh boy. Cody. "Why?"

"You know who 'he' is?" Trace asked, slowly standing and making it hard for Molly to concentrate on mom issues when he was in nothing but a white T-shirt, jeans, and paint.

"Of course she knows," Pru said. "I tell my mother everything."

She and Pru had been talking about Cody Noonan for a good many days now, discussing the pros, which were none, and cons, which were many, of this new boy who'd caught Pru's attention.

"You were right," Pru said. "He's a low-key jerk."

"How'd you finally figure that out?"

Pru looked at Trace. "Superman."

Trace looked skyward at the compliment. "Didn't take superpowers to figure that dude out." He snapped his fingers for Meatball, who looked torn between following the command and sniffing all the other dog smells on Molly's jeans.

"What happened?" Molly made it easy for the dog, walking him closer to Trace.

"Nothing Pru couldn't have handled quite well," Trace said.

"Cody called him a badass," Pru added, then lifted her brow. "It's a quote, so don't give me a Mom look."

"I'm not…" Molly shook her head. "I'm confused. What happened, exactly?"

"Nothing," Trace said, returning his attention to a bucket of brushes that needed to be cleaned.

"Not nothing," Pru corrected. "It was awkward and awful, Mom. I wanted him to leave, but I didn't know how to tell him without sounding, you know, nasty."

"So I did the dirty work."

"Totally got me off the hook," Pru said, coming closer to stand between Trace and Molly. "And I told Trace this afternoon all about the things Cody has said and done, and you're right, Mom. I don't want to have anything to do with him."

Molly let out a relieved sigh. "Sounds like Trace got you there faster than I did."

"Well, he was able to help me see it from a guy's perspective."

"Really." She looked over Pru's shoulder to catch the look Trace sent, but couldn't quite interpret it. Something sparked in his eyes. Fear? Pride? Longing? Something. "That's great." She reached for Pru's shoulder, covered only by a thin sweater. "Don't you need a jacket out here? It's getting chilly."

"Oh, we've been working so hard, I was hot."

"Well, make your mother happy and get your jacket."

"'Kay." She started off, then turned. "Be right back, Trace!"

As she scampered away, Molly waited until she was out of earshot before commenting. "Must have been quite a successful day together."

Trace was sitting on the ground now, pulling paint brushes from the thinner and laying them on a towel. "It was fine," he said, a little gruff.

"Fine?" Molly came closer, and Meatball matched her steps. They both stopped a few feet from the towel, but Trace didn't look up. "Seems like it was more than fine to me. Did you have a breakthrough or something?"

He shook off a brush. "Something."

"Trace."

When he didn't answer and kept his eyes averted, she crouched down to get him to look at her. When he did, she saw the agony all over his face.

"What happened?" she asked softly, her words as tight as the breath in her chest.

"Everything," he admitted on a whisper. "Everything I wanted to have happen. We connected, we communicated, and I told her the whole story of why I was incarcerated. We painted and ate lunch and talked about her friends and boys and her family and dogs. We finished the project, I let her 'interview' me for the paper she's writing, and..." With each word, the shadows of pain deepened on his face. "And now, when she finds out…"

"All that good stuff will be undone."

He closed his eyes. "She likes me, but she isn't going to want me to be…you know."

"It's not like she has a choice about wanting it."

"I know, I know." He shook his head with the same vehemence he used on a brush. "Today was amazing. It was like…*real*. What it would have felt like to be around for thirteen years. I never felt anything like it. Never." He squeezed his eyes shut as if they stung, which only made Molly's heart ache more.

"She's not heartless, Trace. It might throw her, but surely you know by now that she's got a good and loving heart."

He searched her face. "I've never felt anything like love," he whispered. "I didn't know what it felt like until now. I had no idea it could consume you."

Tears sprang into her own eyes. She knew exactly how it'd felt that first time she'd gazed at Prudence Anne Kilcannon and fallen utterly and completely in love. Could it be any different for a father, no matter how much time had passed? "You can tell her that."

"No, no. Once she knows, she won't look at me the same. It'll be distrust and contempt. When it becomes personal, when it becomes family, she'll hate who I've been, where I've been, and be completely ashamed of me."

"You don't know that."

"Yeah, you don't know that." At Pru's voice, they both froze, only then realizing she'd come back outside.

"Pru." They both said her name at the same time.

"I heard you," she said softly, looking from one to the other.

What had she heard? Did Trace ever say the words *I'm her father*? Molly tried to play back the conversation, but Pru's fine features pulled into a look that told Molly she'd heard enough.

"And, honestly, I'm pretty upset with both of you," she said.

Molly reached for her. "Honey, listen to me—"

Pru jerked away. "Why wouldn't you tell me you're that serious? I mean, Meatball can smell the chemistry between you two, it's so obvious. I don't know why you guys don't think I'm old enough to understand."

"Pru, it's not—"

"I heard you, Mom. I heard Trace. He never knew what love was until now?" She clasped her hands and pressed them to her chest, her eyes filling. "Don't you think I want this kind of happiness for you, Mom?"

For a second, Molly couldn't breathe as she realized what Pru thought. They were dating. It was serious.

But it was so much more complicated than that.

Trace pushed up to one knee. "Pru, you need to understand something about me."

"No, you need to understand something about *me*," she fired back. "I wouldn't look at you with contempt or distrust for liking my mom. For loving her. Don't you see that gives us something in common?"

"Oh, Pru." Molly sighed the words. "You do have such a good heart."

"And so do you. And..." She turned to Trace, freeing her index finger from her still-clasped hands to point at him. "So do you. I've seen you with the dogs. With my family. And with my mom. And here, with me. You both need to give me a little more credit."

Neither one of them spoke. But one of them had to. One of them had to tell her the truth now. Molly turned to look at Trace, who still held that classic position of a man on one knee as he looked at his daughter. And there was love in his eyes. Joy, even. Feelings this man who'd had such a rough and unfair life had barely ever known, while Molly had had a lifetime of love and joy.

If Molly opened her mouth and uttered the truth, even Pru, who was showing remarkable maturity and tenderheartedness at the moment, would be thrown for a loop. All that love and joy would be gone in an instant. She wasn't going to clap her hands and pronounce him "Daddy" with a big hug. She would be rocked to the core by the news.

"So, it's okay," Pru finally said in the face of their silence. "I'm fine with it. I'm totally cool."

She saw Trace's shoulders heave with resignation. "Pru, there's more to it than you know."

Pru held up both hands. "Now, *that* I don't need to know." She added a nervous laugh. "What you two do—"

"Pru—"

Molly stepped forward to stop Trace before he made the confession. She took his hand and slowly pulled him up to stand next to her. "I'm really proud of you, Pru," she said softly. "It would be really easy to make this about you, but you're thinking of others and not yourself. Thank you, honey."

"Sure." Then her eyes flashed. "You don't think

260

this disqualifies the project, do you? You two dating? Not just talking or a thing, but actually dating? I mean, technically it happened after we started, but let's keep it on the QT until after the presentation, please? It's really important."

They looked at each other, a world of emotions ricocheting between them.

"Please?" Pru added. "I mean, we can tell the family. We have to tell the family!"

"We don't—"

She cut off Molly's protest. "You need to tell Grandpa, Mom. He made this whole thing happen." She pointed from one to the other. "He's the Dogfather. In fact, Trace, come to Sunday dinner tomorrow night and let the whole family see how happy you are."

"Oh, I don't know," Molly said.

But Trace smiled. "I'd love to, Pru. Thanks. I'll be there." He looked down at Molly and squeezed her hand. "She's right. Everyone needs to know. Together."

Okay, Plan B, then. Which wasn't going to be any easier than Plan A.

Chapter Nineteen

"Hey, handsome."

Trace turned when he heard Molly's voice over the barking, his eyes widening at the sight of her walking down the wide, white kennel corridor. A skirt the color of a ripe raspberry grazed right above the knee, moving flirtatiously over black tights that showed off long, lean legs. Her hair fell in thick waves over her shoulders, bouncing with each step, tempting him to touch it as she got closer.

"Look at that, Tashie," he muttered under his breath to the little puppy resting in his arms. "Doctor's in a dress."

Molly playfully twirled to flutter the skirt and give him a full three-sixty view. "Church clothes."

"You really go to church?"

"Most of the time, with the family. It makes Gramma Finnie happy, and everyone knows a happy Gramma means a happy Sunday dinner." She reached to open the puppy gate and gave him a slow once-over. "You clean up nice, too, Bancroft."

He tipped his head in acknowledgment, grateful he'd spent some hard-earned dollars on crisp new khaki pants and a blue button-down shirt. "I had a feeling Sunday dinner wasn't jeans and Waterford T-shirts."

"No one would mind," she said, coming closer and putting a hand on his shoulder. "But this is nice."

He held her gaze and guided the puppy's face closer to hers. "My Tashie thinks you look pretty," he teased.

Molly tapped the dog's little nose. "Thank you, Tashie. Where's your brother?"

"Taking a test."

She frowned up at him. "What kind of test?"

"Shane took him outside for a few minutes and said he'd be back. I asked if he was testing Bo's therapy skills, kind of as a joke, and he said, yes, which also might have been kind of a joke, I don't know."

"Because everything's a joke to him," she mused, playing with Natasha's ear. "But I saw Chloe, and she said Shane was in my dad's office."

"Do they test training dogs in there?"

"Not usually." She made a face. "Maybe someone wants to adopt Boris."

"I'd hate to separate these two."

"Wait and see," she said. "It could be anything. Are you ready?" She put enough emphasis on the question for him to know exactly what she meant.

"Yes, but I still feel like we should tell Pru first and in private," he said. "I feel strongly about that."

"Well, she's going to leave early and go spend the night at Brooke's," Molly said. "Tomorrow's a teacher work day, so there's no school, and she wants to finish working on her presentation, which is Tuesday afternoon."

He made a face. "If we tell her tonight, she won't write it. She won't enter. She won't win."

"But, Trace—"

He looked over her shoulder as Shane came back down the corridor, the puppy trotting next to him without a leash. "How'd he do?" he asked.

"Awesome." He reached the kennel and nodded to Molly. "This guy's a natural trainer."

A burst of pride kicked him, but he waved off the compliment. "Boris's a sweetheart and easy to train."

"He's going to be an incredible therapy dog. We're moving him into therapy training next week."

Which left Trace...where? "Oh, okay. What about Natasha?" He held the pup a little higher. "Same?"

Shane beamed. "Natasha has a bigger job to do. And so will someone else soon." He gave Trace a meaningful look. "We'll talk at the house."

Trace nodded. "Sure."

"We'll be over in a few minutes," Molly added, inching closer to Trace. "Make sure Trace has a seat next to mine."

Shane's hazel gaze flickered in a little reaction, but he was too cool to say anything. He merely guided little Boris into his kennel and left with a promise to save that seat.

When they were alone, Molly stroked the puppy still in Trace's arms. "Look how peaceful this dog is."

"She's going to be a service dog," he said, knowing that's exactly what Shane had meant.

"And you're going to be offered a job to run our service dog training."

Was that even possible? He blinked as the reality of that hit him so hard it almost knocked him over.

"Do you think so?"

"I know so."

"You were told this? It's a fact?"

She laughed, probably at the sound of desperation in his voice. "I'm not in on those kind of hiring decisions, but they've been talking about this for weeks. I know my father and brothers want to fill this slot and build it into something significant at Waterford Farm. And based on what Shane just said, they're going to offer you a full-time job."

He let out a shaky breath. "I can't believe it."

"Why not? You're a fantastic trainer and you have a touch. Natasha is going to give someone so much happiness, and you are going to take Waterford to a new level for training."

All he could do was stare at her.

"Don't you want to?"

"More than I want my next breath," he admitted. "More than I want anything. Well..." He added a smile. "Almost anything."

"Pru?" she guessed.

"Actually..." He eased the puppy to the side and touched Molly's cheek. "I was thinking about her mother."

Her smile grew as he stroked her skin. "And her mother has been thinking about you. A lot."

He leaned forward and kissed her. Lightly, at first, then deepening it.

Then all that heat got doused by reality. "But what about when we tell everyone I'm Pru's father?" He inched back as another thought hit him. "It might make them change their mind about the job."

She inhaled softly. "I never thought about that."

"This news is going to have repercussions. You have to remember that."

She didn't answer, looking at the dog, thinking. "I don't want you to lose the job, and I honestly think my family can accept anything, but…"

"A little longer, Irish," he whispered the plea. "So much hangs in the balance. A dream job. Pru's contest. My tenuous relationship with her. Even…us."

"Us? What are we waiting for?"

He inched closer. "For everything to be perfect and right, remember?"

She bit her lip, searching his face. "Well, Pru is going to be gone all night…"

Deep inside, something clutched his chest. Tonight. *Tonight.* "Tonight," he whispered. Unless they broke the news and it caused such an upheaval, Molly ran far and fast away from him. Was that possible?

"You're thinking too hard," she joked. "Yes, tonight."

"But your family…"

"Won't be there tonight." She dropped her head against his shoulder and sighed. "But today? This Sunday dinner? Everyone will know there's something going on between us before the first Bloody Mary pitcher is empty. Just accept that."

"Do you think Pru's going to make an official announcement? 'Cause I'm not sure I can handle that."

"You can handle anything," she quipped. "But I don't know if she's going the official announcement route. She's probably already told Gramma Finnie, who's let out a hint to Darcy, who texted our cousin Ella."

His jaw dropped.

"Oh, and sorry." She slipped her arm through his and started to lead him out. "I forgot to mention my four cousins and my aunt are coming. It's a big Sunday dinner when the Mahoneys come, too, which is rare since all three of my male cousins are firefighters, and they usually don't have the same days off."

"How many people will be there?"

"Well, there are twelve of us, including my brothers' wives, one fiancée, and Liam's stepson. Then five Mahoneys, if all four of my cousins plus my aunt are here."

"Eighteen people at dinner?"

"We'll probably do a buffet since we won't all fit in the dining room."

"Eighteen…and they all know I'm head over heels for you?"

Her eyes flashed as she drew back, a sweet smile tugging at her lips. "You are?"

He leaned closer, lifting her chin to his face. "This can't come as a surprise to you."

"What surprises me is that…" She closed her eyes and whispered the rest into a kiss. "I feel the same way."

Right that moment, he couldn't imagine how his life could get any better, but he headed to the house with her, feeling certain that it might.

As Molly suspected, Trace was circled by her three brothers and her father the minute they were inside the kitchen.

"Short business meeting in my office," Dad said. "Molly, you're more than welcome to join us."

For a moment, she considered accepting the invitation, even though training and staff decisions weren't part of her concern at Waterford Farm. However, it *was* a family business, and they made decisions as a family.

But something told her Trace's negotiations should be done privately, and he'd want that time with her brothers and father. So she nudged him toward the other men.

"Go on," she said. "I'll make a pitcher of Bloody Marys and talk to the Mahoneys."

Trace winked at her and headed off with the others, while Molly greeted a kitchen full of relatives. Aunt Colleen was chatting with Andi, Chloe, and Jessie, no doubt discussing the recent wedding as well as the one coming up in April. Darcy and Ella had set up their usual places at the island bar, but the other inseparable couple, Pru and Gramma Finnie, were nowhere to be found.

"They went up to Gramma's apartment," Darcy informed her when Molly looked around. "Gramma's having problems with her new website plug-in."

Molly snorted. "Phrases you don't hear at most family dinners." As she added ice to the pitcher, she frowned again, doing a casual head count. "And the boys?" They all knew *the boys* referred to the three Mahoney men—Declan, Connor, and Braden—who were all impossible to miss. All in their thirties, they'd stopped being boys long ago, but she'd never think of her cousins as anything but.

"My sons wanted to stop at the fire station on the

way over." Aunt Colleen rolled her eyes. "Shocker."

"Meaning they'll be a half hour late," Ella added. "You'd think they hadn't just spent a twenty-four-hour shift with half those guys."

"But they're all off today?" Molly asked. "It's so rare when they get on the same schedule."

"Not rare now that Declan is a captain at the station," Colleen reminded her with noticeable pride in her voice.

Molly smiled at her aunt, so grateful that the woman not only accepted that all three sons wanted to follow in their father's footsteps, but she'd also encouraged them. That couldn't have been easy since Uncle Joe, also a captain, had died well over twenty years ago fighting a blaze.

"Declan will be great in that job," Molly said.

"He's excited about it."

Molly finished mixing the cocktail and poured some drinks, chatting easily with the women when *the boys* arrived and filled the kitchen. Each one of the Mahoney men was better-looking than the next, each tall, strong, proud firefighters.

Connor and Braden had inherited their mother's— and grandmother's—blue eyes, but Declan had Uncle Joe's dark eyes and hair. They all had Kilcannon jaws, strong and stubborn, like her brothers, and the same good hearts. But the fire station came first in all their lives, so those three were single, along with Ella, the youngest Mahoney.

After about a half hour of easy conversation in the kitchen, she saw Trace come in with Garrett and Liam, all of them looking quite satisfied with whatever had taken place in her father's office. Her heart kicked up a notch at the sight of him, knowing what that look had to mean.

Trace Bancroft had been hired by Waterford Farm.

Which meant she'd see him all the time. And so would Pru. She closed her eyes for a moment, hoping they hadn't made a mistake waiting so long to tell her about Trace.

What if she—

"You look awfully serious." Trace was close enough for her to smell the masculine scent of his aftershave and feel the warmth of his whole body next to her.

"Then I better have a Bloody Mary. Want one?"

"I don't think so," he said. "I've been promised a Jameson's at the right time."

"That must mean you have good news."

He held her gaze, his dark eyes glinting with a look she didn't see often on this man. A look of…hope. Yes, that's what he had now. Hope and a bright future, when a few short weeks ago, he'd arrived with nothing but mistakes and a dark past.

Her heart soared with that knowledge, quieting her fears about Pru. Letting him get settled and established with the family before making their foundation-rocking announcement was the right thing to do. It was fair for Trace, who'd had so much unfairness in his life.

She smiled back at him, the urge to reach up and hold his face and plant a congratulatory kiss on his mouth so strong she had to will herself to keep her hands on the counter and off him.

"You'll never guess the perk they offered as a signing bonus."

Lifting her brows, she tried to think of what that might be. "Housing?"

"Actually, I've decided to move back into the house now that it's so nice and clean. No, they offered something even better, Irish." There was enough of a tease in his voice that she knew it had to be meaningful, but she couldn't imagine...

"Oh." She bit her lip. "A Waterford van."

"Until I have my own transportation."

Heat tingled in her chest, mostly because of the way he was looking at her. "Don't you even think about it."

He leaned forward to whisper in her ear, "Comes complete with a dog crate."

She laughed, but then realized the chatter had quieted a bit and...she glanced around, noticing more than a few gazes on them. Oh boy. If Pru hadn't started her whisper campaign, then they were all figuring it out on their own.

And that was fine, because Molly cared about this man. And she didn't want to hide their relationship.

"Come and meet my cousins," she said, sliding her arm through his.

She took him to Ella, who had started the year off with a dramatic "boy cut" of her dark hair that perfectly accentuated her Audrey Hepburn-type of beauty. It was so different from the Barbie-doll blond look that Darcy carried off like a model.

At the introduction to Trace, Ella and Darcy shared enough of a not-so-secret look to confirm Molly's suspicions that they all knew. Even Aunt Colleen, based on that playful gleam in her eyes when she shook Trace's hand, was aware this new man was more than a trainer who'd had a dog under Molly's care for the last several weeks.

They knew about them…and they knew his past.

Realizing that, Molly couldn't love her amazing family any more. And said a secret prayer that their warm and encouraging acceptance of him wouldn't change when they found out he was Pru's father.

Only the Mahoney men seemed in the dark about their budding relationship, treating Trace like any another guest at a Waterford Farm Sunday dinner.

"You're both firefighters?" Trace asked after they shook hands.

"And Braden, our younger brother." Connor pointed over his sizable shoulder to where Braden was deep in conversation with his uncle Daniel.

"I've heard about big Irish families of firefighters."

"Only on the Mahoney side," Declan said. "Kilcannons are the dog people. We save lives and property."

Shane elbowed him as he passed on his way to the Bloody Mary pitcher. "Where would you be without the Dalmatians we get for you?"

Declan laughed, then turned his attention back to Trace. "And you're right about the family. My dad was a firefighter, and there was no question we all would be, too."

"Not me," Ella called out. "I have bigger plans."

"Major plans," Declan said. "When are you going to tell everyone your news?"

"You have news?" Molly turned to her young cousin, always amused by the flighty, funny slip of a girl. Well, the slip of a girl was thirty now and had spent most of her twenties traveling around the world, usually with Darcy. Molly wasn't sure she wanted to know all the adventures those two had had together.

"We sure do have news." Aunt Colleen came over and put an arm around her daughter. They were very close in a way that reminded Molly of how she'd been with her own mother. She swallowed a sudden and unexpected pang of jealousy, realizing at that moment how much she wished her mother was still alive.

Annie would have known what to do and when to tell the family and Pru. The ache squeezed as Molly watched her aunt give Ella an encouraging pat.

"You tell them, Ella. This is your baby."

"Baby?" Gramma Finnie's voice broke through the crowd, eliciting a few gasps and laughs.

"Not a real baby!" Ella exclaimed in her always over-the-top dramatic way.

Darcy tapped her cousin's shoulder. "If you don't tell them, I will."

Ella took a sip of her drink and grinned. "Okay. It's official this week. Mom and I leased space on the west side of Bushrod Square where that old video rental place has been sitting vacant for a few years."

"It's about time somebody put that prime real estate to good use," Molly said.

"Well, we are." Ella beamed at all of them. "Mom and I are opening a franchise of Bone Appetit, the dog treat and specialty store."

"What?"

"Wow!"

"Congratulations!"

The room broke out in hugs, high fives, and noisy toasts to celebrate the news.

"It's all your doing," Aunt Colleen said to Chloe,

who was right in the middle of the cheers. "You've brought so many dogs to Bitter Bark—"

"*Better* Bark," Chloe corrected with the playfully strained patience of a person who made the correction a hundred times a day.

"Well, it's spurred Ella and me to start the business."

"We're proud of you, Mom, because we know you hate change of any kind." Declan, the de facto Mahoney family leader since Uncle Joe died, held up his glass in a mock toast to his mother. "And you, Smella," he added, making her roll her eyes at the childhood nickname her big brothers had hung on her years ago.

"Well, this franchise is one of the fastest-growing businesses in the country," Colleen said. "And Ella and I think we can handle it."

At that moment, Molly felt the lean, familiar arms of Pru wrapping around her waist from behind. "Hey, Mommy."

"Pru." Molly turned, and suddenly, it seemed like another light had come on in the kitchen. Behind her, Gramma Finnie smoothed her soft white hair, which looked particularly stunning with today's midnight-blue sweater set and pearls. The color showed off her eyes and the spark of playfulness in them.

"What are you two up to?" Molly asked in a whisper.

"We were just talking," Pru replied.

"About?"

Gramma's brows rose, and she glanced at Trace, who was still listening to the Ella and Colleen news.

"Of course," Molly said.

Pru inched Molly closer. "Gramma thinks it's a good thing."

Molly eyed the older woman. "I like having your approval." And she especially liked having her help Pru navigate anything difficult about the situation. "And your help with Pru."

"I don't need help," Pru reminded her.

"Then I do," Molly said. "Raising a daughter alone isn't..." Except she wasn't alone, really. Pru's father was standing five feet away. "Thanks," she finished awkwardly, all of them falling silent as the other conversations grew louder.

"And when things settle down at Waterford," Darcy said from her perch on a barstool next to Ella, "I'm going to help you start a grooming business."

"Well, things are not settling down at Waterford anytime soon." Dad took a few steps closer, two shot glasses of golden scotch in his hand. "We have more good news to toast today."

A small cheer of surprise rose while Molly and Trace looked at each other, holding a long, silent gaze.

He gave her a secret wink that made her toes curl tighter than the ringlets in her hair, and all she could do was smile back.

"We're adding a new division to Waterford to extend our training to specialized service dogs."

"Hallelujah," Liam muttered.

"It's about time," Shane added.

"And Trace Bancroft," Dad said, holding a glass to him, "will be heading that division under Shane's management."

While another small cheer erupted, Trace took the glass and nodded at Dad. "I will drink to that, sir."

275

They toasted, and as the glasses parted, Dad added, "You can't call me 'sir,' though."

"Would you prefer Dr. K?"

Dad grinned. "Some people call me the Dogfather." As everyone laughed, Dad threw back his shot, but Molly was the one who felt the heat in her chest.

He couldn't have...*no*. It was impossible. This romance could not be credited to her father, although Trace wouldn't be here if it weren't for Dad.

It didn't matter. He was here. And she was very, very happy about that.

Chapter Twenty

After dinner was over and the family had dispersed to their own homes, Daniel Kilcannon gave Trace the keys to a Waterford van and offered to walk with him to the driveway where they kept it parked. Boxy and spacious, it was more industrial than the old Plymouth Voyager, but the irony of what was being handed to him—along with the pure contentment that had come during dinner—had Trace smiling.

"You sure you don't want to stay in housing tonight?" Daniel asked.

"No, I'm ready to go home. I can get there now, thanks to you, and the place is more than habitable, thanks to Pru."

But the truth was, he wasn't going home...yet. He was headed straight to Molly's house, where they'd planned to meet after dinner once Pru had left for her friend's house.

"But I am leaving Meatball here at the kennel," he added. "If you don't mind. I'd like to get to my house and make sure all of the tools and paint are all put away so it's dog-safe for him."

"Very responsible," Daniel said.

"Thanks again for the wheels, Dr. K. At the salary you've offered, it won't be long until I can get my own."

"No rush," Daniel assured him. "The van sits here at night, and when we need it during the day to move dogs, you'll be here. I'm really happy about this arrangement." He hesitated a moment before adding, "Seems like Molly is, too."

Molly's warning that no man would be good enough for Dr. Kilcannon's daughter echoed in his head. And how could he blame Daniel for being the same protective father Trace knew he'd be with Pru?

Trace cleared his throat before answering. "Molly's done an amazing job of taking care of Meatball," he said carefully. "I'm grateful to you and her for saving his life."

Daniel stared straight ahead as they walked, silent for a few steps before he sighed. "You know, Molly's kind of the glue that holds this family together."

Oh boy. Here we go. "You may think that, sir, but I'm pretty sure a family this tight doesn't need glue."

"We do. We did." He slowed his step, his strong jaw clenching for a moment. "My wife used to have that job, but Molly really moved into the role these last few years."

Trace looked at the man, trying to game where he was going. "And you don't want that to change?"

"On the contrary," he said softly. "I'm afraid she's sacrificed so much to add the job of, well, glue-holder to her already packed schedule."

Nope, definitely not sure where Daniel was going with this, but Trace had learned long ago that sometimes silence was much more effective at getting a person to talk, so he listened.

"I am aware that you two are more than just casual acquaintances," Daniel finally said. "Would you like to know how I know that?"

"I assume you've seen us together."

"I've caught a few meaningful glances and casual touches, yes," Daniel said with a quick laugh. "But what I've really seen is a change in my daughter these last few weeks."

"How so, sir?"

"Hard to describe, really, but Molly always seemed like a content and fulfilled young woman, loving work and the family and being a single mom."

That slowed Trace's step. "Doesn't she still?"

"Of course, yes, but, well, when my wife died and Molly stepped up, as I said, I sensed a hollowness growing inside her."

"I'm sure she misses her mother very much," Trace said. "She talks about her frequently, and your wife sounded like a great lady."

Daniel smiled. "That's an understatement, son. She was one in a million. My best friend, my firm foundation, my...everything." He cleared his throat as if the very words choked him up. "But as Pru grows older, Molly knows she has to have some very difficult conversations with her daughter, and I know she'd hoped her mother would help her through those talks."

Difficult conversations about...Pru's father. Trace could barely swallow, let alone respond. He should tell him now. This was his chance. This was his moment.

"And now I see this change in Molly, like she doesn't feel quite that alone anymore." Daniel stopped as they reached the van, turning to Trace. "I'm crediting you with that change."

"I'm stunned and, honestly, humbled, if you think I could have helped her that way."

Daniel gave him a sharp look. "I know you have. I sense an inner strength in you and a nurturing heart. I think…" He hesitated, then exhaled. "I think you're good for Molly and Pru."

"Pru, yes." He took a slow breath. "I want you to know—"

"Oh, I know," Daniel interjected. "We both know that it's a package deal with my daughter."

"About that package deal, sir." He turned and looked into Daniel's piercing blue eyes, seeing nothing but warmth and respect in his gaze. Respect that would melt away like metal under a burning flame when Trace told him the truth. He'd waited his whole life for a man like Daniel to look at him with respect. Waited to be worthy of a woman like Molly. Waited to make someone like Pru feel proud.

Waited so long, he couldn't bring himself to lose it all yet.

"Yes?" Daniel asked.

Trace shook off the temptation and frowned as he tried to pull together the right words. "I want you to know, sir, that you have my promise that I will do whatever I have to do, whenever I have to do it, at any sacrifice to myself, to make sure your daughter and granddaughter are happy and safe."

"That's all this Dogfather really wants." The older man's smile was slow, and wide, and made his blue eyes dance a little as he handed him the keys. "You drive this van carefully, son."

Trace took the keys and nodded. "I will, and thank you."

He thought about the conversation the whole time he drove to Molly's, where he'd been a few times over the last weeks to pick up or drop off Pru. The whole way, he mulled over the promise he'd just made, thinking about all the ways he could keep it. They'd tell Pru the truth, of course, as soon as the presentation was over. They'd carry her through whatever white water swirled in her life because of it. They'd work together every day at Waterford, and they'd...

As he pulled into the tiny driveway next to Molly's blue car, Trace froze as he replayed his thoughts.

They'd do this. *They'd* do that.

He thought of he and Molly as a *they*. How had that happened? When?

Before he could answer the question, she stepped out of the front door of the quaint two-story house, already changed into an oversized shirt and comfy sweat pants, her curls wild around her face and shoulders.

He couldn't help smiling as he strode toward her, already aching to pull her into his arms.

"What took so long?" she asked, holding the door open to invite him in.

"Had a talk with your dad."

She drew back, eyes wide. "About?"

"You. And Pru."

"What did you say?"

"Not important."

"It is to me."

He paused inside the door, taking a whiff of a citrusy, sweet scent he'd noticed before when he'd stopped in with her to get Pru or pick something up on the way to his house. "Did Pru leave?" he asked.

"She's gone for the night." She lifted her brows in a sexy invitation. "And you are welcome to stay as long as you like."

He slid his hand along her cheek, loving the feel of her smooth skin against his palm. "Truth is, I never want to leave."

She sighed into him and looked up for a long moment, barely breathing.

"So, here we are again, Irish." He grazed his thumb over her lower lip. "Where should we go?"

"Somewhere I can kiss the holy hell out of you all night long."

He laughed softly at the echo of his own words spoken fourteen years ago. "I got a minivan in the driveway."

"Maybe next time." Silently, she led him toward the stairs.

She kissed him all the way into her bedroom, pulling him into a dimly lit sanctuary and folding into his arms to make every dream he ever had seem like child's play compared to the real thing.

For a man who hadn't been with a lover for well over a decade, Trace showed remarkable restraint in the bedroom. But Molly soon figured out that he wasn't holding back to show his finesse as they fell onto the bed and kissed until they were both breathless. He was savoring her.

The realization was as intoxicating as his hands when he slowly pulled her sweat shirt over her head and discovered she'd ditched her bra along with her Sunday clothes. Letting out an appreciative groan, he caressed her skin like she was made of spun silk, his fingers light and reverent. "My sweet, sexy Molly. You're more beautiful than ever."

Every kiss made her blood hum and skin sing. Every whisper of warm air on her breasts made her want to tunnel her fingers into his hair and press him against her. Every pulse of his body against hers made her want to shed all clothes and feel him everywhere.

While he suckled and kissed her, she unbuttoned his shirt, spreading it wide to get her hands on his chest. His muscles bunched under her touch and she whimpered in appreciation of every masculine bulge and cut.

"You had this all set up." Trace took a quick glance around her room as he sat up to help her push the shirt over his shoulders.

Not really. After Pru left, Molly had showered and freshened up, then lit one soft light, made sure the bed was folded back, and threw a few condoms on the nightstand. "You said you wanted everything just right."

He tossed the shirt on the floor and gave her a look of disbelief. "I didn't mean the setting, Irish."

She lay back down on the pillow, looking up at him. "What did you mean?"

"Us," he said without hesitation. "I meant everything needed to be right with us. We needed to trust each other and care about each other and..." He shook his head as if he couldn't finish.

"You said you wanted it to be meaningful," she finished for him, wrapping her fingers around his neck to pull him closer.

"Yeah," he said huskily, falling into the next kiss.

"It is meaningful." She slid her thigh along his leg to punctuate that point. "I don't quite know what it means yet," she admitted. "But I know it's something."

He responded with a long, openmouthed kiss, then worked his way down to her belly, dragging her yoga pants all the way down so she had nothing on but a black silk thong she'd chosen only for him to see.

"Bad girl," he teased, running his finger over the top of it and sending sparks of crazy, sexy pleasure through her.

"You should talk, with all those tattoos."

"Some you haven't even seen."

She dragged her hand over his washboard stomach, finding his navel and a thin trail of hair that led lower. "Show me," she murmured into his ear.

She felt him hiss in a breath when she touched him, both of them too lost to talk anymore. They communicated with touches, kisses, and a slow exploration of every pleasure point they could find.

When the heat had built to the point where the room was filled with nothing but ragged breaths and pleas for more, he sheathed himself and hovered over her, looking into her eyes.

"I know what it means," he whispered.

It took her a minute to force her brain to pick up that thread of conversation and think of something other than the fiery need for him to be inside her. "What?"

"You, going to all this trouble and taking me into your bed and body. I know what it means."

"It means I'm attracted to you, that I trust you, and that I want you here with me tonight. More nights. Lots of nights. Maybe a few days, too." She tightened her grip on his arm, not wanting to beg for him to enter her, but she might if the conversation went on for one more minute.

"It means I'm worthy of you." The words were thick with emotion and spoken with awe.

"Yes, of course you are." She reached up and cupped his face, stunned by the fact that he could doubt that. But then she remembered his history and how many times life had made him feel worthless. "In fact, I'm honored to make love to you, Trace Bancroft."

He closed his eyes as if the words had sliced right through him, finally letting his weight fall and spreading her legs with his hips to slide inside her. They moved in slow silence for three, four, five beats, then both closed their eyes and held on to each other and found the perfect rhythm.

Molly clung to him, pressed her lips against his shoulder, and welcomed this man into her body and heart. When she opened her eyes, her gaze landed on the blue outline of the shamrock on his shoulder, reminding her that in fourteen years, he'd only been with her. The first time had meant enough to memorialize it.

And the second? Maybe *she'd* get a tattoo.

She rolled with pleasure, lost with each stroke of his body deeper into her.

He murmured her name, his breath uneven and desperate, his whole body owning her from top to bottom. Cut by shards of pure pleasure, she finally tumbled into a long, sweet, delicious release against him, and he did the same a moment later, finally resting his whole body on hers in complete satisfaction.

Molly listened to his heart and inhaled the musky scent of sex on the sheets. Stroking his back lightly, circling that shamrock on his shoulder, she sighed as her breath came back to normal and her body began to feel sore in places she'd forgotten she owned.

Deep inside. Way deep inside. Maybe where her heart resided.

What *did* this mean? Trace felt worthy and she felt…full.

"I never realized I was so empty," she admitted on the next soft exhale.

Slowly, he turned his head to look at her. "You were?"

"I know, it's crazy. I have a family the size of a small country, a daughter who needs and loves me, a thriving business, a town full of people who've known me since I was a child, and yet…"

"You felt alone?"

She eased back so she could see his eyes, glittering in the dim light. "I didn't realize how much I needed touching and kissing and…you." She stroked his back again. "I needed you and didn't know it."

"Now you've got me." He kissed her tenderly. "For as long as you'll have me."

"Long," she whispered. "Don't disappear on me again, Trace. Even when things get tough with Pru, and they will. Even if my family doesn't throw their arms around you like you're a long-lost brother when they find out the truth about you being Pru's father. Okay? Don't disappear again."

He searched her face. "It must have been hard for you, huh? When you found out you were pregnant and I was gone."

"It was lonely," she admitted, realizing only this minute *how* lonely. "I needed you. I guess I've needed you for thirteen years and didn't realize how much."

He closed his eyes and wrapped his whole body around hers, cuddling her into him, stroking her hair, and feathering kisses on her face. "I wish life had been different."

"I guess you do, but right now? This is exactly what I want it to be. Just don't disappear again."

"No worries, Irish. I'm in it for the long haul."

She closed her eyes and let his words and mouth and body soothe a wound she hadn't even known she had.

Chapter Twenty-One

"Good afternoon, ladies and gentlemen. My name is Prudence Anne Kilcannon, and I represent Mr. Margolis's eighth-grade class project in community service." Pru closed her eyes and stopped for a long second. "Maybe I should say, 'Hi, I'm Pru.' I don't want to seem like I'm trying too hard."

"There's no such thing as trying too hard." From the sofa in Molly's living room, Trace gestured for the practice to continue. "And you're doing great. One more time through from the top and you got this."

"Or you could stop rehearsing and eat this pizza before it gets cold." Molly lifted the box lid and waved some of the aroma their way. "Pepperoni and pineapple, Pru. It's your favorite."

"Really?" Trace looked oddly excited by that. "I thought I was the only one who loved pizza that way."

So pizza preference was hereditary, Molly mused. Because no one else in Molly's family ate that combination. In fact, her brothers complained loudly about it when Pru handled the ordering on a Kilcannon family movie night.

But Pru wasn't interested in anything but her notes and presentation at that moment. "Mom, you have to let me run through this one more time to make sure I come in under ten minutes or I'll be disqualified."

Molly rolled her eyes. "You are not going to be disqualified, and I'm starving."

"See?" Pru said to Trace. "See what I have to put up with? No regard for rules, no respect for thorough preparation. She just wants to have fun."

Laughing at the exchange, Trace pushed up and held a hand out to Pru. "You need both in life, Umproo. Gotta have fun and be prepared. Also, gotta have pizza. C'mon, let's take a break and make your mama happy."

"Thank you," Molly said with an exaggerated sigh, putting three paper plates on the counter.

Even Meatball got up from his comfy corner spot and came over as if he was part of the party, giving Molly that look that most people would fall for.

"No, baby, I'm sorry. No table food for precious dogs who've lost most of their stomach."

He sank to the ground with a whine.

"Oh my gosh, he's the most dramatic dog," Pru said.

"Usually gets him what he wants," Trace agreed, taking his slice and sitting on a counter stool.

"Well, he can't have pizza. But..." Molly turned to the bag of healthy treats she'd brought home for him. "He can have this!"

At the tone of her voice, Meatball was up, barking, rounding the counter to take his treat and then nuzzle Molly's leg.

"He officially loves you more than I do," Trace said.

At the statement, both Molly and Pru blinked at him. After a second, he realized what he'd said. "I mean, more than he loves me. Not more than…" He laughed and shook his head. "Stuck my foot right into it, didn't I?"

Molly just stared at him, heat on her cheeks.

"You know what Gramma Finnie says," Pru said, waving her pizza slice. "'Sometimes you say what you think and mean what you…'" She frowned. "Wait. It's 'sometimes you say what you mean when you really mean to…'" She took a bite, laughing. "I can't remember. Can you remember, Mom?"

Molly couldn't even remember her name at the moment. Had he just basically said he loved her? "I don't know," she managed. "But I'm sure it's on a pillow or cross-stitched on something else up in Gramma Finnie's apartment."

"How long has your grandma lived there?" Trace asked, clearly eager to change the subject.

"Oh, I'll tell you the whole story," Pru offered.

Molly managed to chew her pizza as Pru delved into Waterford Farm history about Gramma and Grandpa Seamus leaving when Garrett was born, then Gramma moving back in after Grannie Annie died. Molly stayed standing in the kitchen, with Meatball at her feet, watching Pru's animated hand motions and listening to her while Trace sat completely rapt. He barely ate, spellbound by the story and the storyteller, laughing at her asides, smiling at almost every word she said.

He loved Pru, that was evident in his eyes. And he…

Had that been a slip of the tongue, or the truth of how he felt? It seemed crazy, but Molly got it. She could fall in love with him. She was halfway there already. She loved his good heart and his humility. Absolutely adored his simple soul that appreciated every moment of his life and freedom. She hurt for his past and wanted to be part of his future.

She wanted this. The three of them and a dog, all cozied up in the kitchen, being a family, being whole, being complete.

Oh my God. I am *in love with him.*

"Isn't that what Grandpa always says, Mom?" Pru asked, ripping Molly from her reverie, leaving her dizzy with the realization and at a loss about what question she'd been asked.

"Um…yeah."

"I think your mom is suffering from presentation-practice overload," Trace said quickly, pushing back his stool to come around and join her. "You're tired."

Of course she was. They'd slept about an hour the night before, though she wouldn't have given up a minute of their intimate time for something as mundane as sleep. "I'm pretty wiped," she admitted.

"It's getting late," Trace said. "I better take off."

"You need to time my presentation again." Pru jumped off her seat, waving another piece of pizza. "One more time."

But Trace looked hard at Molly, searching her face, trying to read her expression, which was pure shock, no doubt. It was true: She was in love with him.

"I think you got this, Umproo," he said, sneaking his hand around Molly's waist to give her a quick squeeze. "If you practice too much, you won't sound genuine." He leaned closer to whisper, "And you need some rest, Irish."

She smiled at him and nodded.

"Meatman." Trace snapped his fingers. "Let's go, bud."

But Meatball cuddled closer around Molly's feet, making them both laugh.

"He *does* love you," Trace muttered. "Walk me out?"

She nodded and looked down at Meatball, who put one paw over Molly's shoe. "But can he stay with us? I can take him to Waterford in the morning when I go to work."

"He'll be happier here," he said, then mouthed to Molly, "Who wouldn't?"

Smiling, she walked him to the door after he gave Pru a high five and promised he'd be at her presentation after school tomorrow. Outside, he hugged Molly in the driveway, wrapping his arms around her shivering body.

"Thanks for making me feel so at home here," he said, pressing his lips to her ear, which only made her shiver some more, but not from the cold.

"Thanks for being here, for helping Pru, and for…" She leaned back to look at him. "For last night."

"You don't have to thank me for that. Just promise me it won't be another fourteen years until next time."

"Mmm. Fourteen hours, I hope."

He grinned. "Liked it, did you?"

"I like you." She put her cold fingers on his cheeks, immediately warmed. "I…*really* like you."

"I never felt this before, Irish."

Love? She didn't dare whisper the word, but waited for him to say it first.

"I never felt this much hope. I didn't know what

hope was. I've been dead for thirty-five years, until you. And Pru. And now I'm alive again." His voice cracked. "I love...this feeling."

She got it. It was too soon to say anything else, and they still had a major hurdle to get over.

"I love this feeling, too."

He kissed her, long and slow, then got into the van, gave a wave, and drove off. She stood watching the red lights disappear, shivering in the late January cold, utterly content with life.

Was that love? If so, she was in deep and had no desire to ever get out.

It was cold, clear, and dark when Trace rounded the bend at Sutton's Mill and headed for home. He'd found a country station that played oldies and caught the opening notes of a song that took him back to high school, back to a very specific night.

When Dierks Bentley started whining *What Was I Thinkin'?* he laughed out loud.

How could he do anything else? The past twenty-four hours had been the best of his life. This morning, he'd slipped into his studio apartment at sunrise, having somehow managed to tear himself out of Molly's bed. He'd showered, changed for work, and packed up his meager belongings to move them back to his house after work.

Then he'd spent the day as a full-time manager of a division of a company. He'd worked with Tashie and Bo, had two meetings with owners of potential service dogs, and helped Shane with the trainees. Like all the employees of Waterford Farm, he'd cleaned kennels, helped with the dogs, and celebrated when Garrett put on his "doggone hat" and took a mixed-breed dog named Captain Crunch off to a new forever home. Apparently, Marie had been eating cereal that morning.

The best part of the day was hanging with Molly and Pru, practicing the presentation, and feeling so much love it damn near made his heart break. That woman. That girl. Two incredible humans to love, and he did. Both of them. He absolutely—

His thoughts evaporated as he spied lights behind the trees that blocked the front of his little house. He hadn't left a light on, he was sure of it.

Who could it be? No one knew he was there except the kids who'd worked on Pru's project. Was it one of them? That little Cody tool looking for trouble?

Frowning, he turned into the property, the van tires crunching and the headlights landing on a bright blue car parked in front of his door. What the heck? Had Molly beat him here for a surprise good-night?

He'd stopped in town for gas, so maybe she—

Then his vision cleared. That wasn't her hybrid. That was a two-seater sports car, although it was nearly the same color of robin's-egg blue. A Porsche, in fact. Brand-new and crazy expensive.

He knew exactly who owned that car. But no idea what the hell Allen the asshole lawyer could be doing here.

Trace narrowed his eyes at the car and took a slow breath as he tried to imagine what that man wanted. Nothing good.

The driver's door opened slowly, the van's headlight beams bathing the inside of the car in yellow.

But all he could see was one long, lean, shapely leg in skintight jeans and black high heels slide out, followed by another.

Oh, not Allen. His other half.

A woman climbed out of the car and stood right in the light, blond hair spilling, red lips shining, looking like trouble from head to toe.

Trace swallowed as an old fear crawled up his back. Whatever Isabella wanted, he had to handle this right. He couldn't screw up. He couldn't make a mistake. He couldn't be in the wrong place at the wrong time again, just when his life was so *right*.

Very slowly, he unlatched his seat belt and opened the door.

"Hello, Trace." Her voice was low, sultry, and way too welcoming.

"Hey."

She tipped her head and gave a flirtatious smile, taking a few steps forward and looking him up and down like a starving cat eyeing a can of tuna. Damn it. "Your house looks good."

His *house*? She wasn't drooling over his house. "What's up, Isabella?"

"Call me Izzie. All my friends do."

He cleared his throat, which was surprisingly tight, holding on to the still-open van door with that sixth sense that said he might have to make a run for it. "How can I help you, Isabella?"

She flinched just enough for him to know she did not like that subtle insult. "Lotta work been done here."

He nodded, staying still and silent and wishing to hell that she'd state her business and leave.

"She's a good girl, that Prudence Kilcannon," she said.

He sucked in a soft breath at the name. Was that her business? Pru?

She closed the space and got close enough for him to see she wore carefully applied makeup and tasteful jewelry and had a dangerous gleam in her eye.

"Why are you here?" he asked.

"I'm sorry you don't seem a little happier to see me."

"I don't know you," he fired back.

"We could fix that."

Oh man. Really? "Pretty sure your husband would have a few things to say about that."

She made a disgusted face. "He won't be home from the gym for hours, then he'll knock back most of a bottle of red wine, eat dinner without talking about anything but himself, and be snoring by ten."

"Sounds like a man who works hard," he said. "And maybe you should be right there next to him where you belong, Isabella."

Undaunted by the dismissal, she pushed her hair back and took one more step. "I'd rather be here next to you."

He snorted. "You serious?"

"Dead."

Oh *man*. "Look, you're a gorgeous woman and—"

"Thank you."

"—you drive a fifty-thousand-dollar car, have a nice daughter, and I presume your every need is met by your husband. What the hell are you doing coming on to me outside my hovel on the wrong side of town?"

She put a hand on her hip and lifted one side of her mouth in a smile that deepened a dimple. "It was sixty-five thousand, fully loaded. That girl isn't really my daughter. And my husband can't meet my needs without the help of a little blue pill. But I like the gorgeous part. Can we talk about that some more?"

Really? This was happening to him?

"Don't look bewildered, Trace," she said on a laugh. "I've been thinking about you ever since I saw you in town." She shrugged. "I didn't think it would hurt to give it try."

"No harm, no foul, huh?" He shook his head. "Well, no one's hurt, and you can go home now." He stood his ground, pointing to her car.

"I don't want to go home."

He looked her right in her big blue eyes. "I don't want you to stay."

"Just for a minute? We can talk." She closed the space between them, giving him a whiff of expensive perfume. She looked up at him, sex oozing from every pore. "For a while."

If there had never been a Molly and he'd been here floating around like a lost ex-con who hadn't been with a woman in fourteen years, Isabella's offer would have been a sweet one. She was a pretty woman, even with a sheen of desperation. Maybe he'd have taken the comfort she offered.

But everything had changed in the last few weeks. He now knew what he was worth, and it was way more than what this woman was offering.

"No," he said simply, still standing by the open van door, considering his options. His best option was to get the hell out of here. "I'm not interested." He turned to get back into the van, but she grabbed his arm.

"Well, now I know where Pru Kilcannon gets her rule-following trait."

He froze halfway into the van.

"Or maybe they drummed bad behavior out of you during your fourteen years in Huttonsville Correctional Center serving time for killing a man."

He closed his eyes as the words hit their target.

"Because the Trace Bancroft I know had no problem getting it on with women of all ages. Kimmie McQueen for one, and then Molly Kilcannon one night over Thanksgiving break."

He backed out of the van slowly, turning to her, words caught in his throat, fury strangling him.

"Do you forget that I was the one who put you two together that night?" She angled his head, seemingly gaining confidence with all her facts and his silence. "I've always known, ever since Molly came home from college that spring with some vague story about a boyfriend at Chapel Hill. I forgot, frankly, but then a few years ago, my stepdaughter was invited to a sleepover for Pru's birthday, and I took one look at her and..." She lifted a shoulder. "If you're looking for it, the resemblance is there."

"Good for you, Izzie. You're quite the sleuth."

She laughed. "Oh, it's Izzie now. You change your mind about me?"

"No." He practically spat the word, hard enough to make her recoil and narrow her eyes.

"You should drop to your knees and thank your lucky stars a woman like me wants a man like you."

Maybe he would have...weeks ago. Before

Waterford Farm. Before Molly. And before Pru. Because of all of them, he wouldn't give this lady the time of day, no matter what she knew about him.

"I'm leaving now, ma'am," he said with quiet calm. "I think you should do the same."

"And I think you..." She put both hands on his chest and dragged them down slowly. "Should remember your manners. I'm a guest. And I want—"

"No." He grabbed her elbows as the sound of a roaring engine and squealing tires made him freeze, followed by a bath of halogen brights sitting high on a massive truck. Trace fought the urge to push her off him, but fear and history and full knowledge of what a push like that could do to the other person stopped him. He clung to her, fighting that urge, and in that split second, she whipped to the side, her back to the lights. As she did, he saw her reach up and rip her silky top so hard the buttons popped.

What the hell—

"Get your hands off my wife!" a voice bellowed from behind the lights that blinded Trace as Isabella stumbled away, clutching at her torn shirt.

"Oh my God, Allen! You're here!"

"Damn right I'm here." A large silhouette emerged from the headlight beams, nothing but a menacing black shadow moving toward him.

"How did you find me?"

"You think I don't have a tracking device on that car, Izzie?" He stomped closer, headed for Trace, who felt every hair on the back of his neck rise. "You touch my wife, son?"

"No, sir, I—"

"He was trying to push me into that van and kidnap

me, Allen! I came here to find Corinne, and he...he... assaulted me!"

What the holy hell was going on? Trace fisted his hands, tried to breathe, tried to think, tried not to relive every hellacious moment of his mostly hellacious life.

"You're a fool, Isabella." The man growled the words, but kept coming toward Trace, who could make out his angry features now. "I told you he's a convict! I told you he's a murderer and rapist!"

Trace reeled at the accusations, still shocked into silence.

"That's why I came here," Isabella said, her voice rising to an earsplitting whine. "Corinne said she was going to help her friend with a community service project, and I remembered he was here, and I had to come and find her."

"Corinne's at home." He threw enough of a vile look at her to give Trace hope that Allen Phillips didn't believe a word his lying wife said. "And you, boy?" He was about five feet away now, close enough for Trace to see his nostrils flare and eyes narrow. "You need to get the hell out of this town."

Trace tried to swallow, bile rising. "I didn't do anything."

How many freaking times in his life would that be his defense?

"Oh, really? Didn't kill a man outside a bar in Charleston, West Virginia, and spend fourteen years in Huttonsville Correctional Institute?"

Trace didn't flinch.

"Didn't rape Kim McQueen and run out of town when old Bart wanted to kill you for it?"

"No, I didn't."

He snorted. "Like father, like son."

This time, Trace did flinch. How did this asshole—

"I did a little research on you about ten years ago when I handled Bart's divorce. It all came back when I saw you in town. I know exactly what you got away with. I know what you come from. I know what a piece of shit on a shoe you are. And it is time for you to go back to whatever hellhole you want, 'cause you are no longer welcome in Bitter Bark."

He was vaguely aware of Izzie sniveling and backing away, her breath heavy. But most of his attention was on her husband, who was a gym rat and strong, but Trace knew he could take him if he had to.

And then he'd have another crime on his record.

The man closed the space completely, inches from where Trace had backed into the open van door. "Maybe you want to take a swing at me, son." He turned his jaw and offered it. "Go ahead. It's a one-way ticket back to prison, that I can guarantee you. C'mon." He tapped his jaw. "Give it to me, killer."

"Allen. That's enough."

He whipped around to his wife. "Defending him, Izzie?"

"No, but let it go. Nothing bad happened."

"To you, maybe. But what about the next woman? What about Molly Kilcannon? You going to rape her, too? And that sweet little girl of hers—"

Trace's fisted hand moved like it had a life of its own, propelled from his side and through the air, landing hard enough that he heard the guy's jaw crack as he stumbled backward.

"Allen!"

For a moment, Trace couldn't move. His brain went dead. White lights popped like he'd been the one punched. His whole life flashed before him—the job, the life, the woman, the daughter—all gone in the time it took to throw a punch.

The man tripped a little, but rebounded and caught himself as Izzie launched to help him.

"You son of a bitch," Allen said, wiping his face. "You must really want to go back to prison. Call the cops, Izzie."

"No, no, Allen, no."

He glared at her. "You said he assaulted you!"

"He did…not. You can't do that to him. You can't make him go back to jail. It's not right."

Now she thought about what was right?

Allen Phillips gave him a murderous look, his sizable chest rising and falling with fury. "Get the hell out of this town and don't ever come back. Ever, you hear me? If I ever see your face again, I will make it my personal duty to see your ass back in prison. You want to give me that pleasure? Stay. I will make your life and the lives of anyone around you a living hell."

With that, he went back into the blinding lights, slammed the door shut, and drove off.

"You better do what he says, Trace," Isabella said as she walked toward her car. "He's a mean son of a bitch."

"Why'd you marry him?"

She shrugged. "Why do we do anything? I was lonely. Still am, obviously," she added with a mirthless laugh. "Bye."

She climbed into the car, started it up, and drove out of the driveway slowly.

Trace stood stone-still as the lights turned to watery red splotches in his eyes.

He'd made a promise, and now he had to keep it.

Chapter Twenty-Two

Wow. Trace must really be anxious to get to work.

It wasn't even seven thirty in the morning when Molly pulled up to Waterford Farm and spied the dog van inside the front gates, more than a half mile from the house. Only then did she realize Trace sat at the wheel.

Her mind zipped through a list of possibilities, landing on the obvious one. He knew she'd be there early since Pru wanted to get to school at seven that morning to do one more run-through in the auditorium before her after-school presentation. He wanted to meet her…in the van.

For old times' sake? Didn't he realize she'd have Meatball with her?

Still, she liked the way he thought. Maybe they could take a drive after lunch.

"Come on, Meatman," she said to her attentive passenger in the back. "Let's go see your real master." Smiling, she parked way off to the side, well behind the van, and climbed out. The dog followed, bounding to the passenger door.

There, Molly stopped cold at the sight of Trace behind the wheel, head in hands, completely unmoved by Meatball's happy barks.

She tapped very lightly on the glass, and her veins went icy when he turned and she saw red-rimmed eyes, bloodless cheeks, and nothing that looked like a smile on those beautiful lips.

Something was very, very wrong.

He didn't reach for the handle to let her in, so she slowly opened the door and stared at him. Meatball climbed in, heading straight for Trace, who barely acknowledged him.

"Trace?" Her voice was taut, her throat closing up at the abject sadness in his eyes.

"I need to talk to you, Molly."

"Okay." She pulled herself into the seat, nudging the dog toward the back and turning her whole body to face Trace. "What's the matter?"

He exhaled slowly, a ragged, pained breath dragged from deep in his chest. "I'm leaving Bitter Bark."

She blinked at him, hearing the words but hoping she'd misunderstood. Even though she knew she hadn't.

"I almost left without saying goodbye, but—"

"Why?"

"I didn't want to hurt you any more than I have to."

She reached for his arm, but he jerked away like her touch burned him. "Well, that did."

He closed his eyes. "Molly, listen to me."

She didn't say a word, staring at his face. He hadn't slept, shaved, or changed since yesterday. "Trace, what's going on?"

"I am going to ask you to do something for me—"

"Anything."

He turned and shot her a look. "Wait until you hear what it is."

Silenced, she nodded.

"I need you to, I mean, I am *begging* you to never tell Pru I'm her father."

Her heart dropped with a thud into her stomach.

"Trace, I can't do that. I won't go one more day with this—"

"She's my daughter, too," he ground out. "I have a say, don't I? I get a fifty percent opinion in deciding what she knows. Don't I?"

Maybe he did. She'd never thought about it that way. "Why?"

"Because I love her. And I love..." His eyes shuttered. "I love the dream of you, I guess. The job, the life, the... No. *You.* I'm asking this because I love both of you."

She clasped her hands, squeezing tightly, the only way to keep herself from reaching for him, holding him, loving him back. But she didn't want to be rebuffed, even though he just said...

"I'm confused," she admitted with a humorless laugh. "You love us, so you don't want her to know you're her father and you want me to live a lie. Oh, and you're leaving."

"It's not confusing, Molly. Something has kept me from telling her the truth all these weeks. I had to come to terms with it. The fact is, I am what and who I am, and I will never, ever be good enough to be that girl's father or your—" He stopped himself.

"You *are* my lover," she reminded him.

"I'd want more."

Her heart flipped, because hadn't she been thinking the same thing all night? "Then why would you leave? Why would you ask me not to tell her? Why wouldn't you give yourself a chance to live a normal, happy life, Trace?" Her voice rose, strangled by frustration.

"Because I can never live a normal, happy life. I can*not* undo my mistakes, I can*not* erase my past, I can*not* be the kind of father Pru deserves or…or…the man you deserve. People will always judge me harshly, but fairly. And I can't hang that shame on you or her."

She tried to breathe. Failed. "I don't care what people think."

"You say that now. But what about tomorrow?"

"I won't care what people think tomorrow or the next day or the next year. I care about my family, and they have shown you that they don't judge. I don't care what strangers think. You'll show them they're wrong."

He turned to her, agony darkening his eyes. "Okay, let me be blunt. I don't *want* Pru to know. Please. It's my choice as her father, isn't it? If she knows and hates me for it, it will hurt her."

"That won't—"

"And if she knows and I leave, it will hurt her in a different way."

"Why would you leave?" She searched his face, aching for an answer she somehow knew he wasn't going to give.

"I have to," he said coldly.

"Why?"

"It doesn't matter," he said, his dismissive tone cutting her. "What matters is Pru. And you. Please do this for me, Molly. Please make up some great guy who stole your heart but then he died. Tell her he died. Give him a heroic death. Tell her he was strong and smart and good and kind and so excited to be a father he couldn't breathe."

"None of that would be a lie."

He dropped his head back with a grunt. "I knew you'd make this difficult."

"Me? I'm making it difficult?" She practically choked. "You're walking out on me, on her, on a job, on people who believe in you. And you won't even tell me *why*."

He turned and tentatively reached for her hands. "Because I made a promise that I will do whatever I have to do, whenever I have to do it, at any sacrifice to myself, to make sure you and Pru are happy and safe. I have to keep that promise, and this is the way to do it. Trust me, I've been awake all night trying to come up with something better."

A promise? "You made one to me, too," she whispered. "Remember? 'I'm in it for the long haul.'"

He grunted softly. "Molly, please. You two can't be safe or happy with me."

How did he know that? She didn't know what to say to that, not that she could talk. Her throat was closed, her eyes stung, and an old burn of grief and disbelief started low in her belly. She hadn't felt like this since the day Dad called and said he'd taken Mom to the hospital with chest pains.

Totally and completely devastated.

"So, this is what I'm asking you, Molly." He narrowed his eyes, but not in anger, more because she could see them growing moist as he looked at her.

"This is what I, as Pru's father, want most."

"For her to think her father is some dead fictional character?" How could he think that would be better for her?

"I never want her to know I'm her father. Never."

She pressed her knuckles to her lips to keep from crying out. "Trace."

"Please." His voice cracked and tears welled. "Please. It's my request."

"Where are you going?" she finally asked, zeroing in on the easiest of the million questions hammering in her head.

"I don't know. I'll figure something out, but I have to return the van."

"And your job? Tashie and Bo?"

He shook his head, unable to answer.

"You and Meatball are just going to walk out of here?" Her tears fell now, as much in sorrow as frustration.

"Only me," he said, so quietly she could actually hear her heart breaking. Or maybe that was his. "He loves you."

She glanced into the back, where Meatball had stretched out next to the dog crate, taking in the exchange.

"And so do I," Trace whispered, touching her chin. "If I didn't, I'd stay. If I didn't care about Pru's well-being, I wouldn't go anywhere but home with you. Believe me."

Right then, she couldn't believe anything. "Please don't do this, Trace."

"I have to. And you have to promise me you will tell her her father is dead."

"I can't—"

"Molly, promise me!"

She stared at him. "I'm not making any promises I can't be sure I'll keep."

After a moment, he dropped his hand, reached behind the seat, and grabbed his duffel bag. Molly watched in silent shock.

He looked back at the dog, mouthed, "Goodbye," then took one more look at her. "God knew what he was doing when he gave Pru to you," he said. "You are a stunning mother and the most beautiful woman I've ever known, inside and out."

"Then why…" Her voice trailed off, and he gave a tight smile, pushed the door open, threw the duffel bag over his shoulder, and started walking down the road.

Meatball got up to look out the back window, barking a few times for Trace to turn around and come back.

"Shhh," Molly said, automatically reaching for the dog. "He's gone, baby."

He'd left her sitting in a dog van, confused, sad, and very much alone, exactly like he had fourteen years ago.

As the applause filled the tiny middle school auditorium, Pru nodded her thanks and scanned the audience one more time, biting back a sting of disappointment. She could see her mother, of course, who'd come in so late she was in the back row, not with Gramma Finnie and Grandpa, who sat closer.

She loved that they'd come to support her, but where was Trace?

They'd practiced so much, and he'd seemed entirely comfortable with the idea of her telling the school
that the man who lived in the house had been incarcerated—unfairly, in her opinion, but he hadn't wanted her to say so. And the presentation had been great. She hadn't been nervous a single bit.

And based on the applause when she finished? She had this. Nobody else's project had the creativity or scope of hers. The only competition came from David Hellman, who'd worked at a food bank every single day in the month of January, which was ambitious, but not original. Hailey Moore got ten abandoned cats adopted, but Pru was sure she'd stretched her hours. Corinne Phillips had given manicures to old ladies in assisted-living homes throughout the county, which was probably as much fun as it was work, and Joshua Gruen collected travel-sized toiletries and sent them overseas to the troops. The other five who'd made it this far weren't that impressive.

And no one else had made a house livable for a former prison inmate! Yes, he worked at Waterford Farm, but he hadn't when she'd started, and Mr. Margolis had already cleared that.

So now there was nothing to do but wait for the panel of teacher-judges to vote on which three projects got sent to the state competition to represent the county.

From her seat on the stage, Pru peered into the back and saw her mother check her phone for the twentieth time. If Pru had been allowed to bring her phone up here, she would have texted Mom to ask about Trace. He'd said he'd arranged with Shane to leave work early so he could be here.

Maybe he was embarrassed because he was the ex-convict who needed community service? But who cared about that? He was—

"We have our winners," Mr. Margolis announced, taking a piece of paper from one of the judges and heading toward the podium where Pru had just presented. The kids on stage all looked at each other with nervous smiles and whispered *good lucks*.

Pru scanned the audience one more time. Her gaze landed on Gramma Finnie, who gave her two thumbs-up, and next to Gramma, her grandpa beamed with pride. And way in the back, Mom looked…awful. It was hard to see from here, but was she crying?

Pru's chest suddenly squeezed as she put two and two together and came up with…they had a fight? They broke up? If Mom was upset, and Trace wasn't here—

"Every one of these service providers have legitimately invested the minimum of twenty-five hours in the month of January, making them all happy recipients of free passes to Carowinds."

They cheered, along with the audience, the five of them taking one another's hands and holding them up in victory.

"But only three will go on to compete in the state competition and be eligible to win an all-expense-paid trip to the Mouse House in Orlando, Florida!"

That got a big laugh, and all the kids squeezed one another's hands, lowering them but still holding on while they waited for the names.

"Our top three have accrued the most points for project creativity, inclusion of other students, scope of work, and a bonus for positive impact on the town of Bitter Bark."

"Better Bark!" Gramma Finnie called out, making everyone laugh, including Mr. Margolis. "Better Bark," he corrected himself. "Our winners are, alphabetically, Josh Gruen..."

At the applause, Pru squeezed her eyes closed. Still a chance if they did K next.

"David Hellman."

More applause, and Pru let out a breath. They still hadn't passed K. Or N. She looked over at Corinne Phillips, who was staring daggers at Pru. Wow, didn't know she wanted it that bad, Pru thought.

"And Prudence Kilcannon!"

Even though the blood rushed in her head with relief, she could hear Gramma Finnie hooting all the way from her seat. Grandpa was practically standing while he clapped, and Mom was wiping her eyes again, which Pru hoped were tears of joy.

On stage, the kids were congratulating each other, the losers looking dejected.

"Good job," Pru whispered to Corinne, who still looked like she might kill someone. No, not someone—Pru. "Sorry you didn't win."

"Sorry you cheated," she shot back.

"What?"

"Excuse me! Excuse me!" At the voice, the commotion started to die down as people turned around. "Excuse me for a moment, please! We have a problem!"

Everyone looked now, spotting a tall man marching

down the center aisle, waving his hand. Wasn't that Corinne's dad?

Pru whipped around to look at Corinne, who looked every bit as shocked to see her father climbing the stairs to the stage where the judges sat.

"One of these winners must be disqualified for gross negligence and a disregard for competition regulation 14B, as stated on page three of the Community Service Outreach Competition Rules."

That silenced everyone, including Mr. Margolis, who was shaking hands with Josh Gruen. He cleared his throat, frowning from behind his horn-rims, and let go of Josh's hand.

"Can you be more specific, Mr. Phillips?"

"I most certainly can." He settled right behind the podium and raised the microphone like he was going to make a big old keynote speech or something.

Pru stared at him, only realizing then that her head felt light and her palms were officially drenched. She was going to get disqualified because Trace worked at Waterford. She knew it.

She looked at Mr. Margolis, ready to plead her case. He'd told her it was fine. He'd told her—

"There is a strict regulation, spelled out with complete clarity, that service projects cannot be generated by or in aid of a family member."

Oh. Pru exhaled with relief. It was *that* rule. Well, she was in the clear, then. It must be one of the other kids.

"So Prudence Kilcannon is disqualified."

"What?" The word came out of Pru's mouth like a croak.

"How is that possible?" Mr. Margolis asked, stepping closer.

"The recipient of the service is a family member."

"He is not!" Pru said. Yes, he was dating her mother, and maybe she should have told Mr. Margolis that, but their relationship also didn't happen until the project was nearly done.

From the podium, Corinne's father turned and glared at her. He leaned close to the microphone, but stared at her. "Trace Bancroft is your biological father, Prudence. How long did you think you could keep that secret from everyone?"

She heard the collective gasp of the audience. Felt all that blood drain from her head down to her stomach. And was vaguely aware that she swayed a little in shock.

It took everything Pru had to make sense of what he was saying.

"My…" She shook her head slowly. "No, he's not. He's seeing my mother—"

"Yes, he is," Mr. Phillips insisted. "He impregnated your mother just one day before he murdered a man in West Virginia, which would be 'the felony' you glossed over in your presentation. Unless you were referring to his father, a known felon, but still your blood relative."

"Stop it!"

Pru put her hand over her mouth, shocked that the words had come out. Except, they hadn't.

"Stop it right now!" It was Mom, barreling up the little aisle with her hair flying, eyes on fire, finger pointed at Mr. Phillips. "How dare you do this? How dare you shame that child because yours didn't win a middle school competition?"

The audience rumbled, maybe in support, maybe in shock. But Pru still couldn't breathe or think or make sense of anything.

Trace was her father?

And suddenly, she could make sense of *everything*.

"I'm *merely* pointing out a discrepancy and demanding a disqualification." Mr. Phillips's voice was cool and calm, despite the growing chaos around him.

Mom climbed the steps to the stage. "You are *merely* scarring a child for the rest of her life, making a mockery of this process, and establishing that you are, without a doubt, cruel, heartless, and pathetic."

Someone actually clapped. Probably Gramma Finnie. But Pru felt herself hit the chair as she sat down with a thud, staring at the floorboards in front of her.

Trace was her father.

And no one had thought it was important enough to tell her.

"Are you denying the facts, Ms. Kilcannon?" Mr. Phillips's voice was so loud, it was like someone had turned the volume on the PA system up to deafening. "Are you going to stand here and lie like your daughter? Like her convicted-felon father?"

"Why would you do this now?" Mom asked in a harsh whisper.

"I'd have done it privately but my wife just informed me that she has unassailable proof that you and Mr. Bancroft were intimate the night before he committed a murder. While he was on the run from an accusation of rape, I might add."

Pru didn't move. She couldn't look up as seconds of silence ticked by and the whole entire auditorium seemed to hold its breath.

"Is he or is he not your daughter's biological father, Dr. Kilcannon?"

Pru looked up as Mom reached her, seeing everything she needed to know on her mother's face.

"Pru, come on."

"Come on?" Pru demanded, her eyes filling with hot tears. "*Come on?*" She turned, looking from one side of the stage to the other, seeing nothing but a sea of faces, all of them staring at her. David and Josh, and Corinne. There was her grandfather, already in the aisle and coming closer, followed by Gramma Finnie.

She turned to stare at Mom, who looked as stricken as Pru felt.

"How could you?" Pru rasped. But she didn't wait for an answer. Didn't wait for Mom to tell Mr. Phillips he was right. She didn't have to.

She pushed past her mother and ran to the edge of the stage, easily jumping down and lunging for the fire exit door. She shoved it open and ran as far and fast as she could, sobbing the entire way.

Chapter Twenty-Three

Molly spotted her instantly, tearing through the school parking lot, her dark hair flying as she sprinted away.

Her heart. Her poor, broken, little child's heart. Molly's own heart shattered over and over again every time she remembered the look on Pru's face when that monster vomited out words that had needed to be said tenderly and gracefully.

Pru had to be devastated.

As the wind screamed in her ears, Molly could really only hear her mother's voice.

You're only as happy as your least-happy child.

Then Molly simply couldn't be any unhappier. She saw Pru slowing down, gasping for air, bent over. It gave Molly enough time to catch up and thank God that her car was twenty feet away. They had to get out of there.

"Pru!"

She didn't even look up, still doubled over, her narrow shoulders rising and falling with sobs.

"Honey, we have to talk."

Finally, she straightened as Molly ran closer.

"It's a little late, don't you think?"

Catching her breath, Molly slowed her step and tried not to throw herself at Pru for a hug and a plea for forgiveness.

"He's my father." It wasn't a question.

Molly nodded, which only made Pru's eyes close as she gave a soft grunt.

"I wanted to tell you."

Those eyes popped open. "Then why didn't you? Like ten years ago, Mom!"

"I planned on it."

"Right. On our trip to the Outer Banks that never happened."

"Trace showed up at the front door, Pru. Everything changed."

Pru stumbled backward, shock hitting her all over again. "You let him into my life and made me like him...and..." She swiped tears from her face. "Where is he?"

Oh God. Only in that moment did Molly realize that not only had that pompous jerk ripped Pru's heart out with a public announcement, he'd also stolen any chance of Molly honoring Trace's last request. And now, poor Pru had to face one more heartbreak. Her father had left without even saying goodbye.

She couldn't tell her. At the sound of voices, Molly glanced toward the school and saw people drifting out of the auditorium. She couldn't tell her here, anyway. They needed to be alone, home, holding each other.

"Can you get in the car, Pru? I'm parked right over there. I'll tell you everything."

Pru snorted, wiping her nose and keeping her angry gaze on Molly. "Where is he, Mom?"

She swallowed. "He's gone, honey. He…left."

"What? Where? When is he coming back? When can I see him?"

"I don't think he is coming back."

"Mom!" Pru nearly sobbed. "I just found him! I waited my whole life to have a father, and I spent three weeks with him and didn't know it was him, and…he's *gone*? Why? Why would he leave me?"

"He didn't leave you, Pru. He left…us."

"Why?"

"I honestly don't know. I saw him this morning and he just said he'd made someone a promise and he had to leave. He left Meatball."

"He left Meatball?" She reached for Molly's shoulders. "Something must be so wrong with him!"

How like Pru to worry about him. It folded her bruised heart in half again. "I don't know what happened. He wouldn't tell me. He left. He wanted me to promise…"

"What?"

Molly shook her head.

"Mom, what?"

"He wanted me to never tell you the truth. Ever." At Pru's crestfallen face, Molly reached for her. "Because he loves you," she insisted, getting a scoffing laugh in response. "He does, honey. And he was absolutely certain that you'd be ashamed of him and devastated to know your father killed a man."

"By accident! And he served his time. And, Mom, he's a really good guy."

Each word slashed Molly's heart and left a permanent scar. Why did he have to leave and not hear his daughter defend him? Why didn't he believe in his own worth? "He wasn't sure you'd feel that way, honey. I've wanted to tell you since the day he showed up, but every day, he stopped me. He didn't want to lose your respect or friendship. He was sure you'd hate him."

"My own father?" Pru dropped her head, finally not fighting Molly as she wrapped her arms around her daughter. "I did treat him like crap in the beginning."

"This is not your fault, Pru."

"He must have known this was going to happen," Pru said. "He had to have known."

Molly eased back to look at her. "No. He would never have left you to endure this without him if he'd known."

"But Corinne knew," Pru said. "She called me a cheater on stage before her dad ever showed up. How could she know? How could they know what I didn't?"

Molly closed her eyes as a piece of the puzzle slipped into place. "Corinne's mother was there the night...she saw me leave a party with Trace."

"The unassailable proof that blowhard guy has?"

Molly nodded. "I bet she's known for a long time."

"And was waiting for the perfect moment to wreck my life," Pru said dryly, looking over Molly's shoulder. "Oh boy. Here comes the cavalry."

Molly turned to see Dad walking toward them slowly as he held Gramma Finnie's arm and made sure she didn't trip on the uneven asphalt. Wordlessly, Molly walked with Pru to meet them halfway.

Gramma Finnie reached for Pru. "My little lass," she whispered into a hug.

Dad looked from one to the other, his blue eyes full of pain. "I'm sorry, Pru."

"You didn't do anything, Grandpa."

"No, you didn't," Molly said. "The blame for this mess lands squarely on my shoulders. I sat on a secret way too long."

"You know what the Irish say." Gramma tightened her grip around Pru. "Three people can keep a secret as long as two of them are dead."

"Only two knew this one, and that was my mistake. Pru should have been the third."

"No, Molls," Dad said softly. "It was mine."

All three of them glanced at him, one face looking more confused than the next.

"I knew. I knew from the day he came to town. In fact, I knew his name when Pru was not even two and Annie met his mother."

"Grannie met his mother?" Pru's voice rose in shock, and Molly's head grew light and dizzy.

"You knew...when you invited him to Waterford?" she asked her father. "When he showed up with Meatball? You've known all this time, Dad?"

He nodded. "Yes," he said simply. "I met him and instantly knew when he said his name that he was the boy your mother had told me had died. After she thought he died, Molly, that's when she told me. Not a moment before."

"You've known all these years?" Somehow, it was more comforting than a betrayal, which she didn't understand. But her dad knew, he'd accepted, and he'd brought Trace to her.

"When I met him, I felt the man had a right to know he has a daughter. That was very important to your mother, honey. She believed that with her heart and soul, but obviously, she stopped thinking it was a possibility when she was told he was dead."

"Who told Grannie that?" Pru asked.

"His mother," Molly answered. "She wanted to save you shame, too."

"I wish somebody had asked me what *I* wanted," Pru said.

"You're right, Pru." Dad put a hand on her shoulder. "We were all too protective. But when I met him, I thought I'd give him a chance, and I knew he and Molly would know the right thing to do, as parents."

Parents. She'd never been part of that equation before. She hadn't known how badly she longed for it until right now.

More people peppered the parking lot, many of them staring at the grouping of Kilcannons deep in conversation. Automatically, Molly moved closer to Pru. "We should go. We should all get home and talk about this."

"No," Pru said, shaking her head. "I don't want to go home. I want…" She took a breath. "I'm going to ride with Gramma Finnie and Grandpa."

The rejection hurt, but Molly tried to understand how mad Pru must be. They would help her. They would ease her pain. "Okay. I'll be at my Waterford office. Come and find me when you're ready."

Inching back, Pru looked away, like it might be a long time before she was ready. "Sure."

Molly's eyes filled with painful tears. She struggled not to cry, cursing herself and blaming herself and hurting so hard she could barely breathe. "'Kay," she managed.

Pru turned to her grandfather, who put his arm around her and guided her to the van, glancing over his shoulder with an encouraging look to Molly. Gramma Finnie held back and took Molly's hand in her weathered palms.

"What time can't solve, God will fix, lassie."

Molly smiled at the predictable and welcome reassurance, but she was pretty sure that no matter what time solved or God fixed, at least three people had been wrecked by it.

Just wade through that shit, Wally would say. *It may be a little uncomfortable, but it's the only way.*

Up to his eyeballs in "wading," Trace turned the page of the fifth or sixth journal, riveted to the words written by a broken woman who hadn't a clue how to be a mother. Terrified that nature would be stronger than nurture, she'd chosen guilt and fear, instead of love and guidance.

In other words, she'd spent years warning Trace that he was like his father in the hope that he wouldn't be. Why hadn't he seen that?

Because until he'd seen Molly with Pru, he hadn't known what a mother should be. His mother hadn't known, either, based on her desperate journal entries that were as much a cry for help as anything he'd heard during the dark nights in Huttonsville. He'd been too young and self-involved to see that, but reading these diaries, it was like a weight lifted with every new entry.

His head whipped up at the sound of a car pulling

up to the little house. What the hell? Had Phillips come back? Or Molly? A car door banged closed. Then another. Who was here?

Whoever it was, they couldn't get in and he wouldn't go out. Staying low and out of the line of visibility of the front window, which was open an inch, he made his way over to sneak a look outside without being seen.

And he almost moaned at the sight.

There, climbing out of the big Waterford Farm van was Daniel Kilcannon, Gramma Finnie, and Pru. They gathered in a group, talking too quietly for him to hear through the small opening.

Suddenly, Pru stepped away and held something up. "But I have a key, Grandpa. I can go in."

"No, you can't go into someone's home without permission."

"Not someone. My *father*."

Trace sucked in air like a fresh punch had collided with his gut. *Molly, how could you?*

"He's gone," Pru said. "Ditched us all without a goodbye. Why can't I go in and get what's rightfully mine?"

"What makes those journals yours, lass?"

"They were written by my other grandmother!" she fired back. "If he left them, they're mine. Heck, this whole house could be mine. And it's all I've got, Gramma. It's the last piece of him."

And that piece of him shattered like crystal on concrete.

She felt that way? She wanted something of…*his*?

Turning, he looked at the books spread across the floor where he'd been sitting for hours. After the long walk home, he'd collapsed in a fitful sleep. When he woke, something made him take that box out of the closet and start to read.

And now that same something had Pru. A desire for answers, no doubt. Answers that child deserved but he was too scared to give. Shame, that old companion he knew so well, slithered up his belly and wrapped around his throat, strangling him.

"I can't let you go in there, Pru." Daniel put a hand on her shoulder, his look stern and steady, as unwavering as that moral compass the man used to guide his family in everything. He wouldn't even let her use a key to enter an empty house.

"Grandpa, please." Her voice grew soft and cracked. "I fixed that house for him. I…" She looked up to the roof, her lower lip quivering. "I helped him."

Helped him in so many ways, she had no idea.

"If I had known this was where you wanted to go, I wouldn't have driven you, Pru," Daniel said. "You need to get back in the car so we can leave. Your mother's waiting for you."

Pru didn't look convinced, her delicate features fixed in an expression of frustration and determination. She looked like…him. In that moment, Trace saw a glimmer of himself in her.

Hadn't Molly shown him how to be a better parent? Hadn't Wally told him to wade into whatever he had to and get through it? Hadn't Pru taught him what it meant to be a father?

"I need to know more!" Pru insisted. "I need to know who he really is, and what I come from, and why he left."

He owed his Umproo so much more than running away.

Gramma Finnie put her arm around Pru. "Your mother needs you, lass. She's hurting for you."

So much hurt. He'd caused that. And he had to undo it.

"Gramma, I want to…"

Trace didn't hear the rest, only the blood thumping in his head as he made his way to the front door. He stood there for a moment, closed his eyes, and said the closest thing he knew to a prayer.

Let me be worthy of her.

As he opened the door, she was climbing into the back of the van.

"Pru."

He saw her little frame freeze as he took one step closer.

"Prudence Anne Kilcannon…Bancroft." He whispered the last word, letting it fall out like the olive branch he was offering.

Very slowly, she inched back out of the van. He was aware that the other two people watched, but his gaze was solidly on his daughter, who finally turned and looked at him. He saw her swallow, breathe, and, he swore, he saw her forgive. Just like that.

"That's Umproo to you," she said softly.

He wanted to cry. Wanted to drop his head back and weep with wonder that someone, somewhere had blessed him with this child. But he didn't. He wouldn't. Instead, he reached his arms out to her, and she came right to him, slowly at first, then she rushed closer. Without hesitation, she let him hug her, stroke her hair, and feel her cry for him.

"I'm sorry," he said, his throat thick with emotions he hadn't even known were possible. "I'm so sorry for not telling you. For leaving. For hurting you. I'm sorry."

She eased back. "Please don't leave us."

Us. Both of them. His family. He pulled her in again, and over her head, he met the gazes of her grandfather and great-grandmother, both of them holding back as they stood next to the open doors of the van.

Which reminded him of last night and how tentative his grip on security really was.

"Something happened," he said to all of them, easing Pru away. "Last night, when I got home, a woman was waiting for me and...she came on pretty strong. I tried to leave, but her husband showed up."

"Allen Phillips, by any chance?" Daniel asked.

Trace frowned. "Yeah, that's the guy. And, look, I know this sounds like a pattern for me, but he knew my past and he threatened me. And everyone close to me." He looked at Pru, then Daniel. "I made you a promise to keep them safe, so I thought leaving would be the best way to do that."

Pru snorted. "*That's* who told me," she said. "He had me disqualified from the competition, which I won, by the way, and announced to every person in my school that you're my father."

He felt his eyes widen in horror, along with a kick of guilt that he'd blamed Molly. "He did?" Fury shot through him. "He *did*?" Then pride. "You won?"

"Yeah, but it was awful."

"Oh, Pru. I'm sorry." He hugged her again. "I

couldn't take a risk that anyone would hurt you or Molly. But he did anyway."

"But you didn't do anything, did you?" Pru asked.

"Nothing, but..." He gave a rueful laugh. "That doesn't always matter in life. Sorry if that's the first official lesson I'm teaching you."

Daniel came closer. "He threatened you and his wife was a witness?"

"For whatever that's worth," he said. "I'll tell you right now he took a swing at me and I hit back."

"No other witnesses?"

He shook his head and gestured toward their van. "It was right here. I just drove home in that van."

Daniel's brows lifted as he looked over his shoulder at the van, then back at Trace, as if he were reconstructing the scene. "No chance you left any of the van doors open during this encounter, is there?"

The van doors? He vividly recalled the way Isabella had thrown herself at him and Phillips taunted him. From courtroom experience, he could remember every aspect of the scene, including the open door behind him. "Actually, the driver side door was open."

Pru's and Daniel's expressions both morphed from disbelief to something else, something like hope.

"Does the camera have a microphone?" Pru asked, her voice rising.

"Of course."

Trace was legitimately confused now. "A microphone?"

"Then you have a good witness, lad!" Gramma Finnie exclaimed.

Daniel was already hustling to the back of the van, lifting the big door. "I have a security camera so we can monitor the dogs. Sometimes we have to leave them in the van for a few minutes, crated, so for their protection, I had a small camera and mic installed." He gestured for Trace to join him. "See that?" Pointing to a tiny camera with one hand, he pulled his cell phone out with the other.

"There's an app for it," Pru told him. "Grandpa can go back to a certain time and listen and watch."

"Like…" Daniel tapped the phone screen. "Last night? What time?"

"Around eight."

Another few taps, then he held the phone up and hit the volume, the gruff sound of Allen Phillips's voice instantly recognizable as the recording picked up in the middle of their confrontation.

"Maybe you want to take a swing at me, son. Go ahead. It's a one-way ticket back to prison, that I can guarantee you. C'mon…give it to me, killer."

Trace winced at the words, but Pru jumped up and down. "We have proof! We have proof you are innocent!"

He took a step back, reeling. "Are you serious?"

"I bet it's admissible in court," Pru said, lifting her brows. "I've been thinking I could be a good lawyer."

He still couldn't quite grasp what they were saying. "What would you do with that recording?"

Daniel gestured toward the car. "Let the man know he has no power. Support you. Ensure you don't leave Waterford, or Pru, or…" He angled his head.

"Molly," Trace finished, a rush of affection for all these people, most especially the woman who'd changed his life so completely.

Gramma Finnie sidled up to him and patted his

shoulder as Daniel put the phone away and reached to close the raised door.

"Bet you wish you'da had something like that all those years ago when you got into trouble," Gramma Finnie added.

Trace glanced into the back of the van, at the empty crate and the two feet of space next to it, almost fighting a smile at how glad he was they *didn't* have that technology fourteen years ago.

But it made him realize something else. This wasn't the first time his life had changed for the better in the back of a dog-carrying minivan.

"We need to tell Molly," he whispered. "I need...Molly." More than anything.

Chapter Twenty-Four

"So this is what they mean by 'dead' silence." Molly leaned closer to the gravestone, closing her eyes to picture Annie Kilcannon the way she remembered her best: laughing. And she so would have laughed at that.

But her mother's wind-chime laugh was silent, as it had been for more than three long years. And Molly had never needed to hear it more. Out here, in the valley, surrounded by winter-brown grass and a sleet-gray sky, the only sound was a light whoosh of wind in the bare trees and the soft snoring of a dog pressed against her legs, keeping her warm.

Stroking Meatball's head, Molly closed her eyes and tried again.

"Mom. I need help. Advice. Encouragement. Maybe a little agreement that, once again, I made a huge and stupid mistake. Tell me what to do."

Meatball huffed and rolled over, able to do that without moaning now. The wind died down, so not even the branches above her moved. No birds chirped in the middle of winter. No wayward squirrels sneaked out for air. There wasn't even a distant dog bark, which could sometimes be heard even this far from the house.

If Mom was here, in spirit, she wasn't making a sound.

"I don't know who else to turn to," Molly said softly, aching for her mother's touch one more time. "I know you wouldn't have agreed with the decision not to tell Pru. I didn't, either. But I let him..." She shook her head. "No, no. You'd tell me not to blame someone else for my decisions. That, I can still hear you say."

But Annie would have said it with humor and love, handing Molly a cup of coffee and gesturing for her to come out to the porch for some girl-talk time. Oh, what Molly wouldn't do for five more minutes on the porch with her mother.

"I've never felt so alone," she admitted in a ragged voice. "Not since you left us. And before that? Not since that day I discovered I was pregnant. This is like that, Mom. That same agony that...that..." Her voice cracked, and she dropped her head, fighting a sob. "Mom, I want him back, and that's the truth. I don't care what he did or where he's been. It's made him who he is, and I like that. More than like it. I can see us sticking it out, raising Pru together. But he didn't."

Because you're only as happy as your least-happy child.

Finally, she heard Mom's voice in her head, saying the words Molly had heard a thousand times, sometimes with a sigh, other times with an easy laugh. But this time...she thought about Trace.

Pru was his child, too. No, he hadn't been able to guide her through the first thirteen years of life, but he'd given her life. And if she wasn't happy, neither would he be. So it hadn't been fear that kept him silent these weeks, or lack of courage to face the truth. It had been love.

He loved his daughter and would do anything to protect her, exactly like Molly would.

He'd even *leave* her. That was the one piece that didn't fit. Why would he do that?

A fresh wave of tears threatened, making Molly moan and Meatball lift his head, concern in his normally sweet expression. He had his own bit of sadness, too, no doubt missing Trace.

"What would you have done, Mom?" Molly asked, still longing for the answer. Her mother had agreed that Pru didn't need to know the details of her conception and who her father was when she was still a child, but Pru had been ten when Mom died, and there'd been no great need for a revelation yet.

But once he showed up, what would Annie have done? Protect her child. At all costs. Annie's mothering had grown from that one focal point: protect the child. And that's what Molly and Trace had done.

Or had they protected themselves? Wasn't that the reason he gave—the convoluted, frustrating reason— for leaving? Because he'd promised to protect them?

She tunneled her fingers into Meatball's fur, getting warmth and comfort from all that was left of Trace's brief visit to Waterford Farm. Once again, her gaze traveled the gravesite, and the hole in her heart that her mother had left behind burned with pain.

"So what should I have done?" she asked, lifting her head. "What should I do now?"

"Give him a chance, Mom."

Molly sat bolt upright, whipping around as Meatball jumped up with a bark. She half expected to see Annie Kilcannon emerge from the woods. But it was Pru who ambled closer, making Molly blink with surprise and disorientation, because the only way to get to the path in those woods was by a road that ran the perimeter of the property.

And Pru surely didn't drive out there.

Meatball rose and barked, trotting to Pru, his tail swooshing. But then he darted right past her, into the woods.

"Meatball!" Molly called, standing up to go after him. "Pru, don't let him go back there alone."

"He won't be alone." Pru glanced over her shoulder. "My dad's back there."

Molly froze. What? "Trace is here?"

Meatball's barks grew quiet, the way they would if he were getting nuzzled and loved by his master. Molly tried to steady her breath and clear her head, but there were too many questions.

"You talked to him? He's here? He knows you know? Is he okay? Are you..." Her barrage trailed off as Pru wrapped her arms around Molly's waist and pulled her in for a hug. Suddenly, she felt very much like Meatball must—comforted, assured, loved.

"It's okay, Mom," she whispered. "It's all okay. We all know everything, and it's cool." She backed away and looked up. "In a way, I'm glad you waited so long. I got to know him and that was fair. That guy has had so much unfairness, you know?"

"Oh, Pru." She stroked her daughter's hair. "You are so much like my mother."

She leaned back and gave a grin full of braces. "I'm so much like *my* mother," she said. "Who happens to be the world's greatest mom."

The echo of words spoken years ago drifted into Molly's head, like a musical promise that by the grace of God and a lot of help was fulfilled.

You'll be twice the mother I am.

Molly looked toward the gravestone with a tear-filled smile, silently thanking Annie Kilcannon for her strength and example. Just then, Trace and Meatball emerged through the trees. His hands tucked into jean pockets, his worn cloth coat open, his eyes dark, intense, Trace focused on Molly like she was the only thing in the world he cared about.

Silent, they stared at each other for a long moment.

Pru stepped to the side, her arm still around Molly. "You guys need to talk," she said. "I'll take Meatball for a walk, okay?"

Molly exhaled, nodding. "Okay."

Pru kissed her on the cheek and whispered, "I really like him, Mom."

"Me, too," Molly muttered.

That made Pru laugh as she walked to Trace and slipped her fingers into Meatball's collar. She said something to Trace that Molly didn't hear, but they both laughed at what Molly started to suspect was one of many inside jokes they would share in the years ahead.

And just then, in that moment, she could have sworn she heard Annie laugh, too.

As he finished the story, Trace closed his fingers around Molly's narrow, cold hands and brought them to his lips, saving the most important part of what he had to tell her for last. "I'm so sorry, Molly. I'm sorry I made you cry, but now you understand I thought I had no choice."

She held his gaze, her hazel eyes taking on a jade tone as they finally cleared of tears and filled with understanding.

"You always have a choice," she said.

"When you have backup like the Kilcannon family."

"You always have the Kilcannon family." She turned her hands around to thread their fingers and bring his knuckles to her lips. "You're Pru's father. You're part of the clan whether you like it or not."

He almost laughed, shaking his head. "Why would I not like it? I never had a family, and even if I had, there aren't many in the world like yours."

Her sigh was deep and content and sounded like it came from the bottom of her very soul. "We shouldn't have underestimated Pru."

"We? You never did. I did." He peered into the woods where she'd disappeared earlier, his heart almost bursting with affection for that kid. "And I never will again. As long as I live, I will never doubt Pru."

"I learned that years ago."

He let go of their joined hands so he could put his arms around her. "And what about us, Irish?"

She looked up at him, a question in her eyes. "Is there an us?"

"There's something, that's for sure. Don't you feel it?"

"Of course I feel it." She narrowed her eyes. "What do you think it is?"

That made him laugh. "You're the doctor."

"This isn't an illness."

So true. "Well, we share a child, for one," he said. "And we are intensely attracted to each other, for another. What would you call that?"

"Healthy, normal, and kind of fun," she said without hesitation.

"And I wake up every day thinking about you and go to sleep every night wanting you, and pretty much every hour, minute, and second in between, you're on my mind. Is that healthy, normal, or fun?"

"It's a crush."

He snorted in derision. "We can do better than a crush."

"An affair?"

"Not classy enough for my girl."

A slow smile lifted the corners of her lips. "Well, I guess I can be your girlfriend."

"Girlfriend. Hmm." Pulling her closer, he put a kiss on her forehead. "We can start there and see where it takes us."

She tilted her head up. "Can it take us to a kiss, or do I have to initiate this one?"

"This one's all me." He lowered his head and kissed her, tasting the salt of dried tears and feeling the tenderness of her mouth. "But it's not going to be enough," he murmured into the kiss.

"This kiss will have to suffice with Pru somewhere in the woods."

"That's not what I meant." He traced her lower lip with his finger, slowly, intentionally. "Girlfriend.

It isn't going to be enough."

She searched his face, silent.

"I know what I want to say," he whispered. "And how much I want to say it, but I'm not sure how you'll take it."

She lifted a brow. "Speak the truth, Trace Bancroft. Did you learn nothing about Kilcannon women in the last few weeks?"

"No kidding. Okay, the truth." He held her gaze and took a slow breath. "I'm in love with you and I'm not going to be completely happy until a certain two Kilcannon women are Bancroft women."

Her eyes flashed a little, but not in fear and certainly not in anger. But...promise. "Then you'll be happy to know you're halfway there."

"What?"

"Your name is on her birth certificate."

He drew back, feeling another jolt of emotion he wasn't quite prepared for. "It is?"

"She's never seen it. I have the only copy in a safe-deposit box in town. I never planned to lie about who her father was, Trace. I just waited."

Prudence Anne Kilcannon Bancroft. The sound of it was like music to his ears, even if it was only half the song he wanted to hear. He put his arm around Molly and turned her around, anxious to take her back to Pru and have the three of them be together with all that truth surrounding them.

"How'd you know where to find me?" Molly asked.

He glanced at the graves nearby. "Pru and I knew you'd be here. They said you left the office, and we both knew you'd come here. She suggested driving to get here faster." He tugged her into his side as they walked into the woods. "Did your mom help you?"

"Not as much as you did," she admitted, heading toward the road on the other side of the trees where he'd left the Waterford Farm dog van. The back of the van was open, and Pru sat inside with Meatball stretched out next to her, the crate pushed aside to make room.

"Would you look at that, Irish?" Trace whispered.

Molly laughed and elbowed him. "Some things need to stay secret," she warned as Pru jumped out of the van.

"I had the best idea, you guys." She looked so fresh and young and untouched by the drama. His girl was resilient. Beautiful. Brilliant. And came with a mom he already loved.

"What's that, Umproo?" he asked.

She grinned. "Let's go to the Outer Banks this weekend. The three of us. And Meatball, of course."

Trace looked at Molly, who beamed a smile brighter than the sun that peeked out to warm them.

"I love that idea," Molly said, breaking out of his grip to head toward Pru. "And I love you." She planted a kiss on Pru's forehead while Trace took a moment to drink in the beauty of it all.

His girls. His family. His home.

Epilogue

W aterford Farm was doused in April sunshine and bursting with as much joy as spring flowers the afternoon that Shane and Chloe got married in an outdoor ceremony, surrounded by friends and family. And dogs.

In fact, Ruby had stolen the show as she lumbered her way down the aisle and stood next to Shane, sporting a pale pink collar that matched the summery dresses that Molly and the other bridesmaids wore.

As the reception began in earnest, Molly slipped from her bridesmaid duties into her role as the natural hostess of the home, greeting guests, checking on catering, and keeping the event moving along so Shane and Chloe could just relax and have fun.

Under the massive tent spread out on the front lawns of Waterford Farm, dozens of tables were spread but the dance floor was still empty. At the head table where most of the Kilcannons were gathered, Molly inched next to Liam to remind him it was nearly time for the best man's toast. Next to him, a very pregnant Andi sipped a glass of ice water and kept one eye on her husband and one on her son,

Christian, who was, at the moment, escorting Gramma Finnie to a seat at the table.

"Once Chloe and Shane finish talking to the Mahoney table, you should get out there and toast."

Liam rolled his eyes. "Garrett should have been best man. I hate public speaking."

Andi laughed and leaned into him. "Just do it the way you practiced and everyone will love you as much as I do."

"I don't want everyone to love me that much," he cracked, putting an arm around her.

They shared a laugh and Molly joined in, anything that remotely resembled a pang of jealousy over her brothers' good fortune in love all gone now. She had love of her own and she'd never been happier.

At the far end of the table, Trace was deep in conversation with Pru and, when she sat, Gramma Finnie, saying something that made them both laugh. And all three of them turned to look at Molly with an expression she didn't get, but knew the conversation was about her.

She gave them a pretend scowl, but that made Pru smile and Gramma Finnie look kind of smug, like she was in on something and Molly was out. Trace just gazed at her with so much love she nearly reeled from the impact of it.

"No toast yet," Garrett said, sidling up next to them. "Dad went inside a few minutes ago and hasn't come back."

"He did?" Looking around, Molly hadn't realized until just that moment her father wasn't at the party. "He was just talking to Linda May by the cake."

"He talks to that baker a lot, don't you think?" Andi asked with an unmistakable gleam in her eye.

Liam narrowed his eyes at her. "Linda May's not his type."

"I think he secretly likes Marie," Garrett said.

"Are you out of your mind?" Liam shot daggers at his brother.

Molly held up both hands. "One wedding at a time, guys. Why did Dad leave, really?"

"Beats me," Garrett said. "But he bolted and looked damn serious."

A tendril of worry tugged at her heart. Why would Dad walk out a few moments after Shane and Chloe came in to rousing applause and the post-ceremony festivities started? What could be more important than that to him?

"It doesn't make sense," Molly mused as Chloe and Shane reached the small group.

"Everything makes sense," Shane said, his typical smartass grin wider than ever. "She married me."

Chloe beamed, but her attention was on Molly that second. "Is something wrong?"

"It's time for the toast and Dad went inside."

"No, there he is," Liam said. "And based on the look on his face, something's up."

He was smiling from ear to ear, trotting down the steps of the patio with a bounce in his step.

"I'm telling you, it's Linda May," Andi muttered. "Every time I go in the bakery below my office, he's in there. No one needs that many croissants."

Her brothers shared a look, but Molly's attention was on her dad, who suddenly stopped, looked skyward, and surreptitiously wiped an eye. The others might have missed that move, but Molly had seen her Dad shed secret tears before.

"Hang on a sec," Molly said. "I'll go get him." Without waiting for an argument from her siblings, she took off, grateful that Chloe picked knee length dresses so Molly could move with ease and speed.

"Everything okay?" she asked as casually as possible when she approached Dad, who hadn't made any effort to come closer to the wedding.

"Everything is okay," he said. "It's never been better."

Really? Because his eyes were definitely wet. But there was joy on every angle of his face. This was more than another Dogfather success in the wedding department. For a moment, she suddenly wondered if Andi wasn't right about Linda May. She was here and—

"Aidan's coming home."

Molly froze and let that sink in. "He is? For good? When?"

Dad exhaled as if he'd been holding the news in for a long, long time. "Yes. Yes. Soon. A few weeks. He's definitely not re-upping his contract but there's the small matter of a dog he wants to bring home."

Charlie's dog. Aidan had talked about the boxer for hours when he was home for Christmas; not being able to bring him back to the States was a big part of his decision to re-up or not. "Dad, we know how to get a dog home from Afghanistan. There's a program in Europe that will help and Cilla Bartlett can help." The travel agent they used in town was a miracle worker when it came to arranging transportation for dogs, even from war-torn countries.

"I've already called her," he said. "And I'm sorry for missing so much of the wedding."

"But for such a good reason." She hugged him, her own tears threatening. "We'll be a whole family."

"A growing family." He hugged her a little tighter. "That is, if the conversations I've had with Trace lately lead to anything."

Her heart flipped. "Conversations?"

He laughed, the heartiest she'd heard in ages. "Let's just say you can chalk up one more success for the Dogfather."

"Oh, Dad." She took his arm and kept stride as they walked back to the tent together. She strongly suspected today was the day, maybe tonight, after Chloe and Shane left for their honeymoon. Trace would never want to steal their thunder. And speaking of thunder, her heart was doing exactly that. "I haven't been this happy in years."

He gave her arm a squeeze. "Music to my ears, Molls."

"You should feel like this," she said under her breath, knowing the conversation about Dad getting back into the dating scene was his least favorite topic. "I know people in love want everyone else to feel like they do, but we all want you to have this kind of completion."

He glanced away, silent.

"I know you had it once, but don't you think..." She slowed her step. "You're still a young man, Dad. With so much life ahead and love to give."

Finally, he turned to her, his blue eyes misting. "She was my life, and I gave her all the love I had."

"The supply is endless. As one of six kids, I know that for a fact."

He planted a smile on his face and focused on the tent. "Liam ready to give that toast now?"

She understood the change of subject. Didn't like it, but understood it. "We're waiting for you."

Moving with purpose, he headed into the tent. "When he's done, I'll share the news about Aidan." His gaze moved around the whole reception, suddenly intense. "Any single women here?"

Molly almost tripped. "Dad, really? You're ready?"

"Me?" He choked softly. "No, for Aidan. I have another project to work on."

Of course he did. Molly didn't push the issue, but let go of Dad's arm when they reached the table and settled next to Trace, who was deep in conversation with Gramma Finnie and Pru.

The talking stopped when Liam stood and tapped his glass, took a mic, and made a characteristically brief but heartfelt toast, followed by Garrett, who added some more brotherly humor. Dad took over from there, toasted the couple one more time, and sent them off to the dance floor.

Not long after that, the family was called to join them, and finally, Trace pulled Molly into a slow embrace and moved to the beat of the music.

"You look pretty in pink, Irish," he whispered into her ear. "Can't wait to take it off you."

She laughed. "Shhh. My family is everywhere."

"Don't worry. I won't embarrass you."

"You never do," she assured him. "In fact, I never feel anything but pride around you."

She saw his expression soften, his eyes warm at the compliment. "I still can't believe you love me."

"So much," she assured him. "So very much."

He held her gaze and tightened his grip. "I love you, too."

"This I know."

"And I'm about to prove it to you."

Her eyes widened. "Here? On the dance floor?"

He laughed at her horror. "And steal the thunder from Chloe and Shane's day? Not a chance. But I do have a very special gift for you, and I'd like to give it to you today, in private, when you're ready."

A special gift. A talk with Dad. A look that said…forever. "I'm ready anytime, Trace Bancroft," she whispered, holding his gaze. "Anytime."

"Then now." He glanced around, then gracefully guided her to the edge of the dance floor and ushered her away from the crowd. "Come with me," he said under his breath, taking her hand.

They walked slowly at first, toward the back of the tent where catering trucks and many of the guests' cars were parked. Once out there, he broke into a fast walk, threading through cars, making her laugh as they made their secret escape.

"Where are we going?" she asked breathlessly.

"To get your special present."

"In the parking lot?"

"Yup." After passing a few more cars, he turned her around and put his hands over her eyes. "Can't look yet."

Confused and giddy, she played along, letting him lead her blindly through cars. This certainly wasn't what she was expecting, but…

"I've been working on this for months, Molly," he said into her ear as he brought her to a stop. "Remember how I promised Shane I'd get my own wheels and return the Waterford van?"

Under his fingers, she frowned and fought that first little squeeze of disappointment in her chest. "I remember," she said.

"Well, I wanted them to be special. Affordable. Meaningful."

His car. That wasn't what she'd been hoping for. "Of course you do."

"So about two and a half months ago, I had your father do a little digging…" Very slowly, he lifted his hands, but left them blocking her view. "And we hit pay dirt. The buyer still had it, and I refurbished the whole thing in the back of my house for the last two months."

"Refurbished…what?"

He moved his hands to reveal…red. Well, maroon. A shiny, oversized, wine-colored…Plymouth Voyager minivan.

"Oh…" And the surprise dawned on her. "This is it? The very van?"

He stepped closer to the beast with a look of joy and pride and utter accomplishment. "I found it, Molly! It's twenty-two years old, but I replaced the engine, brakes, and leather. And I even got us…" He reached for the latch and pulled up the back door. "A dog crate."

Laughing, she covered her mouth in disbelief. "It's…beautiful."

"No, it's hideous, but I got it for a steal, and did all the work myself, and it's functional, and…" He grabbed the metal side of the crate and gave it a good shake. "I welded the crate myself. I hope it carries many happy dogs."

"Trace." Shaking her head, she stepped closer, trying not to feel let down by this news. "It's perfect for dog training."

"And spacious," he added with a wink.

She smiled up at him, hoping he didn't see that she'd had her heart set on a totally different surprise. "I can't believe you've been working on this and I didn't know."

"It's been behind that mess of bushes in my backyard for months. Pru helped, of course. And your brothers all pitched in parts and some time, and everyone kept the secret from you."

"Why?"

"So you'd be completely surprised."

She laughed. "Well, I sure am."

"Really? I don't think you're too excited," he said, a bit of a tease in his voice. "Maybe you should look a little closer."

A frown tugged as she peered into the opening in the back, noticing he'd replaced the carpet, and the upholstery had been refurbished, too. "It's nice, Trace. You did a great job."

His smile kicked up a little as he leaned in and flipped the latch on the dog crate, opening it slowly.

And then she saw the little black box resting on the pillow that lined the crate.

"Oh…" Her throat tightened, making it hard to say anything.

Wordlessly, he leaned in, snagged the box, and presented it with a flourish.

"Trace."

"Let's do this right." Very slowly, he got down on one knee and flipped the lid open, making her gasp at the ring inside. A single diamond, with two smaller ones next to it. "It reminds me of you and me and Pru," he whispered.

The shiny stones melted as her eyes filled with tears.

"Molly Kilcannon, you have given me a life I never dreamed possible. I am so in love with you, sometimes I can't breathe or think straight. I love your curls, your smile, your heart, your soul, and your amazing brain. I want to be by your side from this day forward, till death do us part, raising our daughter, having more kids, and surrounding ourselves with dogs and family and memories like this."

The words of his beautiful speech spilled over her, like petals plucked from a flower, like rain, like sunshine, like love.

"Will you marry me, Irish?"

She bit her lip, closed her eyes, and laughed with pure joy. "Yes. I love you and I'll marry you, Trace Bancroft."

As he slipped the ring on her finger, she guided him back up and put both hands on his cheeks. "And I'll kiss you first forever."

She stood on her tiptoes, pressed her lips to his, and he pulled them both into the back of the minivan where, once again, their lives changed forever.

Don't miss the next book in The Dogfather series:

Ruff Around The Edges

The old dog is up to new tricks again! This time, Daniel Kilcannon guides his youngest son to do what's right, even if that means giving up a dog who feels like a piece of Aidan's heart. Once Ruff is safely transported from Afghanistan to Bitter Bark, the last thing Aidan wants to do is honor a dying request that the dog be given to his best friend's little sister, Rebecca Spencer. But Aidan is a Kilcannon and he'll do what's right. The only problem? Ruff has a whole different idea of where he belongs, and he doesn't like this woman they call "Beck." But Aidan likes her. A lot. So once again, a pupper is smack in the middle of a life-changing, heart-wrenching, happy-tear-inducing romance set into motion by The Dogfather.

Find out the day *Ruff Around the Edges* releases! Sign up for my newsletter—you'll get previews, prizes, and a personal note the day the next book is released!

www.roxannestclaire.com/newsletter-2/

I answer all messages and emails personally, so don't hesitate to write to roxanne@roxannestclaire.com!

Fall In Love With
The Dogfather Series...

Watch for the whole Dogfather series coming in 2018!
Sign up for the newsletter for the next release date!

www.roxannestclaire.com/newsletter/

SIT...STAY...BEG (Book 1)

NEW LEASH ON LIFE (Book 2)

LEADER OF THE PACK (Book 3)

SANTA PAWS IS COMING TO TOWN (Book 4)
(A Holiday Novella)

BAD TO THE BONE (Book 5)

RUFF AROUND THE EDGES (Book 6)

DOUBLE DOG DARE (Book 7)

OLD DOG NEW TRICKS (Book 8)

The Barefoot Bay Series

Have you kicked off your shoes in Barefoot Bay? Roxanne St. Claire writes the popular Barefoot Bay series, several connected mini-series all set on one gorgeous island off the Gulf coast of Florida. Every book stands alone, but why stop at one trip to paradise?

THE BAREFOOT BAY BILLIONAIRES
(Fantasy men who fall for unlikely women)
Secrets on the Sand
Scandal on the Sand
Seduction on the Sand

THE BAREFOOT BAY BRIDES
(Destination wedding planners who find love)
Barefoot in White
Barefoot in Lace
Barefoot in Pearls

BAREFOOT BAY UNDERCOVER
(Sizzling romantic suspense)
Barefoot Bound (prequel)
Barefoot With a Bodyguard
Barefoot With a Stranger
Barefoot With a Bad Boy
Barefoot Dreams

BAREFOOT BAY TIMELESS
(Second chance romance with silver fox heroes)
Barefoot at Sunset
Barefoot at Moonrise
Barefoot at Midnight

About The Author

Published since 2003, Roxanne St. Claire is a *New York Times* and *USA Today* bestselling author of more than fifty romance and suspense novels. She has written several popular series, including The Dogfather, Barefoot Bay, the Guardian Angelinos, and the Bullet Catchers.

In addition to being a nine-time nominee and one-time winner of the prestigious RITA™ Award for the best in romance writing, Roxanne's novels have won the National Readers' Choice Award for best romantic suspense three times, as well as the Maggie, the Daphne du Maurier Award, the HOLT Medallion, Booksellers Best, Book Buyers Best, the Award of Excellence, and many others.

She lives in Florida with her husband, and still attempts to run the lives of her young adult children. She loves dogs, books, chocolate, and wine, especially all at the same time.

www.roxannestclaire.com
www.twitter.com/roxannestclaire
www.facebook.com/roxannestclaire
www.roxannestclaire.com/newsletter/

Made in the USA
Middletown, DE
29 May 2018